THE MUSIC OF LOVE

Denise watched as Tom slid from the seat and closed the door. He walked like a proud tiger or a conquering hero. His broad shoulders rocked gently with each step. He had never looked more handsome or sturdy. No longer did she worry about the effects of professional separation on their personal lives. The expression on his face when he had greeted her in the Olney Theater's grand hall and the warmth of his lips on hers had erased all doubt. Nothing could come between them.

Tom led the way although Denise could navigate the turns in her sleep. His mind was more on the incredibly impressive woman in the car than on his driving. After many years of searching, he had found his ideal woman, his soul mate, and his partner. One day, he hoped that she would be his forever.

The evening had offered even more than they had anticipated. It had been an evening of surprises and affirmations that had lived up to their expectations and surpassed it. The night had been perfect for love . . . and murder.

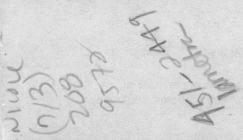

BOOK YOUR PLACE ON OUR WEBSITE AND MAKE THE ARABESQUE ROMANCE CONNECTION!

We've created a customized website just for our very special Arabesque readers, where you can get the inside scoop on everything that's going on with Arabesque romance novels.

When you come online, you'll have the exciting opportunity to:

- View covers of upcoming books

- Learn about our future publishing schedule (listed by publication month and author)

- Find out when your favorite authors will be visiting a city near you

- Search for and order backlist books

- Check out author bios and background information

- Send e-mail to your favorite authors

- Join us in weekly chats with authors, readers and other guests

- Get writing guidelines

- AND MUCH MORE!

Visit our website at
http://www.arabesquebooks.com

THE MUSIC OF LOVE

Courtni Wright

ARABESQUE

★BET BOOKS™

BET Publications, LLC
http://www.bet.com
http://www.arabesquebooks.com

ARABESQUE BOOKS are published by

BET Publications, LLC
c/o BET BOOKS
One BET Plaza
1900 W Place NE
Washington, DC 20018-1211

All Kensington Titles, Imprints, and Distributed Lines are
available at special quantity discounts for bulk purchases for
sales promotions, premiums, fund-raising, and educational or
institutional use. Special book excerpts or customized print-
ings can also be created to fit specific needs. For details,
write or phone the office of the Kensington special sales
manager: Kensington Publishing Corp., 850 Third Avenue,
New York, NY 10022, attn: Special Sales Department, Phone:
1-800-221-2647.

BET Books is a trademark of Black Entertainment Television,
Inc. ARABESQUE, the ARABESQUE logo, and the BET
BOOKS logo are trademarks and registered trademarks.

First Printing: March 2003
10 9 8 7 6 5 4 3 2 1

Printed in the United States of America

One

The parking lot was almost empty when Denise Dory reported in for duty at almost noon. For the first time in her career, she had slept in and arrived at the precinct late. She had worked on a stakeout until long past the closing time of the local bars and returned to her apartment after four-thirty in the morning. She had not changed clothes or stopped to pet Max, her feline companion, but, instead, gone directly to bed without even cleansing her face of the day's grime and sweat. As soon as her head had hit the pillow, she had fallen into a deep sleep. When her alarm had sounded at six, she had been too tired to face the day. Instead, she had hit the off button, pushed Max, the purring cat, onto the floor, and covered her head with the sheet to block out the sunlight as she snuggled into her pillow and went back to sleep.

Feeling deliciously wicked at arriving long after most of the others had already left the office to begin their day's work of investigating murders, robberies, and assorted lesser crimes, Denise strolled into the silent squad room. Everything looked the same as it had the previous day, but, somehow, the tone of the room had changed. The aroma of the slightly burned extra-strong coffee, her partner's signature brew, mingled with the cloying fragrance of mixing aftershaves and perfumes as it had the previous days. The drab utilitarian gray and green colors dotted with memo-laden bulletin boards of important notices, most wanted lists, and items for sale had not changed. The desks, in various states of disarray, remained the same. As usual, Ronda, the efficient, usually overworked department secretary, sat outside Captain Morton's office like a protective pit bull. However, something felt strangely different.

Taking her cup of coffee and walking toward her desk, Denise again studied the room. Everything was exactly as it had been when she left for the stakeout the previous evening. Her partner, Tom, sat hunched over the folders on his desk as always. His broad shoulders strained against the white of the slightly snug shirt, stretching the wrinkles from the wrinkled permanent-press fabric. His canine partner, Molly, lay dozing at his feet with one massive German shepherd paw casually draped over her nose. Her lids fluttered and her paws jerked in a dream of hot pursuit of a helpless rabbit. Everything appeared the same but different. Denise scowled as she identified the change that she, instantly, did not like.

Walking past her partner and tossing her briefcase onto her desk, Denise turned to Tom and asked, "Whose idea was it to play music in here?"

Without taking his eyes from the report he was drafting, Tom replied, "The captain's. This is one of the ideas he brought back from the human resources conference he attended last week. It's supposed to relax us, relieve some of our stress, and make our job more enjoyable. Works for me."

"Do you like it?" Denise queried incredulously of the man who did not like to listen to music in the car while he was driving. He claimed that even symphonic music interfered with his concentration.

"No, but I've gotten used to it. It grows on you quickly. I couldn't stand it when I first came in this morning," Tom replied with a shrug. "Now it only bothers me when it stops. The silence makes me crazy. For dental office white noise, it's not bad."

"As long as the captain isn't piping in any subliminal messages the way they used to do in the grocery store, I guess I can learn to live with it." Denise chuckled as she hastily typed the report that was due in fifteen minutes.

"Ready for lunch?" Tom spoke loudly over the background music that was so low that it did not demand the effort.

"Lunch? I just got here," Denise replied, turning her body slightly toward his desk.

"But I didn't, and I'm hungry. I waited for you, sleepyhead. I managed to report for duty on time despite the late hours," Tom commented as he put the finishing touches on his report.

"What can I say? I'm a slacker. And you're a . . . brownnoser? Denise responded with raised eyebrows and a chuckle as she returned her attention to the detailed report of last night's successful sting operation. "Let me finish this first. The captain said he wanted to see me as soon as I finished this report."

Both Denise and Tom had to submit independent versions, part of departmental policy. Usually her copy contained the meat of the case with all the detail while his served as an outline. Hearing the printer pump out a single page at Tom's request, Denise knew that this report would not be different from their usual effort. Her partner was definitely a man of few words.

Denise and Tom had been a team long enough to know each other's quirks and sore spots. Their deepening personal relationship served to cement the professional commitment and make them a more effective partnership despite everyone's predictions to the contrary. The office skeptics had started a pool on the length of time their romance would be able to withstand the pressure of their work lives. The longest prediction was three months. Their relationship had already survived six with no signs of wear.

While they worked almost exclusively together when they needed a partner, each had a professional identity separate from the other. Tom and his canine partner, Molly, made headlines often for their successful drug busts. Denise had attained a certain level of celebrity for her involvement in national cases that took her away from the usual jurisdiction of the Montgomery County Maryland Police Department in a nearby Washington, DC, suburb. Their work together had become almost legendary, almost the reverse of the notorious Bonny and Clyde. However, regardless of their professional duties, they always made time for each other and their thriving personal relationship.

Collecting her five-page report, Denise inserted his and her efforts into the file folder that contained the photographs and notes of the case. Leaving Tom working angrily to unhook the chain of paper clips that, as usual and without explanation, filled the caddy on his desk, Denise walked to the captain's office. Looking at the large clock on the wall, she saw that they had finished their work with five minutes to spare.

"Finished?" Ronda asked as she extended her hand for the report, which she efficiently placed in the pile that would shortly join the others on the captain's desk.

"Finally. The captain said he wanted to see me," Denise replied, helping herself to one of the peppermints that Ronda kept in a little candy dish on her desk.

"He's expecting you. You can go in," Ronda said as she motioned with her head toward the closed door.

"Do you know why he wants to see me? He's not sending me away again, is he?" Denise asked, wary that the captain might assign her to another project that would take her far from home and force her to live from her suitcase for months. Captain Morton only summoned her to his office when he wanted to assign her to a special case that would pull her from her usual duties and Tom.

"Not a clue. He's been especially quiet this morning," Ronda responded as she pressed the button that would signal Denise's arrival.

"Wish me luck," Denise stated as she headed toward the door.

"Sure, but you'll land on your feet as always," Ronda replied with a chuckle.

"You never know . . ." Denise commented as she braced her shoulders for the latest meeting with the captain.

Captain Morton was a very reasonable man . . . most of the time. He tried not to assign more work than his dedicated team could handle. He constantly reminded the chief that his people had lives away from the precinct, and he insisted that their work not interfere in family time. However, over the years, some cases had required personal sacrifice of his officers, and they had risen to the challenge without too much complaining.

"You wanted to see me, Captain?" Denise asked as she entered the office. Official black-framed photographs of state and local dignitaries lined the wall while candid family pictures in casual frames littered his otherwise organized desk.

Motioning to the well-used chair with the tricky spring, Captain Morton replied with a smile and a nod, "Have a seat, Denise. I'm on hold. I'll be with you in a minute."

Denise carefully sat in the offered chair being mindful of the spring that always poked into the rump of anyone who visited the captain. Although he was aware of the problem, he preferred to keep the chair as it was rather than repair it. He claimed that the possibility of being jabbed kept his detectives alert during meetings with him. No one dared to snooze or daydream while in the captain's company.

"I'm still here, Chief," Captain Morton stated into the receiver. "Right. She's here now. You know that Denise and her partner just closed a case last night. That's right. That one was in addition to the designer murder case and all of the other work on their plates. Okay, but I think she's about due for a break . . . maybe even a vacation. I know, but we can't afford to overwork her. Fine, I'll tell her, but she won't like it. You know that Denise doesn't like these high-profile cases despite her reputation."

Denise could tell from the one-sided conversation that the captain would once again assign her to a special case, one that would probably put her in the public eye and danger once again. At the very least, the assignment would make her so busy that she would see little of her friends. From the tone of the discussion, she knew that he had tried without success to give her a much-needed break, but the chief would not hear of it.

She had learned not to mind the inconvenience of having to put aside her regular cases in order to devote her attention to the more demanding ones. However, Denise could never get used to working on cases without Tom. She trusted him completely to watch her back. Without him, she felt lost.

"Well, Detective Dory," Captain Morton began in his formal tone that left little room for negotiation, "the chief wants to thank you and Detective Phyfer for a job well done on the case you wrapped up last night or, rather, this morning. She's very appreciative of your hard work. A letter of commendation is on its way for your files. As always, I knew you'd pull it off. You're the best detective in the state."

"Thanks, Captain," Denise replied softly, "but don't forget that Tom was instrumental in the success of the case."

"I know, but you were the leader of the team," Captain Morton insisted as he picked lint from his tone-on-tone gray suit. "The chief was so impressed that she wants you to work on a case that she's affectionately calling 'the Music Man Murders.'"

"Let me guess. Someone's killing musicians," Denise interjected in a less than enthusiastic tone of voice. The chief had a way of trying to make especially troublesome cases sound cute. The last case involving jewelers had almost cost Tom his life. Denise did not find the thought of this one at all humorous.

Smiling, Captain Morton replied, "That's right. However, this case involves more than simply random killing. Someone's targeting the nation's best professional musicians in all fields of music. The killer or killers seem to have a grudge against anyone who composes, plays, or directs music in any way. No one is safe . . . not composers, conductors, Hollywood types, or Broadway musicians."

"Do we already have a murder weapon or a list of suspects?" Denise asked hopefully as she accepted the folder he handed her. As usual, the contents consisted of few pages.

"Unfortunately, no. The three deaths have appeared to be accidental. However, the pattern suggests murder," Captain Morton replied as he watched Denise skim the three sheets that contained all of the information to date on the case.

"No murder weapon, a series of murders, and no suspect. So far, this is a typical case for us," Denise said with a tired smile that barely concealed a yawn.

"Look, Denise," the captain began, "I know you're tired of being assigned cases like this, but, when the chief calls, I listen. Besides, you'd be bored with any other kind. You're one of those people who thrives on challenge."

Rising, Denise retorted with a tired chuckle, "Give me a chance for a little boredom once in a while."

Smiling, the captain joked, "Look at the bright side; all of these murders, so far, have happened locally. Maybe you won't have to travel this time."

"Good. I'll leave my suitcase in the closet. Maybe it'll collect a little dust," Denise said with sarcasm. "I haven't seen my friends in so long that they probably think I've moved."

Chuckling, the captain replied, "Go get 'em, tiger. I'll expect frequent reports for the chief. By the way, the chief made all the arrangements with the other jurisdictions. You won't have to notify anyone. They'll be expecting you in their turf."

"That's good . . . saves me some time and hassle. I just hope she hasn't shared anything with her cocktail party friends," Denise quipped, remembering the leaks on one of her last cases.

"Don't worry about that," Captain Morton responded with a smile. "She's learned her lesson after blowing your cover last time."

"By the way, is that Internet-monitoring equipment still connected?" Denise asked more out of curiosity than concern.

"No," Captain Morton stated with a shake of his head. "The chief decided to trust rather than to monitor. She knows that my officers are good people and wouldn't abuse the Internet while on duty. She learned that monitoring often causes more trouble than leaving well enough alone."

"Glad to hear it." Denise chuckled as she covered a yawn. "At least this time the suspect won't know my plans at the moment that I make them."

"Ask Tom to cover your caseload for you," Captain Morton interjected as she walked toward the door.

"Okay, but I hate to dump work on him," Denise agreed reluctantly. "He's already busy with the canine study."

Losing interest in the discussion and turning his

attention to the pile of work on his desk, the captain replied, "He's a big boy. He'll handle it."

"Right," Denise commented. "See you later, Captain."

Denise returned to the squad room humming. Although she was not looking forward to working on a case without Tom, this one at least held a little charm. Maybe she would have a chance to attend a few free concerts. The last big case had taken her to New York and the theater. Maybe for this one she could go to the Olney Theater or Carnegie Hall. The price of tickets had become so high lately that she had abandoned one of her former passions. Besides, Tom hated the going to the symphony almost as much as he hated the theater.

As she approached her desk, Denise's mind worked feverishly on a way to tell Tom that she would have to push their caseload onto his shoulders. Every time the captain assigned one of them to a special project, the other had to cover and manage all open cases. The arrangement worked fine as long as they could manage the inconvenience and no one felt used. Unfortunately, the arrangement did not always work.

Lately, however, Denise was the one who was always dropping cases on Tom's shoulders. Although he did not complain too loudly, she wondered if he was beginning to regret teaming with her. Perhaps he would prefer a less high-profile partner. Maybe he would like a partner who had time for lunch periodically or one who worked on the meat-and-potatoes kinds of cases, too. She also wondered if he would prefer a girlfriend who was not always on the run, arranging stakeouts, and tracking down suspects.

Tom looked up as Denise returned. The smile that had played at the corners of his mouth when he first saw her vanished as he looked at the folder in her hand. He knew from experience that the captain had assigned Denise to another of those cases that the chief would monitor personally. It always meant bad news and loads of publicity every time the chief became involved.

Remembering his involvement in Denise's last big case, Tom involuntarily shuddered. He had inadvertently eaten poisoned rolls and almost died as a result of his partner's work on that case. If Denise had not become worried about not seeing him and come to his apartment, he might have become one of the killer's victims. He hoped this case would not put either of them at risk. The time before that, poisonous mushrooms almost put an end to him. Being partners with Denise often proved a dangerous arrangement.

"Well?" Tom asked as Denise slipped into her chair.

"Well what?" Denise replied as she stretched her tired body.

"What's in the folder?" Tom demanded, pointing to the flat manila folder on her desk.

"Nothing much," Denise answered as she massaged her temples to rub away some of the fatigue that made her eyelids feel heavy. "By the way, the chief sends her regards for a job well done. She really likes our work on last night's stakeout. The captain says she's impressed by our ability to close a tough case so quickly and professionally."

"Okay. Now, you've given me the good news, now what's the bad?" Tom asked as he leaned farther forward. The muscles in his bare arms bulged as he pressed his palms together.

"The chief calls this one the 'Music Man Murders.' Cute, ha?" Denise replied as she read the few pages of the skimpy preliminary report.

"Any clues so far? Jewelry? Gold charms?" Tom inquired, reminding her of the killer's mode of communication in the last case. Denise had received so many packages that the members of their unit had begun to wonder if she had a wealthy lover.

"Nothing really," Denise commented in a tired voice.

"The report just states that in each case the conductor's baton lay beside the body. Doesn't seem like much of a clue to me."

"Any description of the deceased?" Tom inquired as he leaned forward and plucked one of Max's hairs from Denise's shirt. He really was not interested in reading the report but in sniffing the faint whisper of the perfume she had started wearing lately.

Reading the reports, Denise replied, "The first one had been a conductor exclusively. The second was a violinist and conductor. The third served as the adviser to the symphony orchestra and a guest conductor. Two lived in this area, but the third lived in Baltimore. I'd say that our killer dislikes conductors."

"What's the name of your perfume again?" Tom asked as he inhaled deeply of her fragrance, more interested in Denise than in her new case.

"Love Notes. Why?" Denise inquired absently. She was more interested in the cases than Tom's question.

"Ironic, don't you think? Love Notes and you're on a musical case," Tom joked with a wicked wink.

"You're a nut!" Denise exclaimed as she turned her attention to Tom and his seemingly silly statement. "Love notes are sweet words, not music."

"Oh, well, it could mean both," Tom insisted with a grin.

Denise chuckled. "Let's hope the killer doesn't make that connection and start sending me perfume. I have all I need for a while. I haven't opened the bottle you sent me for my birthday two days ago yet. It was really sweet of you to remember that I liked it. The surprise gift on my desk was nice, too."

"I didn't send you perfume for your birthday, and I definitely didn't leave anything on your desk," Tom stated flatly. "I bought you that little pearl necklace."

Fingering the necklace that gently caressed the hollow of her neck, Denise replied, "Then who did?"

"Is the box still in your desk?" Tom demanded, growing more interested in the case and the intruder into the temporary quiet of their lives.

In reply, Denise opened her desk drawer. At the back, she had placed the unopened box of perfume. Pulling it into the light, she examined the package carefully. The original wrapping was still intact. Knowing that Ronda had already sent the box through the X-ray machine as part of standard operating procedure in the police precinct, Denise carefully unwrapped the box while Tom watched.

Lifting the lid, Denise exposed the large oval gold bottle with the embossed security seal on the twist-off top. Placing it on her desk, she pulled the satin lining from the box. Pressed between the lining and the box was a white business card on which the sender had written a message.

"Read it aloud," Tom instructed with more than a little irritation that someone was again sending Denise messages and gifts. He was especially annoyed because the gifts were always more than he could match on his police salary. No other man should send gifts, especially expensive ones, to his girl.

Looking from Tom's scowling face to the paper, Denise read, "'One note and one note only. Listen to the classical radio station every day at three-thirty starting on Friday.'"

"What does that mean?" Tom growled as he took the carefully typed business card from Denise for a closer look.

"It means that I'm about to have an education in classical music," Denise replied as she pulled her radio from the bottom of her desk drawer.

"What?"

Explaining her hunch, Denise responded, "I think the suspect plans to provide the clues to the murders through the selection of music on the radio station.

That's ingenious since anyone can phone in requests to the station, making it almost impossible to connect one person to the selection."

"It's sick, that's what it is," Tom stated angrily. "How did he know that the chief would assign you to the case? She could have assigned anyone."

"I guess he assumed that she would. I usually get the high-profile ones. Funny thing though. We wouldn't have talked about the perfume if I hadn't been assigned to this case. I never would have known that you didn't give it to me. I hadn't even opened the box," Denise asserted.

"I don't like this at all," Tom declared. "Just what you need is another perpetrator who knows that you'll work on a case. Now there's someone else watching you. This is too much."

Shrugging her shoulders, Denise replied, "I guess that's what newspaper coverage brings. Every nut with a bone to pick thinks that I'll be assigned to his case and give him plenty of media coverage. I guess these people count on the press giving them some level of legitimacy. They're no longer simple murderers; they're people with a cause."

"Some cause!" Tom rebutted heatedly. "Most of them kill for greed, not to advance a cause. They don't like the other guy. The other guy drives a car that they can't afford. The other person receives public acclaim and they don't. Besides, it doesn't matter why they committed the deed. It's only important to them that they did it and to us that we catch them. In some way, they want us to catch them. The jails are full of people who felt justified in taking the law into their own hands and count on us to affirm their sense of right. I bet that, if we didn't catch them, they'd feel miserable."

"I won't argue against that very sound logic," Denise mused, changing the subject. "I wonder what motivates this killer."

"He's someone who disagrees with something in the music world. I doubt that he's a deejay. That'd be too easy. He's probably someone who feels slighted," Tom stated flatly.

"He's undoubtedly planning to use the station to communicate bits of information to me. Anyone can phone in musical requests and state the times for the deejay to play them," Denise replied. "I think the suspect will give clues to the case through the music the deejay plays."

"How do you know which classical station he'll use?" Tom asked as he tossed Denise the card.

Smiling, Denise declared, "That's the only easy part of this case. There's only one classical station in the DC area. The other one's in Baltimore."

"How do you know that?" Tom sneered as his mood deteriorated even further. The combination of fatigue and irritation at having someone stalk Denise put him in a very foul mood.

"I listen to it whenever I'm not in the office or with you," Denise stated, frowning at Tom's sullen mood.

"You never told me that," Tom growled accusatorily.

Patting his hand, Denise replied, "It never seemed important. There's a lot of little stuff you don't know about me. I'm sure that I haven't learned everything about you either."

"No, that's not true," Tom stated flatly. "I'm a very simple person, totally uncomplicated. What you see is what you get. There's nothing you don't know about me."

"I guess that's the difference between us." Denise smiled at his innocence. "There's still tons of stuff for you to learn about me."

"It looks as if I'm not the only person who's trying to get into your head," Tom snarled.

"I love having men vying for my attention," Denise

teased, knowing that nothing she could say would lift Tom's mood. He was simply building up to a good sulk.

"Women!" Tom growled as Denise turned her back and went back to work.

Having her sit in front of him was both a benefit and a curse. Their proximity made discussing cases easier than if Denise's desk had been across the room. However, sitting near her constantly interfered with Tom's ability to concentrate. From the very beginning of their partnership, he had found being close to her a temptation. Her soft brown skin always glistened with health. Her eyes always sparkled with life and energy. Her lips constantly intrigued him. Since their relationship changed from being simply partners to tentative lovers, Tom had found sitting behind her an even greater distraction. The curve of her back and the slenderness of her waist invited his caresses. He had learned to exercise considerable restraint because of the proximity of their desks.

Denise chuckled at Tom's irritation as she adjusted her radio to the classical station. She had learned early in their partnership that he was a man of few words. However, when he said them, she listened. Often the words he spoke and their meaning were miles apart. He grumbled when he meant to speak softly. He often barked when his feelings were most on edge. Denise knew that at that moment, Tom was especially troubled by what he perceived as a threat to his ability to defend her from the attentions of the murderer. If he could send her a bottle of her favorite perfume, he could reach her in other ways. Tom was not happy with the reality that the murderer had penetrated their little world, learned intimate little details, and used them to make contact.

Tom was a surprisingly complicated man who saw himself as transparent. He wanted to fill all of her needs and tried very hard to accomplish his goal. He was strong and sensitive without being maudlin. He understood when she needed quiet and often sought it himself. He enjoyed her company but did not push himself on her. He was a dedicated police officer who would protect her to the death, fighting with great abandon. However, he was a tender lover who used his silence to allow his body to speak words of love.

Denise and Tom made a perfect pair. She was outgoing and gregarious; he was the strong silent type. They enjoyed each other tremendously, appreciated the same weak jokes, and relished spending time strolling through parks, eating picnic meals, and lounging in front of the television. Their personal relationship had progressed well despite the demands of the job and Denise's celebrity status. Even their differences, her enjoyment of the theater and classical music and his of anything in the sports arena, drew them closer as they accepted each other's ability to stay true to their own preferences.

Denise adjusted the little radio until the station was clear. She enjoyed listening to the deejay give the historical and biographical information before playing the musical selection. Some of her friends had complained that they thought the daytime deejay talked too much, but she did not agree. The material he shared enriched her listening pleasure and provided insights into the epoch, the genre, and the musician.

At that moment, the deejay had started playing a Beethoven sonata. Turning to the files she needed to update before handing them to Tom, Denise allowed herself to feel the music. Although she kept the volume low so as not to disturb Tom, she closed her eyes and swayed to the gentle sound of the strings. The plaintive melody seemed to speak to her soul.

Denise knew that Tom did not share her interest in classical music. He much preferred R&B or jazz. While

the background w... on
they were together, they
to soul, music that spo ke to
...e. Although they had giv en up
...e knew that he would always prefer
either of those to the mellow sounds of strings and orchestral harmony. Once when he had ridden in her car,
he had asked if he could change the station from her
classical selection. When she replied in the negative, he
had quickly fallen asleep to escape what he called "mood
music."

Remembering that the classical station maintained a
Web page, Denise quickly typed in the address to read
the day's selections. At the specified hour today, the deejay would play cuts from famous Broadway shows.
Frowning, Denise wondered if the lyrics or the titles or
both would hold the clues.

Following a link, Denise searched for names of the most
prominent conductors and performers in the genre. She
was not surprised to find the names of the three deceased
musicians among them. Scanning the list more carefully,
she saw that more than only the names of classical
musicians appeared on the page. The names of Broadway
and film lyricists and composers, country stars, R&B
greats, soul trendsetters, and opera singers also appeared
either as links or on the same page. The murderer had a
vast musical arena from which to draw. So far, he had stuck
to the classical world. She would have to wait for the three-
thirty selection.

Tapping her on the shoulder, Tom asked, "Are you
ready for lunch? I'm hungry."

"You're always hungry." Denise laughed. "Give me a
minute to—"

Before she could finish the sentence, Tom had

...on the kno...
sketchbook, Denise quickl...
room and into the street. At...
morgue. Perhaps she would fi...
sketchbook would come in handy f...
tails of the interviews and anything else she mig...
discover.

TWO

The morgue was not especially one of Denise's favorite places to visit. Not only was it unpleasantly cool, but the personnel who manned it were, at best, macabre. They hardly smiled, and their idea of humor missed the mark. Within the last few years, the staff had begun to change for the purpose of bringing in people with a fresh outlook on forensics. No one envisioned that the morgue would ever become the social center of the police department, but everyone wanted a more welcoming atmosphere for the living.

However, Denise thought that Dr. Sally Childs and her associates were almost as strange as the former staff. They were younger and new to the bureaucratic red tape that had burned out their predecessors but obsessed with pathology. When invited to precinct functions, they threw a wet blanket on the festivities by wanting to discuss their work exclusively. They seemed to live and breathe embalming chemicals. The detectives made a concerted effort to steer the conversation away from bodies to other activities but were unsuccessful. The pathologists only wanted to share news on the latest forensic procedures. After a few attempts at socializing with them, the detectives, as a group, decided to omit their names from the department guest list.

Not even the freshly painted interior could add charm to the uninviting domain of the pathologists. Although new colorful prints covered the walls and music played from the ceiling speakers, the morgue lacked charm. The new receptionist smiled more than the former one, but she possessed a personality that quickly explained the reason she had selected a career in pathology. She looked like a character from the latest walking-dead movie, complete with heavy black mascara, clinging black crepe dress, long blue-black hair, and opaque black stockings. At least, her smile was welcoming.

Smiling, Denise approached Jane Blues, who immediately greeted her as if they were the best of friends. They had so few live guests in the morgue that the receptionist was happy to have company. After exchanging casual conversation, Denise settled down to business.

"Is Dr. Childs free?" Denise asked, nodding toward the boss's door. "I'd like to examine the bodies."

"She's in conference with the chief at the moment," Jane replied as she repaired a chip in her black nail polish, "but she told me to give you these copies of the preliminary reports if you stopped by."

"Is there an office somewhere that I could use?" Denise inquired as she accepted the three thin folders from the outstretched deadly pale hand. "I'd like to study these."

"Sure, use that one. The new hire hasn't arrived yet," Jane instructed as she indicated the office to her right and pushed the black bangs from her heavily lined eyes.

Smiling her thanks, Denise opened the door to the vacant office. The smell of fresh paint mixed with the residual stink of embalming chemicals rushed out to meet her. Stepping back to allow the fumes a chance to escape, she decided that nothing could make the morgue anything but eerie. Denise almost expected Dracula to materialize from the shadows.

Each report contained not only pathology information but also a brief biography compiled from the

Internet. Spreading the report on the first victim onto the desk, Denise saw that the murderer had cut down Michael Hornblatt in his prime. At thirty-five, he was one of the youngest conductors to take the baton of a major orchestra. He had earned a master's degree from a prestigious music school as well as a degree in engineering. After graduation, he had studied under the most famous conductors, learning his craft quickly. He had arranged the score for several films, conducted in Europe, and composed a symphony that had debuted last year to critical acclaim. He and his girlfriend had owned a condo in one of the most famous buildings in Washington.

The autopsy showed no trauma or entry wounds. His girlfriend had phoned the police, stating that she could not awaken him. According to the paramedics report, he was DOA at the closest hospital. Mr. Hornblatt appeared to have died in his sleep of apnea that deprived him of oxygen.

Turning to the report on Ms. Sylvia Butler, Denise read that she had served as the first chair in the national symphony for the last five years. Following her graduation from a prestigious conservatory in Baltimore, she had risen to the honor while in her thirties. Ms. Butler had made a name for herself in the music business by composing and recording several albums of violin music. She had been a member of a chamber ensemble as well as a solo performer. When not serving her function as the lead musician in the orchestra, she attended cooking classes at one of the most famous culinary schools and was one of the most famous black restaurateurs in the area. She was single and lived alone with her Abyssinian cat as company. Her next of kin lived in a little town near the Amish country in Pennsylvania. When she did not arrive at rehearsal, the orchestra secretary had phoned the building superintendent, who had used his key to provide the police with entry to her apartment.

The officers had discovered Ms. Butler dead at her kitchen table, a cup of cold hot chocolate sitting untouched in front of her.

The third victim had been married to the same woman for thirty years and was the father of three children, all of whom lived far away. Gordon Scroll had received his degrees and gained his experience exclusively in Maryland. He had built an addition to their home that served as the office in which he composed the music and lyrics for many award-winning Broadway shows. He and his wife had traveled extensively now that their children had grown up. When he did not leave the office for dinner at the usual time, his wife had searched for him. She had found him sitting at his desk as if daydreaming. When he did not respond, the distraught wife phoned 911. The doctor pronounced him dead on arrival from unknown causes.

While closing the folders and stashing them inside her briefcase, Denise reflected on the careers of each of the deceased. The connections were sketchy at best. Two of the three were men. Two had been involved in classical music. The Broadway composer was male.

Their personal lives yielded little more. Two were unmarried, but one lived with his girlfriend. The woman lived alone. The oldest of the three lived with his wife in the family home although the children had grown up and moved away.

Not even their names suggested a connection. The last name of one was from the top of the alphabet, while the others appeared at the bottom. . . . So much for the killer's clues.

Denise gathered her belongings and left the disquieting confines of the morgue. Waving to Jane Blues, who waggled black-painted nails without pausing in her animated telephone conversation, Denise returned to the squad room. Armed with the names and dossiers of the deceased, she needed to escape the cloying stink of paint and embalming chemicals. Perhaps a whiff of Tom's famous coffee would help to clear her head and organize her thoughts.

As she walked the short distance from the morgue to the precinct, Denise could almost feel her good mood and health returning. The fresh air helped to remove the smell that clung to her clothes and hair. Walking among the living dispelled the gloom of death. The morgue was definitely a place in which she could not spend long periods of time.

Once inside the squad room, Denise took deep breaths of the smells of humanity. Molly's slight dog odor mingled with the fragrance of Tom's coffee and Ron's aftershave as well as the assorted other smells of busy officers. The fragrance of copier ink mixed with new-furniture smell to make the room come alive with the personalities that inhabited it. The squad room smelled of life, and Denise loved it.

The camaraderie of the squad room buzzed with vitality. People shared information, exchanged jokes, and debated the relevancy of details as part of the job and the result of working closely together. The room resounded with productivity and energy.

Pouring her last cup of thick brew for the day, Denise returned to her desk. Tom and Molly were out of the office, making their little space seem massive in its emptiness. Denise was not especially fond of the dog, although a grudging friendship had formed as a result of Tom's brush with death from poisoned food while working on a case with her. She and the dog had protected him as best they could from further danger in their own unique ways. Denise missed the large animal when it was not lying on the floor at Tom's feet. Molly's presence was strangely comforting. Perhaps it was the size of Molly's glistening, white teeth or the depth of her warning growl

that had established the animal's position as the third
partner.

Studying the small amount of information that she
had gained from her visit to the morgue, Denise decided
to visit Mr. Hornblatt's girlfriend, Ms. Butler's secretary,
and Mr. Scroll's wife in her search for clues. Perhaps
those women would be able to share additional information that would give her a starting point for the
investigation. She needed a clue as to the connection between the deceased. Their positions in the world of
music did not shed enough light on the murderer's motives. Without this connection, the Music Man Murders
appeared to be three random acts of violence that the
chief had united without cause.

Leaving Tom a note stating her whereabouts, Denise
drove to Mr. Hornblatt's condo in the Bethesda section
of Maryland. She passed impressive houses on carefully
manicured lawns before she turned onto Wisconsin
Avenue and traveled south to the tall white apartment
building on the right. According to the dossier, Hornblatt and his girlfriend had occupied the penthouse,
complete with pool and jogging track. Her utilitarian
blue suit and sensible shoes would look dowdy in such a
setting.

The doorman summoned a valet, who parked Denise's
car as he ushered her inside the cool lobby. She caught a
glimpse of her fairly nondescript but serviceable car as it
rounded the corner and vanished into automobile heaven
populated by Mercedeses, Jaguars, Bentleys, and Rollses.
She was not the only one out of place in this environment.

Stepping carefully so as not to disturb the silence of the
lobby, Denise glanced at the glistening marble, shining
brass, and sparkling chandeliers that adorned the massive
reception area. An elegant gray-haired man stood behind
the mahogany desk on the right, waiting to serve in any
way possible. On the left a marble and crystal alcove

housed the residents' brass-fronted mailboxes. Colorful oriental rugs dotted the marble floors.

After phoning upstairs, the receptionist summoned a porter, who silently escorted Denise to the elevators. Using his passkey, the man unlocked the special express elevator that served the penthouse. He bowed and walked away as the door closed with a whisper, leaving Denise alone in the coolness of the elevator.

Even the elevator's decor was breathtaking. A tapestry-upholstered chair stood in one mahogany-paneled corner for those who did not wish to stand on the ascent. Reproductions of grand masters adorned the walls, and a smaller rendition of the lobby chandelier twinkled overhead. From the carpeted floor to the antique emergency telephone, the elevator was more elaborate than Denise's apartment or that of any of her friends.

Before Denise could thoroughly enjoy the ride, the door opened in the foyer of Mr. Hornblatt's condo. As the housekeeper guided her to the living room, Denise stole quick peeks at the furnishings. She decided instantly that music could be a lucrative profession for those who made it to the top. The number of original works of art hanging on the walls, sitting on pedestals, and lying on the floor was mind-boggling. With a shrug, Denise decided that she should have taken her piano and violin lessons more seriously.

Settling in the elegantly appointed sunroom off the living room, Denise waited for Ms. Freedman to appear. The housekeeper had said that the woman was almost inconsolable following Mr. Hornblatt's death and had seen almost no one since that horrible morning. She had looked at Denise in an almost accusatory manner as if to say that the detective was violating the sanctity of their mourning period and was not a welcome guest.

Denise did not have to wait long before a strikingly beautiful blond woman entered the room. She wore all black, including the very dark designer sunglasses that covered her eyes. Sitting straight-backed in the straight gold leather chair, Ms. Freedman sighed deeply and twisted the handkerchief between her well-manicured fingers. With the exception of the movement of her alabaster hands, she could have been any one of the stately statues that adorned the room.

"What can I do for you, Detective Dory?" Ms. Freedman sniffed delicately.

"I'm sorry to impose on you at a time like this, but I need to ask a few questions," Denise responded softly.

"Whatever you wish, but I don't understand your reason for visiting me," Ms. Freedman said, dabbing at the corner of her right eye. Denise would have loved to be able to see the eyes behind the dark glasses.

"I'll come right to the point. We don't believe that your fiancé died of natural causes. The evidence suggests that Mr. Hornblatt and two other musicians might have been murdered," Denise stated.

"Murdered? Who'd want to kill Michael?" Ms. Freedman exclaimed behind her dainty handkerchief.

"That's what I'm trying to uncover," Denise replied gently. "We have no clues except the connection of their profession. I'd like to ask a few questions, if you don't mind."

"I'll help any way I can, but I don't understand why anyone would target musicians of Michael's caliber," Ms. Freedman insisted with an indignant sniff.

"May I sketch while we talk?" Denise asked as she reached for her bag. "I use my drawings instead of a tape recorder."

"Help yourself," the bereaved fiancée replied with a wave of her jeweled hand. The ring on the third finger sparkled dazzlingly in the sunny room.

"I understand that you phoned the police when you

couldn't awaken Mr. Hornblatt," Denise stated as she sketched the woman's profile.

"That's right," Ms. Freedman replied, settling comfortably into her seat with a feigned lack of interest in Denise's actions.

"Did you find him on the sofa or in his office?" Denise asked as she smoothed the details of the shadows in the woman's face.

"No, he was in his room," Ms. Freedman simpered without changing her position. She had obviously sat for many portraits. "I went in to wake him, but he was dead."

"It must have been a great shock to you, finding him dead in your bed," Denise said commiserating with the distraught young woman.

"Oh, it was, but he wasn't in my room. Michael maintained his own bedroom. He was in the habit of getting up at all hours of the night to work on his music and didn't want to disturb me. We've never shared a bedroom. Besides, I need all the closet space I can get," Ms. Freedman replied matter-of-factly as if the arrangement were routine in her social circle.

"What kinds of things did Mr. Hornblatt do to relax?" Denise asked, hoping to find an entrée into a meaningful discussion with the woman.

Shifting her position slightly, Ms. Freedman replied, "He never really relaxed. His mind was always churning out ideas. However, Michael was a health nut. He exercised every day and took handfuls of vitamins. He even drank a special concoction that he processed fresh every morning."

"Would you happen to know the ingredients?" Denise asked as she studied the composed face that belied the sniffing.

"Of course, I drink it, too," Ms. Freedman commented in a tone that showed her distaste for the questioning. "It actually tastes quite enjoyable. It contains tomatoes, carrots, celery, cucumbers, green peppers, and any other vegetable or fruit that he'd have the grocer deliver. Michael adds seasonal fruit, too, when they're available."

"He always brought you a glass?" Denise inquired as she sketched Ms. Freedman's full face and neck.

With a tiny smile appropriate for the grieving fiancée, Ms. Freedman responded, "Always. Even if I weren't quite awake, he'd bring me a glass. Fresh ingredients lose their potency if they sit for long periods. Michael wanted me to benefit from the fresh ingredients also."

"Did you say that the grocer delivered your shopping?" Denise inquired without looking from the other woman's beautifully made up face.

"Oh, yes. Doesn't everyone order groceries over the Internet these days?" Ms. Freedman quipped with a slight shake of her shoulders for emphasis and the first sign of true emotion. "We're busy people. Neither of us has the time to push a basket down lines of produce. Michael was always busy with his music and never had the time for such things. I was too occupied with social activities to bother with something so . . . ordinary."

Lifting an eyebrow at the deliberate snub of the working-class necessity of life, Denise changed the topic and asked, "When you went into his room that morning, did you see anything unusual?"

"No, he was lying on his bed as if asleep." Ms. Freedman sniffed again, regaining her composure as the grieving almost-widow. "When I called to him from the door, he didn't stir. Michael's a very light sleeper and always responds immediately. Besides, he never naps. I knew immediately that something was wrong. I thought he might have had a headache. I never thought for a moment that he was dead."

"What did you do next?"

"Why, I walked to the bed and touched him," Ms. Freedman replied as if Denise's question were totally irrelevant.

"Actually, if I remember correctly, I gave him a little shake to wake him. When he still didn't respond, I shook him a little harder. His body just sort of flopped. It was horrible. I knew from police movies that he was dead."

"Then what did you do?" Denise asked, ignoring the tightly clasped hands that rested heavily on Ms. Freedman's lap.

"I called the police, phoned downstairs to let the desk know that I'd soon have a guest, and waited at the door for them to arrive," Ms. Freedman stated with a little nod of her head that gave a sense of logic to her statement.

"Did his room look rearranged in any way?" Denise inquired, noting the subtle changes in the woman who no longer sat as if for a portrait.

"No. As always, sheet music was everywhere . . . on the floor, the dresser, the bed," Ms. Freedman replied, straightening her back a little and rearranging the crease in her perfectly tailored slacks as if aware that her demeanor had slipped.

"I always imagined that artists were very neat people. Was Mr. Hornblatt a contradiction?" Denise inquired, as she watched for further changes.

"He must have been an exception to that rule, Detective, because Michael was a total slob." Ms. Freedman chuckled as she eased back in her chair. "I always straightened his room in the morning while he was taking his shower. He would never have been able to find anything if I hadn't taken it upon myself to help organize him."

At that moment, an apricot-colored little Pomeranian bounded into the room with a conductor's baton between its teeth. Laughing, Ms. Freedman rose and extracted it from the little dog that sat at her feet waiting patiently for the cookie that she pulled from her pants pocket. Balancing on its tiny hind legs, the little canine pirouetted and appeared to bow in anticipation of its treat. With the cookie between its teeth, the little dog left the room as quickly as it had appeared.

"That's Michael's dog, Gizmo," Ms. Freedman explained as the smile faded from her lips. "She was always with him. She's very lonely without him."

"Is that a toy that she brought you?" Denise asked as she motioned toward the baton.

"Oh, no, it's one of Michael's," Ms. Freedman replied. "I told you that he was a slob. She probably found this under his bed."

"Do all musicians own these?" Denise inquired, fingering the slickness of the wood.

Shaking her head, Ms. Freedman stated, "No, but all conductors do. This one wasn't very expensive. It certainly wasn't one of his favorites. That's the one he balanced between his fingers while he worked. He kept the valuable ones locked away in the music room where Gizmo couldn't find them. Tooth marks would ruin the elegance of the baton."

"Might I be able to see his collection?" Denise asked, slipping her sketch pad into the case.

"Certainly, but I don't see the connection," Ms. Freedman responded as she insinuated herself from her chair.

"Honestly, neither do I, but I can't overlook anything at this point," Denise said as she rose and followed Ms. Freeman into Mr. Hornblatt's music room at the end of the long hall.

As they walked, Ms. Freedman pointed out the important works of art on the walls. She appeared eager for conversation and relished being able to differentiate between the truly priceless art and the promising but relatively unknown artists. To Denise, all of it looked as if it should have been in an art gallery rather than in a private home.

The display of art continued into the music room but changed to a musical theme that dominated the works from the paintings to the sculptures. Along one wall, Mr. Hornblatt had hung a display case holding batons of every possible wood. Some even appeared to have gold handles and silver tips on their white shafts. Jewelers had carefully studded others with precious gems that sparkled under the bright display light. Peering closely, Denise saw that a heavy lock protected the contents of the case.

"These are fabulous," Denise commented as she studied the contents of the case. "I can see why he'd want to keep them away from the dog."

Smiling slightly as became a bereaved fiancée, Ms. Freedman stated as she indicated a particular row within the case, "Those are especially valuable and collectable. Very famous conductors had owned some of them, as you can see from the plaques. Michael really prized all of them for their provenance as well as the precious metals and gemstones. Some of his less valuable favorites are on his desk."

Denise gazed at the secondary collection, lying on a velvet cushion on the corner of Mr. Hornblatt's desk. Although they were less stunning than the first set, Denise could tell that these were not the ordinary conductor's orchestral baton. Several of these displayed brass tips and semiprecious jewels.

"Wasn't Mr. Hornblatt afraid that someone would steal his collections?" Denise asked as she carefully held one of the batons that Ms. Freedman placed in her hand.

Shaking her head, Ms. Freedman replied, "As you saw, the case has a very good lock. No one who really knew collectibles would have wanted any of these on the desk. Anyway, an elaborate alarm system protects the entire condo. Michael didn't worry much about theft."

"One of them seems to be missing," Denise stated, pointing to an impression in the pillow.

"It's in Michael's bedroom," Ms. Freedman responded,

sniffing again. "That's the one I found on the bed next to the body. I just haven't returned it yet. I simply could not bring myself to enter that room again."

"May I see the baton and the room?" Denise asked, turning toward the door.

Leading the way to the bedroom, Ms. Freedman replied, "Sure, but I don't see why. It looks like the others. There's nothing special about it."

"Why did he keep it if there's nothing special about it?"

Dabbing at her cheeks as if to wipe away tears, Ms. Freedman stated with a hint of a smile on her lips, "Michael was a very sentimental man and a bit superstitious, too. It's the baton he used during his debut years as a conductor. Michael didn't have any money then and bought the cheapest one he could find. He used it when he conducted his first symphony. He conducted the recording of his first album with it. If he was working on an especially difficult composition, he would hold it for inspiration. I guess it was special in that way but not collectable like the others and not a throwaway like the one that Gizmo liked to carry."

Leaving Ms. Freedman standing in the doorway and stepping into the immaculately clean bedroom, Denise found it difficult to believe that the room had ever been strewn with untidy papers. Tom's apartment was always one step above junky with his bedroom being the most appalling. Mr. Hornblatt was either incredibly neat or he employed a very efficient housekeeper. The room looked as if it were ready for a magazine photography session with layers of pillows on the bed, glistening wood floor with oriental rugs, and more priceless art on the walls.

Calling over her shoulder, Denise stated, "This room is quite impressive . . . very neat."

With an answering sigh, Ms. Freedman responded, "Neither Michael nor I had anything to do with that. As soon as the police gave us the okay, Mrs. Franklin, our housekeeper, spent a day cleaning that room. She said that she needed to do one last thing for poor Michael."

"Was she in the apartment when you discovered the body?" Denise asked as she continued to take in the luxury of the room. With quick strokes of her pencil, she recorded all that she saw.

"No, Michael died on her day off." Ms. Freedman sniffed with indignation. "I had to handle the entire ordeal myself."

Turning her attention from Ms. Freedman's efforts at martyrdom, Denise busied herself in the examination of the baton that lay on the nightstand beside the massive king size-bed. Not a wrinkle or an impression marred the surface of the intricately stitched gold spread that covered the matching sheets. Mrs. Franklin was certainly a skilled bed maker. A soldier could have dropped a quarter on the surface without fear that it would not have bounced back to him during even the toughest inspection.

Ms. Freedman had not underestimated the unimpressive appearance of the baton. It looked like any other dark-wood-handled conductor's baton without any distinguishing ornamentation. If she had not remarked on Mr. Hornblatt's sentimental attachment to it, Denise would have thought it simply any struggling conductor's accoutrement.

However, the baton was special to Mr. Hornblatt and deserved Denise's closer examination. Slipping on a pair of latex gloves that she kept in her bag, she carefully picked up the baton. It was lighter than she had expected, especially after holding the others. The finish showed use, and a slight chip in the white shaft marred the finish on the end. The baton was definitely not of the same quality as the others. However, the oil from Mr. Hornblatt's hands had given it a rich sheen.

"The police have already dusted the baton and the

room for prints," Ms. Freedman stated flatly without entering the room.

"Good. I'm sure they were very thorough," Denise replied without looking behind her. "Would you mind if I take it with me? I'll be very careful with it. I'd like to run a few more tests on it, if you don't mind."

"I don't know what you expect to find, but you're welcome to look," Ms. Freedman commented with a stifled yawn. She was obviously growing tired of Denise's company now that she was no longer the subject of the sketches. "The coroner said that Michael died of apnea," she continued. "He had always snored heavily, producing a sound similar to that of a tractor-trailer truck's horn. I suppose it finally caught up with him."

"What was Mr. Hornblatt wearing the night he died?" Denise asked as she stashed the baton safely inside a plastic bag before slipping it into her briefcase.

"He wore a tux while conducting a concert at the Olney Theater that night," Ms. Freedman replied slowly as she remembered the details of the fateful evening. "He returned home by eleven. We talked for a few minutes and then went to bed. Michael always slept in the nude, Detective."

"Is the tux here?" Denise asked as she stepped toward the closet, hoping for a clue.

"The police have already checked the closet, Detective," Ms. Freedman stated matter-of-factly as she gazed at her cuticles. "Michael kept them at his office in the Olney Theater. They were his work clothes, you see. He had others here, but he never mixed the two. He wore jeans or slacks to work and back. Unfortunately, the police haven't returned them to me. Perhaps you might find it for me."

"I'll do what I can. Did he appear ill or subdued when he returned?" Denise asked as they walked toward the front door.

"Not at all," Ms. Freedman replied with a touch of cheerfulness in her voice, clearly pleased to be free of Denise's company. "The concert had been a big success. It had been sold out for weeks as a matter of fact. Michael was very popular. He was in a great mood when he came home. He said he was a little tired, but that's not unusual after the workout of conducting."

"He went to bed immediately after returning home?" Denise inquired, standing under the sparkling chandelier in the massive marble and gold foyer.

With her hand on the front doorknob, Ms. Freedman replied, "At first, I thought he did, but then I heard Michael at the piano while I was getting ready for bed. He had just started a new composition and probably wanted to work on it awhile. I fell asleep to the sound of his playing. Strange, I didn't find any sign of work the next day. He must have given up and decided simply to play the piano rather than compose. Michael did that sometimes when the Muses weren't with him. Still, I should have seen some indication of his night's work. I didn't even find any balled-up paper in the trash can."

Sensing that Ms. Freedman had reached the end of her patience with the intrusion into her mourning period, Denise thanked her and left. The young woman had been most helpful in her own way. Denise hoped that the baton in her bag would provide more information. Her contacts at the FBI might find something on the baton that her fellow officers had missed.

Following the winding roads through the park, Denise returned to the squad room feeling that she had not accomplished very much. She had seen the deceased's home and his collections, interviewed his fiancée, and taken possible evidence for further study. However, she felt as if the pieces were not fitting just right. Something was definitely missing. Denise thought that, by sharing them with Tom, she might find the missing components. She always enjoyed sharing tidbits with him.

Tom, as usual, sat bent over the pile of papers that never seemed to leave his desk. Between his regular case-load and the ones associated with the canine study, he always had files to close. He appeared in court more often than any other detective in their unit, arrived at the office early every morning, left late every day, and took work home in the evenings and on the weekends. Yet, the harder he worked, the more there seemed to be for him to do.

However, he never complained, yet he never rejoiced once he had completed the work. Tom simply plugged along. Until his professional and personal partnership with Denise, work had been his companion. He had grown accustomed to working at strange hours to ward off boredom and loneliness. After their partnership, he had tried to reduce his workload, but it would not let up. It appeared that he had established an unbreakable pattern.

After the romance bloomed between Denise and Tom, he began to learn to relax and put work in its proper place. However, he still slipped into his old patterns if she did not give direction to their personal life. As a matter of fact, if Denise did not plan their weekend activities, he would never leave the office. Unless she planned for them to spend the evening together, Tom sneaked work home, thinking that Denise did not see him.

Denise, however, lived a full life after hours. She did not mind staying late to finish a project, but she drew the line at taking work home with her. She worked out at the gym almost every evening to relieve the tensions of the day. She enjoyed reading mysteries and romances, working counted cross-stitch, and spending evenings with friends. She felt that relaxation helped improve her performance and efficiency. Work was something she left on her desk when she left the precinct in the evenings.

"Are you busy?" Denise asked as she tossed her bag onto the desk.

"No," Tom replied in his usual gruff manner. He continued to work on the stack of papers that littered his desk.

"You should have come with me. The grieving fiancée was a knockout. However, her grief looked anything but genuine. Not a single tear spoiled her perfectly applied makeup," Denise began, knowing that he would listen without shifting his attention from his work. "According to the coroner, Mr. Hornblatt died of apnea, which his fiancée agreed was possible because he snored heavily. However, they maintained separate rooms, so we have no eyewitness proof."

"Okay, so the man was a night trumpeter. I've been known to blast a few, too, so you say," Tom asked as he placed a completed case in the out-box for Ronda to file.

Shrugging her shoulders, Denise replied, "It's just that Mr. Hornblatt lived with a stunningly beautiful woman but didn't share the bedroom with her. She said he worked at all hours and didn't want to disturb her beauty sleep. I don't understand why they would live together and maintain separate rooms. That's like leading separate lives."

"It's not the way I'd want to live, but I guess it worked for them," Tom commented and then added, "Why do you question it?"

"I didn't see a single thing in that condo that looked like her," Denise stated with hands raised in frustration. "The art was stunning but very conservative. She didn't seem the type to enjoy pieces like that. The color schemes were masculine without any hint of a feminine presence."

"Maybe she just moved in and hasn't painted yet," Tom offered with a shrug.

"Not according to the dossier on Mr. Hornblatt,"

Denise rebutted. "According to the police information, her name has been on the deed since they first bought the condo three years ago."

"I guess she's just not a get-involved kind of woman," Tom suggested.

"I'd agree if she hadn't been so protective of his baton collection," Denise stated as she pulled the baton from her bag. "Ms. Freedman watched it like a hawk. She didn't want me to have this old baton analyzed."

"Do you think she could be a suspect?" Tom asked as he peered through the plastic evidence bag for a good look at the battered baton.

Shaking her head, Denise replied, "No, not yet. Not until I interview the partners of the other two. Maybe she's just a reserved person who felt that my efforts were intrusive. She was polite but not welcoming. She appeared more ready for a photo shoot than a visit from the police."

"Maybe she was anxious to remove you from the condo before you found anything. Everyone knows your reputation," Tom suggested with pride in his partner.

"Sweet, but I don't think that was the reason. I got the distinct impression that she was expecting someone, just not me. She was dressed more for going out than for staying at home. Even the ultrarich sometimes let down their hair. I certainly hope this baton provides a lead," Denise commented as she recollected Ms. Freedman's appearance. "I'll interview family and friends of the others tomorrow. Maybe I'll find something that ties them together."

Grumbling loudly and distractedly, Tom said, "I wish I could find the bum who links all of my paper clips together. I spend my good time untangling them, and the wiseacre does it again."

Laughing, Denise replied, "You will one day. You're closer to making a collar than you know."

"That's what you always say and, so far, I haven't caught

anyone. Let's go. It's getting late, and I'm hungry. I'll work on these later," Tom growled as he tossed the untangled clips into the caddy. Placing both in his desk, he locked the drawer and gathered his keys and ID folder.

As always, Tom covered the distance between their desks and the door in record time. Molly stood patiently at his side. The expression on her face matched Tom's perfectly. The dog almost appeared to be tapping her paw impatiently. With his hand on the doorknob, Tom waited for Denise to join him.

"I'm coming. Hold your horses!" Denise commented under her breath as she rushed to lock her sketchbook inside her desk.

"You're the slowest woman I've ever known," Tom declared as he gazed out the window at the darkening sky.

"You always get a jump on me, that's all," Denise rebutted as she joined him at the door.

"I wouldn't be able to if you weren't so poky," Tom commented as they sprinted down the steps and into the evening air.

"Are we eating alone tonight or do we have to double-date with that partner of yours?" Denise asked as she approached her car.

"We'll eat at my place," Tom replied without allowing Denise's cut at his canine partner to irritate him. "Molly's a little sluggish today. I don't want to leave her alone."

Opening her car door, Denise commented with a chuckle, "Sometimes I think you're more interested in that dog than you are in me."

"No, I'm simply a thoughtful partner," Tom replied as he waited for Molly to ease into the backseat.

"I don't know. You hardly ever hold the door for me," Denise said as she peered over the top of her car.

"If Molly had hands, I wouldn't hold it for her either." Tom laughed as he walked toward the driver's side of the car.

"Whatever." Denise chuckled as she pulled from the space.

"Let yourself in. I'll be too busy to answer the door," Tom shouted as he waved good-bye. The lines of his usually stoic face flowed into a gentle smile as he studied Denise's profile.

Denise eased into the heavy traffic with a wave of her hand, leaving Tom standing beside his car. She hated to admit it even to herself, but she was a little jealous of the dog. Molly spent twenty-four hours of each day with Tom. She only had him for a few precious hours after work. Sitting in front of him in the squad room did not count. They were so busy that they hardly noticed each other. Denise looked forward to their evenings alone, but tonight, she would have to share the precious time with Molly. Knowing that it was not possible for the dog to feign illness, Denise nevertheless wondered if Molly was jealous of her, too, and only pretending to be sluggish to keep Tom at her side.

Whenever Tom came for dinner at Denise's apartment, Molly had to remain at home. Denise's cat, Max, had established his turf and did not welcome a canine guest. Their first encounter had proven that Denise's apartment was Max's territory, and the scratch on Molly's nose was proof of his determination to keep it that way.

With a sigh, Denise stepped into her apartment. As always, Max met her at the door with a deep purr, a heavy flop onto the carpet, and an upturned tummy waiting for a rub. Stroking the furry white belly, she decided to shower and change before going to Tom's for dinner. If she were lucky, they would at least snuggle while watching television before one of them started to fall asleep. For a new couple, they had already established set patterns usually reserved for the long married.

Three

Dinner at Tom's was always uneventful. He always prepared steaks grilled on his balcony, potatoes cooked in the microwave, and string beans overcooked in the oldest stainless steel pan known to man. He never remembered to purchase steak sauce, sour cream and chives, or almonds, preferring salt and pepper to spices.

Fortunately, Tom's expertise in the kitchen was not the reason that Denise ate dinner at his apartment at least once a week. Dinner with Tom and Molly had become a routine to which Denise looked forward even with her slight irritation at the dog's presence. Dinner at Tom's was on a par with the famous greeting card; she dined there when she wanted the very best company and companionship she could find.

The familiar aroma and loud barking greeted Denise as she slipped open the door, using her key to gain admission. Since Tom's brush with death, she had retained a copy of the key although she rarely used it unless instructed. They both enjoyed their privacy too much to want each other to pop in unannounced. However, the exchange of keys had marked a change in their relationship and a cementing of their bond. Although she rarely used it, Denise could not imagine ever returning the key.

"Is that you?" Tom shouted from the kitchen over the sound of slamming pot lids and cabinet doors.

"Who else would it be? Surely, no other woman has a

key to your apartment." Denise chuckled as she arranged the red carnations she had brought to brighten the dining room table in the inexpensive vase purchased from the same florist.

"You never know. I might have decided to build a harem." Tom laughed, always happy to banter with Denise on their more intimate terms.

"Live dangerously, you mean. Between Molly's bark and my bite, another woman wouldn't stand a chance," Denise replied, as she snuggled against the massiveness of Tom's back. She breathed in the muscular scent of him that mixed with the sweetness of the onions and mushrooms that he was braising in the pan.

"Keep it up, Dory, and you'll ruin the dinner I've slaved over," Tom responded with a pleasant huskiness in his voice.

Stepping back, Denise stated, "Me? Never! You know that nothing keeps me from a good, home-cooked meal."

"That's not what you said last week," Tom reminded her with an intimate chuckle and a wink over his left shoulder.

"That was different," Denise quipped as she poured the chilled red wine into the waiting glasses. "I hadn't seen you in a month, remember? That trip to DC had taken me away for too long."

"Yeah, I remember. I hate those cases away from home. It's lonely when you're away," Tom added with a sincerity and warmth that made Denise smile.

"I should go away more often if absence makes you miss me," Denise replied from the dining room.

Laughing, Tom commented as he placed the plates on the table, "I didn't say that I missed you; I said that it's lonely here without you. Molly's not good for snuggling; she sheds too much."

Smiling, Denise eased into her customary chair and stated, "Just like a man to take the romance from the moment. You couldn't leave it that you missed me just a little, could you?"

Looking deeply into Denise's eyes, Tom replied with a mock playfulness that barely concealed the depth of his emotions, "Sure, I can, but I don't want you to get the idea that you're the most important person in my world or that I wouldn't be able to function without you. I'd hate for you to think that I love you more than my life or that I'd take a bullet to save you. A woman would take advantage of a man if she thought that kind of thing."

Resting her small hand on his strong, massive one, Denise replied softly as the tears glistened in her eyes, "I can understand your position. I feel the same way. I wouldn't want you to think that you've become the center of my world and that I fall asleep every night thinking of you and wake up every morning with you on my mind. You don't need to know that I love you with every fiber of my being. You might get a swelled head if you knew. A girl's got to protect herself from conceited men."

Leaning together across the small space that separated their chairs, Tom drew Denise into his arms. As their lips touched, all joking faded away to be replaced by the reality of the warmth of their touch, the aroma of their skin, and the tingling of their nerves. Nothing else mattered, not the sleeping dog that lay on the floor between them, the unsolved murders, or the filet mignons cooling untouched on the plates. At that moment, their world, their touch, and their love were all that mattered.

Breaking their embrace, they turned their attention to the delicious dinner that Tom had prepared. Even without the sour cream and chives or the extra seasonings, he had prepared the steak perfectly. The merlot and flowers added a particularly festive touch to the meal.

As the evening ticked away, Denise and Tom chatted about cases and colleagues. At times, they simply enjoyed the soothing jazz in the background. They did not

feel the need to maintain a steady stream of conversation. They were completely comfortable with the silence
that embraced and warmed both of them.

It was not until they had blown out the candles and
stacked the dishwasher that Denise began to feel any
nervousness about spending the night at Tom's apartment. Since they had been professional partners and
romantic lovers for a while, Denise did not feel the awk-
wardness that accompanies a new relationship. The
tension originated from Denise and the new case that
she had just started.

Placing the leftover string beans into the refrigerator,
Denise slipped into Tom's open arms. As they stood in
the middle of the kitchen with Molly snoozing in the
doorway, Denise tried to relax against his strength and
take comfort in his closeness, but she could not. The
new case weighed too heavily on her mind. She had suc-
cessfully pushed it to the back of her mind during
dinner, but it now appeared unbidden. Before she could
rest that night, Denise knew that she would have to discuss it with Tom.

Lightly placing a kiss on her upturned lips, Tom studied Denise's face. Smiling slowly, he said, "Okay. I can tell
when we're not alone."

"I'm sorry, Tom," Denise replied as she hugged him
tightly, "but you're right. I was thinking about the case.
The chiefs Music Man Murders are really getting to me.
I know I've just started working on the case, but there's
something about it that just doesn't add up."

Leading her gently to the sofa, Tom stated, "Let's talk
it out. There won't be any sleep or anything else this
evening until we deal with this case. I didn't slave in that
kitchen for the sake of taking a cold shower, which, by
the way, don't work."

Chuckling, Denise took her place next to Tom. The
nearness of him and the warmth of the wine provided

instant comfort. Resting her head on his shoulder, she began stating her concerns while he listened attentively, occasionally tracing the arch of her brow or kissing the softness of her cheek.

"I think Ms. Freedman's demeanor bothers me more than the seemingly disconnected nature of the murders despite the chief's attempt to hold them together. I don't think I've ever met a more composed grieving fiancée or widow. She was scary."

"Maybe your interview tomorrow will start to put the pieces together," Tom commented absentmindedly as he rubbed his lips against her forehead.

"Remember the cat show murder from last year?" Denise inquired with a sigh. "That woman was cold but not completely heartless. She managed to press out a tear as we handcuffed her."

"That was different," Tom interjected without stopping his slow, tantalizing progress down her cheek to her lips. "That woman was facing life. This one only sent a conductor baton away for an evening or two."

Relaxing deeper into the sofa, Denise sighed and said, "True, but she didn't react the right way to my questions. She was more concerned about posing for my sketches than in solving the possible murder of her fiancée. I have a distinct impression that Ms. Freedman isn't alone tonight."

Gently opening the unbuttoned top of Denise's crisp, white blouse, Tom purred more like a cat than a tiger, "If she isn't, I bet she isn't thinking about you at this moment."

Involuntarily arching her back from the pure pleasure of his lips on the hollow of her throat, Denise replied, "That might turn out to be her undoing."

Chuckling softly, Tom commented, "That's exactly what I had in mind . . . undoing the last of these buttons."

As his fingers gently caressed her warm flesh and his lips

found their place on hers, Denise pushed all thought of Ms. Freedman and the Music Man Murders from her mind. Slipping her arms around his neck, Denise pulled Tom toward her as she slowly reclined on the extra-wide blue leather sofa she had helped him select. Her fingers tightened their grip on his shoulders as the heat of his kisses ran the full length of her body.

Tom's fingers gently traced the familiar terrain of Denise's body. He lingered just long enough at each curve and hollow to allow his lips to finish the work his touch had started. As Denise's breathing became jagged and the pressure of her hands more demanding, Tom tightened his strong arms around her body and pulled her to his chest. In one graceful movement, he rose to his feet and headed toward the bedroom door.

Walking past Molly, who wagged her tail from her position of sentry at the apartment's door, Tom stated, "See you in the morning, girl."

"Good night, Molly," Denise called from her position against Tom's chest.

The dog did not whimper or try to follow them. She was content in her role as the protector of the home. She would sleep in the living room and leave the bedroom to her master and his lover.

Four

Denise went directly to Ms. Butler's apartment the next morning without stopping in the office. As arranged, the building superintendent waited for her with the key in his pudgy hand and a leering smile on his face. Despite being accustomed to this treatment, Denise immediately bristled and felt the set of her shoulders become rigid and her face stern. She wanted the super to understand that she was all business. She was a detective like any other and demanded the respect that the men always received from each other.

Reading her rigid posture correctly, the super immediately changed his facial expression and stated, "I'll lock the door as I leave. Take all the time you need, Detective."

"Thanks," Denise muttered absently as she began to sketch the layout of the apartment. The cold shoulder and professional demeanor had disarmed yet another potentially obnoxious man with inappropriate thoughts about professional women.

The condo was large and tastefully decorated as was the lobby through which she had quickly walked. The table in the foyer held the first of many African artifacts and established the motif that Ms. Butler continued throughout the home. Ms. Butler had decorated the separate living room and dining room in priceless antiques with African-print upholstery for accents. Kente cloth in various patterns and shades provided the unifying force

for the rooms. Candles clustered on every tabletop while
plants softened the rooms' corners.

Free of the superintendent, Denise wandered first
into the immaculate kitchen. With the exception of the
dish full of cat food on the floor and the ring on the antique dining table from the cup of hot chocolate that Ms.
Butler had been drinking when she died, the room
could have belonged to a model home. An impressive as-
sembly of cooking utensils hung from the walls and filled
the drawers of the bleached pine cabinets. The pantry
contained carefully labeled containers of cereals and
grains and cans of stacked vegetables and sauces. The
impressively clean stainless steel subzero refrigerator
held the essentials of milk, juice, and yogurt. The
microwave and professional range appeared new and
unused. Ms. Butler certainly separated her personal and
professional lives. No one would have guessed from
looking at her kitchen that she was one of the most famous restaurateurs in the area. She obviously did all of
her cooking at the restaurant.

Running her finger along the spotless countertop,
Denise sighed. Her kitchen would not look that clean
even if she spent all day every Saturday for a month
working on it. Some people simply had the knack, but
she was not one of them.

The living and dining rooms offered no clues to Ms.
Butler's death. They were as orderly as the kitchen with-
out even a magazine to hint at the occupant's hobbies.
Only the African art suggested any outside interests.

Stepping to the wall of windows, Denise peered outside at the view of the park. From the twentieth floor, she
enjoyed a breathtaking view of the treetops and the sky.
She could understand Ms. Butler's choice of location
completely. To wake up every morning to this view must
have filled Ms. Butler with great joy.

Walking along the hall, Denise discovered that Ms.

Butler had created a formal television room from one of the extra bedrooms. In this room, Denise caught her first glimpse of the woman's personal life. On an elegant antique cherry credenza, Ms. Butler had placed a myriad of silver-framed family photographs that showed her graduation from college, her position as first chair in the orchestra, and her with her beloved cat. Her healthy warm brown complexion glowed from the pictures as she smiled for candid and posed shots. Photos of people who strongly resembled Ms. Butler nestled among the framed newspaper clippings on the ebony marble mantle tinder which a gas fire would burn in the winter.

Behind the heavily carved doors of the armoire, Ms. Butler had hidden the sixty-inch television. She had arranged seating groups for both conversation and viewing convenience in this formal space. Again, Ms. Butler had softened the corners of the room, but nothing could add warmth. The room was stiff despite the television. Denise could not imagine anyone eating popcorn or watching a football game in that room.

As she wandered into the guest bedroom, Denise continued to sketch the apartment. Ms. Butler had decorated this room in shades of gold and orange. As with the others, it was impeccably organized and coordinated perfectly. However, nothing about it would invite a guest to kick off her shoes or nap on the silk-covered ornate four-poster bed. Everything was too precise, too perfect. Denise would have been afraid to sleep there for fear of disturbing the perfect harmony of drapes, spread, and carpet.

Ms. Butler's bedroom was much the same. Everything matched as if a designer had arranged the room, and no one had lived in it. The throw pillows lay at perfect angles on the bed, resting against the headboard but not obscuring the view of the carvings. The subtle print in the afghan across the foot coordinated perfectly with the colors in the room. The silver brushes on the dressing table sat on a spotless mirrored tray. Denise could not even find a hair belonging either to Ms. Butler or the cat in the bristles.

Opening the closet door, Denise saw that Ms. Butler had arranged her clothes by color and her shoes by style with the black flats occupying a space separate from the black heels. She had relegated tennis shoes to a space in the corner as if to prevent the odor or casual appearance from affecting the others. Even the cluster of scarves on the wall rack to the left hung under little numbers that related to the outfit with which she intended to wear them. Ms. Butler obviously never selected her clothing for the day on a whim but preferred to dress with the help of her color-coding and the little numbers on the hangers. From the appearance both of Ms. Butler's closet and her apartment, Denise decided that she was a woman who left little to chance.

Denise felt almost relieved to see that the music room, however, told a very different story. Sheet music lay everywhere. Every piece of furniture was white with it. Sketching hurriedly, Denise saw that some of it carried Ms. Butler's name as the composer. File cabinet drawers filled with music stood partially open. In this room, it looked as if Ms. Butler never put anything away. Ms. Butler's violin lay on the table as if she had only just stepped away to answer the phone. CDs of classical music cluttered the floor under the stereo table. Posters and photographs of musicians, plays, and celebrated performers covered the walls.

Unlike the rest of the condo, Denise could tell that Ms. Butler lived in this room. Although as well decorated as the other rooms, the music room felt lived in and comfortable. The deep blue leather furniture carried the impression of reclining bodies. The woman obviously spent most of her time here practicing and composing, and her cat must have stayed with her. Cat fur covered the top of the ottoman, showing that the beloved Abyssinian lounged here while its owner worked. An empty soda bottle sat beside a plate containing the crumbs of Ms. Butler's last meal. Everything wore a slight dust reminiscent of fingerprinting activity, as did the other furniture; however, this time, cat fur mingled with the powder.

Turning to leave, Denise noticed something protruding from behind the music cabinet in the corner. She walked toward it, being careful not to step on any of the music that dotted the carpet. Taking a firm grip on the corners, she inched the heavy cabinet across the thick carpet to expose a baton that looked exactly like the ones at Mr. Hornblatt's home. With a scowl, Denise wondered why a violinist, composer, chef, and restaurateur would need a conductor's baton. Perhaps a visit to a music supply store would supply the missing pieces.

Slipping the baton into an evidence bag that she extracted from her sketchbook, Denise carefully returned the cabinet to its original position. With the exception of disturbing a little of the cat fur, she left the room in much the same condition as when she arrived. Walking from the silent room, she wondered who was taking care of the cat. Perhaps she should visit that person for more clues into Ms. Butler's identity.

Returning to the foyer, Denise used her cell to phone Ronda, the precinct's secretary, to ask her to set up appointments with Ms. Butler's friends and family. With luck, she would be able to interview them that day. The apartment had told her nothing except that Ms. Butler was a very organized, controlled person. Denise could clearly see that no one had entered by force or attacked Ms. Butler while she worked. The apartment showed no sign of a scuffle. Even the comparative mess in the music room had the feeling of work-in-progress rather than of someone riffling through the drawers. Content with her findings, Denise flipped off the light and left Ms. Butler's world to return to her own.

During the drive to the precinct, Denise reflected on Ms. Butler's orderly life, at least, the appearance of order. In a room accessible to visiting friends, the woman maintained total composure, but, in the space that she occupied alone, she allowed chaos and creativity to reign. Yet, as she pulled into her assigned parking space in the crowded lot, Denise thought it strange that nothing of Ms. Butler's other life showed in the apartment. According to the dossier, she was a great chief and the owner of a much-touted restaurant, yet none of her love of cooking showed in the immaculately clean kitchen.

Still thinking about Ms. Butler's sense of order in contrast to her own casual approach to life, Denise almost fell over the sleeping Molly, who had taken the opportunity of her absence to spread into her rival's space. Muttering under her breath about colleagues and their canine companions, she stepped gingerly over the outstretched paw and approached her desk. One day the pilot program to which Tom belonged would end. Until then, she would have to bite her tongue and put up with the furry beast.

Watching her set her cup of coffee on the desk, Tom demanded, "What'd you find out?"

"Nothing except the woman was very neat with the exception of her music room," Denise replied and then added, "And this."

"Another baton?"

Placing the plastic bag containing the baton on her desk, Denise said, "It was behind a corner music case. I guess the cat must have batted it there although I still don't understand why a violinist and composer would need one. Anyway, our investigative force didn't see it."

"You think there's some connection with the other

murder?" Tom asked, paying more attention to the movement of Denise's lips than to the words she spoke.

Perching on the edge of her desk so that she could face Tom, Denise responded, "I don't know. It could be a coincidence or a lead, but it could also be a deliberate effort to confuse the investigation. Maybe the murderer leaves the batons for me to find. This might be his way of creating a red herring for me to contemplate, giving him time to plan his next attack. The batons might mean nothing, but I don't want to take any chances."

"By the way, our FBI contact phoned while you were out," Tom instructed with a smile as he gazed at Denise's shapely legs. "Joe says the baton tests clean of the usual substances."

"Oh, well," Denise replied with a sigh. "I was hoping for a clue."

Tapping his index fingers together, Tom continued, "He did say, however, that, when the technician X-rayed the baton, he discovered that it's hollow. Our contact said that he thought they were solid wood."

Stretching her back in a very feline way, Denise stated, "In addition to taking a trip to the Amish country, we'll have to visit a music store. I pretty much decided that I needed to do that while in Ms. Butler's apartment, but now I know that I need the extra help."

"I can understand the music store, but why the Amish country?" Tom queried, watching Denise sink into her chair. "Why are we going there?"

"For the shoofly pie, of course," Denise joked with a chuckle.

"You know I don't like that stuff . . . too sweet. I prefer a different kid of sugar," Tom teased with a wink.

"I'll buy you a triple scoop of homemade ice cream if you'll help me with the interviews," Denise cajoled, leaning over his desk seductively.

"You've got a deal, but I think you can offer better

than that." Tom laughed, a low, rolling sound from deep inside his chest. "Now get back to work or we won't be able to leave for lunch."

Laughing, Denise commented, "Is food all you ever think about? I would think that, after the trouble your appetite got you into at the designers' dinner, you'd be less interested."

Growling, Tom retorted, "No, as I remember from last evening, but a man cannot live by work or love alone. Besides, it's not my fault that the suspect had poisoned those rolls."

"If you hadn't been such a pig, you wouldn't have eaten so many of them," Denise stated as she turned to her desk.

"They were very good rolls," Tom insisted stubbornly. "Besides, my illness helped solve that case. You should thank me."

"Whatever."

"I hate it when you do that!" Tom fumed. "It stops all conversation."

"Exactly."

Muttering under his breath, Tom turned his attention to the work on his desk. He worked steadily until the dog at his feet became restless, signaling a need for a walk and their lunchtime. Clearing his desk as was his habit before leaving the office, Tom slammed the file cabinet drawer as the signal that he was ready to go.

Denise collected her bag and sketchbook. During the silence, she had made an appointment to see Mrs. Scroll, the widow of the Broadway show composer who had lived in Bethesda. Although his death had also been from unknown causes, Denise hoped that his widow might be able to shed some light on the cases that the chief had connected under the title of the Music Man Murders. At any rate, she would interview Mrs. Scroll to learn more about her husband's habits.

Lunch was Tom's treat. He and Molly took off at top speed for a brisk walk to the park with Denise bringing up the rear. Whenever it was Tom's turn to pay, they always ate pizza while sitting on a bench overlooking the swan pool or strolling along the path that wound deep into the nature center. Tom loved being outside rather than stuck in an office or a restaurant. Besides, the pizza was not only inexpensive and generous but the best in town.

By the time Denise had finally caught up with them, Molly was content to walk at a much more leisurely pace at Tom's side. His forehead glistened with perspiration as he handed Denise a foil-wrapped slice and a cup of soda. With a boyish grin, he led her in silence along the path that went deep into the woods past the herb and rose gardens.

The center of attention in that section of the park was always the cool, calm, sophisticated swans. The swans barely acknowledged the attention of the spectators as they searched for fish in the recently stocked pond. Their shimmering feathers and arched necks gave them a nobility that they shared with no other birds. Joining the others on the path along the pond's bank, Denise and Tom marveled again at the majesty of the swans.

Molly, too, sensed the serenity of the pond and lounged peacefully at Tom's feet. She had enjoyed the brisk walk and having Tom all to herself and was ready for a nap. She enjoyed the serenity of the woods and the freedom from the office, too.

Watching the peaceful swans suddenly turn vicious when a particularly appetizing fish swam within range reminded Denise of the murder cases she had investigated. In all of them, perfectly normal people suddenly changed because of greed or jealously. Very few were truly "crimes of passion," causing her to doubt if that kind of spontaneous reaction occurred in the modern-day life in which people maintained day timers and electronic calendars that programmed their every action. Even the athletic activities of children responded to a calendar. Kids never played outside anymore in pickup games. These days they dressed in the appropriate uniform and waited for their parents to drive them to the field. Games of alley ball no longer existed.

Denise allowed her mind to wander over her past cases. In all of them, the perpetrator had acted after carefully planning the attack. Whether for direct personal gain or to advance a cause, the murderer had gone to great lengths to stage the crime. She wondered if the same was true of this case. It certainly appeared as if the Music Man Murders would follow the same pattern. She wondered if their FBI contact would be able to find a commonality involving the batons now that he had two of them to analyze.

Glancing at her, Tom saw that Denise was deep in thought. She had eaten her pizza methodically but without comment. She usually scolded him for giving Molly a pepperoni, but, this time, she did not notice.

"Something bothering you?" Tom asked as he tossed the trash into the nearby can.

"This case."

"Why? You've only just started working on it. Give it time," Tom advised as they slowly walked back to the office.

"I usually have a hint of a clue by now," Denise objected quietly.

"Not all cases solve themselves, you know," Tom replied soothingly. "You might have to work a bit on this one."

"I don't expect it to solve itself, but I'd like a little help from the deceased," Denise commented. "So far, I'm batting zero. They were nice people with friends and family. All of them were musicians at the top of their fields. I can't even see what the murderer would gain by killing one of them."

"Maybe he wants their job," Tom offered as he stopped Molly from sniffing the fire hydrant.

"I don't think that's it," Denise rebutted with a shake of her head. "They're all too different. A Broadway composer, an orchestra first chair and violinist who also composed, and a symphony conductor who composed and arranged on the side the way they all do. I don't see the connection yet. Other than their love of composing, I don't see the connection."

"Maybe the baton will provide the clue," Tom suggested as they rounded the bend and headed through the gate. Leaving the quiet of the park behind was the hardest part of returning to the office.

Shrugging her shoulders helplessly, Denise replied, "I hope so, but I'm not banking on it. Maybe this afternoon's interview will give me something to go on."

Reaching the precinct, Denise stated, "I'm off. Wish me luck at Gordon Scroll's. Maybe his home won't be as neat. Maybe I'll find a clue."

Walking her to her car and holding the car door open, Tom stated, "If not this afternoon, maybe our trip to the Amish country to interview Ms. Butler's family will do it. Don't worry, Dory, you'll solve this one, too."

His confidence causing her mood to lighten, Denise joked, "You're starting to drool over that shoofly pie already."

"Not that sweet stuff!" Tom exclaimed. "I'm a meat-and-potatoes kind of guy. I want to cut into a slab of beef or spoon out some of that chicken noodle casserole they make up there. That's my idea of eating."

"You might want to leave room for a roll or two," Denise teased as she started the engine.

Narrowing his eyes in feigned annoyance, Tom

replied, "Will you ease up on the rolls, Dory? I bet I'll never live that one down."

"Probably not!" Denise exclaimed with a laugh.

"I'll see you at your place for dinner. Make it good . . . but then, dessert's always good whenever we get together," Tom shouted as she pulled away from the curb.

Ignoring his last comment and waving her hand, Denise pulled into the traffic and headed toward the home of Gordon Scroll, award-winning Broadway composer and lyricist. Checking her map, she caught a glimpse of her reflection in the mirror. Her brown hair, usually so carefully trimmed, looked a bit scraggly around the edges. Denise decided that she would stop at the salon before going home to start dinner. A quick check of her functionally short nails confirmed that she could use a manicure, too.

Chuckling, Denise decided that she would have her brows plucked, also. Not that Tom would notice. He never saw subtle changes, but he might notice if she died her hair blond. She was in need of a change . . . something to jump-start this investigation. Maybe a complete makeover would do the trick.

Driving along the quiet road, Denise wondered if Tom would notice changes to her appearance. They had been professional partners for a while but lovers for only a short time. Perhaps the romantic side of their relationship was still so new that he would notice. Perhaps he was still attuned to the little things about her. He appeared to consider her just another element in his environment just as a comfortable chair is a part of the scheme of life. It was entirely possible that Tom had already compartmentalized their personal life and made it part of the picture of his world.

Too practical to dye her hair, Denise pushed that idea from her mind. She did not have the time or the inclination to go for the touch-ups, which was why she wore her hair short. She just did not have the time for the maintenance long hair required. Perhaps, one day when she had the time, she would buy a blond wig. If Tom did not notice, the other detectives and Ronda certainly would comment on the change.

Suddenly, Denise found herself in Great Falls, the location of Mr. Scroll's home. Pulling into a quiet side street on which huge homes stood, Denise slowed the car and checked for the house number. She need not have bothered scanning the mailboxes. She could not miss his house if she had tried. A handy craftsman had shaped the Scrolls' mailbox to look like the treble clef sign. In a very upscale, conservative neighborhood like this one, Denise wondered at the neighbors' reactions. It certainly was unique and quite artsy.

Walking up the long slate walkway, Denise surveyed the neighborhood. The houses were among the largest she had ever seen in the Washington metropolitan area. Actually, they were more like mansions than houses. She would have expected to see this kind of dwelling in Hollywood or in New England but not in the suburbs of Maryland. Not even old Potomac, the crème de la crème of neighborhood, boasted homes of this level of grandeur.

The houses were straight from the pages of the current architectural magazines and were almost too spectacular to believe. Massive balconies spread across the front of some models, while flowering hedges and stone driveways decorated the entrances of others. Eight-foot-tall fences blocked the view of swimming pools in most yards and lighted tennis courts in many others. Tall columns on stately porticos appeared to be the decorating style of choice although a few were stone-front Tudors. Meticulously manicured lawns with topiary surrounded all of them.

Almost before she could press the button, a butler answered the doorbell. Dressed as he was all in black, his

face and attire stated that the residents of the house were
in mourning. In muted tones, he ushered her to the living room in which he instructed her to wait. Denise
almost expected Dracula to appear from the shadows at
any moment.

Unlike the living rooms in the splendidly decorated
apartments that Denise had visited recently, this one was
palatial. Denise felt small and childlike in the surroundings. Not knowing where to look first, she took in the
excess of luxury, knowing that she could not absorb everything in one visit. Mr. Hornblatt's home had contained
fabulous art of stunning quality but not by the most easily
recognized artists. This elaborate mansion housed works
by masters of their craft who were known to everyone.
Everywhere Denise looked, she saw Faberge eggs in special cases, paintings by grand masters, and sculptures by
artists normally seen only in the National Gallery of Art.
Mr. Scroll's pockets had been very deep indeed.

The accessories were also of a grandeur that Denise
had only seen in movies and magazines. The chandelier
in the foyer must have cost three times as much as
Denise's annual salary. The carpets that lay on the magnificent wood and marble floors exhibited intricate
patterns and colors that shouted expensive original, not
bargain reproduction. The crystal vases on marble-
topped tables overflowed with huge arrangements of
flowers of every color and description although white
calla lilies appeared to be the favorite. Denise remembered reading that they made excellent cut flowers that
lasted well although she could not imagine that anyone
with this level of wealth would worry about the expense
of throwing out spent flowers.

The house reminded Denise of the setting of an old
Katharine Hepburn movie. She expected Dinah, the
strange little sister, to enter, pirouette, and break into
song at any moment. She would then flounce toward the

concert grand piano that sat in the corner of the room and bang out a rousing rendition of "Lydia, the Tatooed Lady." She would then vanish into the depth of the house from which she had appeared.

Chuckling at the memory, Denise leaned forward to peer through the wide French doors, at the expansive manicured yard that led to the pool and the changing pavilion. Wealth and its trappings stood everywhere to the point of being pretentious and almost stereotypical of the lifestyle of the ultrarich. Feeling as if she occupied a choice seat at a play, Denise could hardly wait for the action to begin and the characters to appear on the elaborate stage.

Without a sound, Mrs. Scroll glided into the living room on the thickest oriental carpet Denise had ever felt under her feet. Taking a seat opposite Denise, Mrs. Scroll looked quite melancholy despite the healthy glow of her complexion. Her nails had been freshly manicured and her hair meticulously styled. Her figure, despite her having three grown children, was trim and athletic in the soft gray dress that stopped at her shapely calves and exposed her slender but muscular arms. According to the dossier, she was fifty-five, but she looked twenty years younger.

"I'm sorry to trouble you, Mrs. Scroll," Denise began in somber tones in respect for the grieving woman, "but I need some help in a murder case that might be connected to your husband's death."

Gazing steadily at Denise, Mrs. Scroll replied softly as she twisted the fine linen handkerchief, "I'm willing to help, Detective, but I don't see the connection to my husband. The coroner said that he died of unknown causes. Isn't that the same thing as natural causes?"

"Unfortunately, it isn't," Denise responded in a sympathetic voice. "The coroner meant that he couldn't isolate the cause of death, which could be anything other than natural. Two other famous musicians have also died mysteriously. I'm hoping to find the similarities among them."

Speaking through quivering lips, Mrs. Scroll commented, "I certainly hope you find that a strange virus my husband contracted from his recent travel abroad was the cause. I'd hate to think that someone killed him. He was such a wonderful man."

"Would you mind if I sketch while you tell me about the trip?" Denise asked as she opened her sketchbook. "I do this instead of taking notes."

"Feel free if it will help your efforts," Mrs. Scroll agreed softly. "The trip was business for my husband but a little vacation for me. I always accompany him on his trips now that the children have all grown up and moved away. Anyway, we went to Russia on this one. I suppose it's strange that I didn't fall ill. The Russian government had invited him to conduct their symphony in show tunes . . . a celebration of American music mixed with Russian artistry. The concert was quite lovely and very well attended. Their musicians are so dedicated to their work and such professionals. After the concerts, we did some sight-seeing and then came home. We were only there for ten days."

"Where did you stay?" Denise asked as she sketched without taking her eyes from Mrs. Scroll's elegant face.

"Our accommodations were top drawer," Mrs. Scroll replied, waving off the thought of poor living conditions. "This was a musical goodwill mission in a way . . . an exchange of musicians. While we were in Moscow, one of their renowned musicians performed at the theater in San Francisco. We lived wonderfully in an apartment that overlooked the river. The accommodations couldn't have been more delightful. Priceless art and tapestry lined the walls, and extensive collections dotted the rooms. I understand that visiting corporate executives usually stay in that apartment. It certainly speaks well of the Russian economy even if not truthfully."

"And the food?" Denise asked with a new respect for the woman who appeared to be more than simply window dressing for a prominent composer.

"Plentiful and very tasty," Mrs. Scroll stated without hesitation. "I was expecting less than five-star accommodations and restaurants, but I was very pleasantly surprised by the welcome. Even the weather cooperated during our trip. My husband was very pleased, too, and considered the trip a huge success.

"What did he do upon your return?" Denise asked, hoping to find anything that would connect to the other murders although she knew that neither of the others had spent any time out of the country.

"My husband has a show opening on Broadway at the end of the year," Mrs. Scroll stated with pride at her spouse's accomplishments. "They're in rehearsals now and needed one more song. As soon as we came home, he started working on it. As usual, he locked himself in his office. When he was working, Gordon hated to be interrupted for anything other than creature comforts."

"I'd like to see his office if I might," Denise requested as she closed her sketchbook.

"Of course, but the police have already searched the room. It was most heartbreaking to have them tramping around in my husband's office. They dusted everything with that awful powder and took photographs of Gordon's most prized possessions as if they were simply objects of curiosity rather than the products of a lifetime's effort," Mrs. Scroll responded with great sadness.

Following Mrs. Scroll to the back of the huge house, Denise replied, "I'm sure they didn't mean to imply disrespect while doing their job. Unfortunately, we sometimes disconnect from the people involved in the case while investigating a murder. I think visiting his

would give me the feel for his work location. It might help
me to make the connections I need for this case."

"You'll find the room just as it was the night he died,"
Mrs. Scroll said through her tears. "I told the housekeeper to leave it for a while. I'm in no hurry to remove
memories. I only yesterday sent the score he finished
that night to New York. I couldn't bear to enter the
room without Gordon being there. It's hard after being
married so long to be without him. I had always thought
that we'd live a long life together."

Denise smiled in solemn camaraderie with the woman
who had lost the man she loved. She remembered her
fear at finding Tom lying unconscious on the floor and
her worry while nursing him back to health after the
episode with the poisoned rolls. For a while, Denise had
been afraid that their dreams of living happily ever after
might come to an abrupt end.

Opening French doors that led from the massive family room to the composer's office, Mrs. Scroll stepped
aside to allow Denise to enter. Finding the absence of
her husband too much to bear, she sank into a chair in
the main room and muttered that she would give Denise
space to do her work. Smiling gently, Denise surveyed
the room from the door and then proceeded to study
the room that had inspired such creative genius.

Unlike Ms. Butler's office, Mr. Scroll was incredibly
neat. Although the concert grand piano's keyboard
cover was still up, everything else was tidy as if expecting
company. Pencils and a few sheets of music paper sat
on the piano bench ready for use. The shutters were
open to allow natural light to illuminate the keys. Plants
softened the corners and hung in front of the south-
facing windows. Wicker furniture in welcoming clusters
invited people to sit while the composer shared the fruits
of his labor. A best-selling novel rested on the table. Its
brass page marker glistened in the sunlight. Massive

stereo speakers sat on opposite sides of the room connecting the sophisticated system to both itself and the piano. Photographs of famous composers, musicians, and conductors smiled down from the off-white walls. The room was elegant, yet relaxed.

Denise slowly walked the perimeter of the room. Everything in it held a purpose and had a place. Nothing was superfluous in any way. It was a room for work and leisure. Only the tape on the tile floor that had once outlined the body marred the perfection of the decor. Once Mrs. Scroll was able to allow cleaning of the room, the last trace of intruders would vanish also and allow the room to regain its customary inviting atmosphere.

Turning toward the door after finding nothing out of the ordinary in the room, Denise noticed a baton resting against the piano's music stand. Slipping on her gloves and extracting a plastic bag from her briefcase, she eased the monogrammed cedar-handled baton into the evidence bag. Following a hunch, she picked up the pencil, too.

Turning for one last look at the room, Denise spotted something under the wicker sofa. Bending low, she pulled out another baton just like the first only minus the engravings. She slipped this one into an evidence bag, also.

"Did you find anything?" Mrs. Scroll asked as Denise joined her in the family room.

"Only a baton on which I'd like to run some tests if you don't mind," Denise replied as they walked toward the front door.

"I'd like to have it back when you finish, please," Mrs. Scroll stated softly. "It's the only one my husband owned. It was a present from the Russian Symphony Orchestra's conductor to him. They even went to the trouble of engraving his name and the date on it. The baton meant a lot to Gordon and to me. More now, I suppose. That was our last trip together."

"I'll take good care of it," Denise promised. "You said it's a one-of-a-kind object? I found another one under the sofa."

"Really? Someone must have given it to him because Gordon didn't own any others," Mrs. Scroll commented confidently. "Whenever he conducted, he always borrowed one. He didn't see the need to own things that he seldom used. Gordon was very meticulous about his person and his music room, as I'm sure you noticed."

"Yes, I did. That's what makes the other baton such an interesting find," Denise replied with a little smile.

As sadness flooding her face once more, Mrs. Scroll stated, "You may keep that one, if you'd like. I only need the other one back as soon as possible. There won't be any others, you see."

Deciding that this was the perfect time to leave the grieving widow, Denise thanked Mrs. Scroll and left the house. Taking a deep breath of the flowers that bloomed in profusion in the neighborhood, she pushed aside the heaviness of mourning and moved into the world of the living. She was almost overwhelmed by the irony of Gordon Scroll's situation. All the wealth in the world had not been able to save him from an untimely death at the hands of a murderer.

Walking to her car, Denise thought about the information that she had gathered after visiting the homes of the three victims. So far, the batons were her only link between them and a very weak one at that. Perhaps the FBI lab report on the four batons would provide the information she needed.

Glancing at her watch, Denise discovered that it was time for her to listen to the classical station as instructed in the note left on her desk. She turned on the car radio and settled into the seat. Perhaps the musical selection of the day would offer a clue to the murderer's identity.

As she drove toward the precinct, Denise listened to the

gentle sounds of symphonic music that seemed a fitting conclusion to an afternoon spent in the home of a deceased composer. Easing from the quiet neighborhood streets onto the congested main thoroughfares, she enjoyed the heavy strains of a Mozart requiem that seemed to be an appropriate eulogy for the victims. In her mind, she envisioned each one of them conducting the magnificent piece.

Rather abruptly and shockingly, the music changed from classical to show tunes as the emcee switched to a selection from a musical that promised a brighter tomorrow. Almost against her will, Denise felt the exquisite melancholy of the Scrolls lift from her shoulders. She was able to detach herself from the case and the grieving woman.

Humming to the music, Denise realized that the lyrics that played through her head carried a personal message, one directed at her by an outside source. Suddenly, she knew that the murderer was telling her that she had done all she could for the moment. The next day might provide more information and a clearer picture of the events that led up to the murders.

For a few minutes, Denise could not pull away from the intersection. Horns blared behind her as motorists impatient for home forgot to be polite. A few even switched lanes to pull around her car. Not one of them asked a woman alone if she needed help. They were all too focused on their own needs to think about hers.

Slowly pulling away from the stoplight, Denise marveled at the facility the murderer had shown in selecting the perfect music. Even without singers belting out the lyrics, the music was so familiar that she could hum almost every word. She knew the song by heart. It was almost ingrained in her soul, just as the Mozart requiem had been. Whenever she heard the selection from the well-loved music, it spoke to her about a future that promised more than the present had delivered. The murderer had made his selection well.

The lyrics echoing in her head told Denise that she had indeed done all she could until the murderer made his next move. She had conducted the appropriate interviews, gathered the batons as evidence, and learned little tidbits about the victims. Her FBI contact would find nothing that the murderer had not intended for him to discover. She knew the report would read that the batons were simply as they appeared . . . pieces of wood painted black with white tips with or without engravings.

Yet, Denise knew that they meant so much more. They might not have been the instruments of murder, but they were the murderer's signature just as clearly as the music contained his message. She had learned nothing truly substantive for her effort because he was not ready to share more with her. This murderer was adding batons to her collection just as the other one had added charms to a bracelet.

As the selection ended, Denise knew that tomorrow would be another day, and she would find more clues that might bring the pieces into focus. She only had to wait for the murderer to expose himself. Until then, she might as well go home and fix dinner for Tom.

Five

The sun shining through the window awakened Denise. She stretched her arms over her head and yawned contentedly. Max purred loudly and snuggled against her side. A good night's sleep always set the pace for the next day. As the energy coursed through her body, Denise knew that this would be a wonderful day.

The aroma of brewing coffee and toast drifted into the bedroom. Breathing deeply, Denise smiled and looked toward the empty pillow beside her. Cradling it, she inhaled Tom's aroma, the mixture of sleep and aftershave. She felt content as a woman always did after a night of sleeping in the arms of the man she loved.

"Coffee?" Tom asked, appearing in the doorway fully dressed in slacks and an open-neck shirt. He carried a tray containing two steaming mugs of coffee and plates of hot, buttered toast.

"Love some," Denise purred, stretching languidly again. "You've been busy this morning."

"That's more than I can say for you," Tom teased as he deposited the tray on the side of the bed he had vacated an hour earlier.

"I wouldn't still be in bed if you hadn't kept me awake so late," Denise replied with a sweet smile.

"We went to sleep late, if I remember correctly," Tom teased over the rim of his coffee mug.

"That didn't keep you from arising early and

demanding your morning delight," Denise replied with a smirk as she munched the abundantly buttered toast.

"I didn't realize that I had forced you into being an active participant in my morning exercises." Tom chuckled deeply. "You seemed rather energetic with only a few hours' sleep."

"Well, that's true," Denise teased as she ignored the blush that covered her cheeks. She was not quite as comfortable with their sleeping arrangements as Tom but she was learning to appreciate the benefits of their romantic partnership. "I was awake then anyway. Your snoring probably awakened the neighbors."

"You did your share of disturbing the peace, if I remember correctly." Tom beamed at their easy banter.

Wiping her fingers on the paper napkin Tom had provided, Denise replied, "Let's go to the Amish country. I need to interview Ms. Butler's family. We can spend the day and eat dinner there."

Collecting the dishes, Tom agreed. "Sounds good to me as long as I can bring Molly with us. She's about due for an outing."

Brushing the crumbs from her nightgown into the bedside trash can, Denise replied, "Fine, as long as she doesn't get in the way. I don't know why you're so attached to that big, slobbering beast."

As Denise walked toward the bathroom and a quick shower, Tom responded, "She's not slobbering. Shepherds don't slobber, and she's a great partner. She never makes demands on me and always understands when I'm late for dinner. You should try the canine corpse some time."

Poking her head from the bathroom, Denise retorted with a grin, "That's okay. I already have a slobbering beast for a partner. I don't need another."

"I don't slobber either," Tom growled with a chuckle. "I don't think the moisture on your pillow would support that statement," Denise commented as she closed the door and turned on the water.

Smiling, Tom returned the dishes to the kitchen while Denise took her shower. He considered joining her but thought better of it. Their relationship had just reached this new level of intimacy, and he did not want to take the chance of breaking the fragile thread. There would be plenty of time for leisurely showers in the days, months, and years to come in fact. Besides, he could read Denise like a book. Now that she was out of bed and on the move, she was all business. She would see a romantic interlude in the shower as a disruption to the flow of her day.

Denise appeared dressed in cream-colored slacks and a soft off-white silk sweater. She had brushed her freshly trimmed hair away behind her ears and added large gold earrings that hugged her face. Around her neck, she wore the gold necklace Tom had given her. As was her habit, her wrists were bare except for her watch. As expected, Tom had not noticed the very slight change in her hairdo.

"Ready when you are," Denise announced from the door with her briefcase hanging from her shoulder.

"Coming. I just need to straighten up a bit," Tom replied, as he and Molly exited the kitchen into the dining room.

The roomy living room and dining room combination seemed small with Tom standing in it. His habit of scattering the newspaper while reading it had left sections around the room. Discarded coffee cups from a morning of reading while she slept sat on every table. Molly's leash hung over the front doorknob. Tom's tennis shoes waited at the door, as he plodded along in his stocking feet. Denise noticed that everything changed when he visited, and she was glad it did. She liked the increased sense of relaxation that his presence provided. While she

waited, she reluctantly tidied the kitchen. She hated to
see the comfortable appearance of use vanish behind
cupboard doors.

"Ready," Tom stated, as he joined her at the kitchen
door.

Glancing past him, she saw that he had returned the living room to the pristine condition in which he had found
it. Sadly, the apartment no longer looked lived in. All signs
of their time together had vanished. Even Molly stood at
the door as if ready to close this episode in their lives.

Being familiar with the route, Denise drove the back
roads of Pennsylvania into Amish country while Tom
and Molly slept. She sang softly to the music that played
on the radio or glanced quickly at the passing countryside. She loved this section of the state and thrilled at the
road signs advertising towns with the quaint names of
Intercourse, Paradise, and Bird-in-Hand.

Along the route, shops selling antiques, hexes, food,
and treasures of the Amish country dotted the scenery.
If she had time, she would stop in Bird-in-Hand at one
of her favorite shops that sold intricately patterned
quilts. The last time Denise visited the area, she had purchased the quilt that lay on her bed. Its shades of rose
warmed her bedroom year-round.

The familiar aroma of cow manure blew through the
windows as soon as they entered the fertile farmland. Fat
ears of corn reached their silky tassels to the sky. Carefully tended barns, often painted red and trimmed in
white, dotted the landscape. Men and children dressed
in simple black and white garments worked in the fields
while the women toiled inside the houses.

The familiar Amish horse-drawn buggies slowed traffic to a crawl. Stern-faced children rested briefly from
their chores as the cars slowly passed. Horses stuck their
heads over fences and stared at the no longer menacing
intruders. With the exception of the visitors who pointed

and marveled at the change in lifestyle, all was sedate and quiet.

Tom and Molly, fresh from their naps, looked out the window at the old-fashioned communities that refused to allow the new ways to interfere with the old. Occasionally, Molly would growl or bark at the cows in the pastures. Tom appeared less than impressed by the aroma that pervaded the area despite Denise's explanation of the wonderful produce they would enjoy because of it.

"I'm hungry," Tom stated, as they passed yet another restaurant despite the cloying manure smell.

"It's all in your mind," Denise rebutted with a chuckle.

"No, it's in my stomach. You should hear this growling. Feed me!" Tom repeated, pointing across the road to the family-style restaurant.

Stopping the car in the parking lot of one of the most well known of the Amish country restaurants, Denise looked at Tom and smiled. He was so like a child in some ways and very much the man in others. She found the combination very endearing.

While Denise waited, Tom fed Molly and then took her into the woods behind the restaurant for a brief walk. When they returned, the dog settled into the backseat while they wandered through the stores and into the restaurant. Stopping along the way to buy a shoofly pie at the bakery, Tom was indeed a happy man. Despite his denial of his love of them, these sticky sweet pies were his favorite. Denise, however, preferred pecan, and, while he was not looking, she purchased one for the office, if it survived that long. She stashed both in the cooler she had brought for the purpose of keeping the treats away from Molly's drooling mouth.

Their lunch was delicious and so plentiful that both agreed that they would not need anything for dinner except a slice of pie and a cup of coffee. The restaurant's smorgasbord contained artfully arranged meats, vegetables, breads, and salads. In another section, desserts ranging from cakes to pies to ice cream filled glass-front refrigerated cabinets.

Carrying overflowing plates, they managed to find a table for two in the corner. Cutting into the succulent meats from which oozed flavorful juices, they ate with gusto. Tom, who loved good food, appeared enraptured by the combination of spices. Denise, a picky eater, wondered if she could be able to get a doggy bag to carry the remainder of the food home with them. Both admitted that, even if they did not have interviews to conduct, the food compensated for the lengthy drive.

Neither spoke during the meal. Denise was busily composing the questions she would ask during her interview of Ms. Butler's family, while Tom was happily submerged in mashed potatoes and gravy, beets with orange sauce, prime rib au jus, and butter-laden biscuits. He was planning his pending assault on the turkey with all the trimmings and the chocolate cream pie that he had seen in the dessert area.

By the time they had completed the feast, the afternoon sun was casting lengthy shadows on the cornfields. Consulting her watch, Denise saw that they needed to leave immediately for Ms. Butler's sister's farmhouse a few miles down the main road. As she drove, Tom slumped in his seat. He was so full that he could not keep his eyes open and was asleep before they even left the parking lot. His snoring joined the sound of the tires on the road as they continued their journey.

The farmhouse sat in the middle of a dense field of corn. According to information that Ronda had prepared for Denise, Ms. Butler's sister, Ria Martin, was one of the few blacks who lived in the quiet Amish area. She had once been an attorney in New York City, but she had decided to trade her law practice and city life for the rural setting when her last child had graduated from college.

Her husband had willingly agreed that the country life would suit him just fine after a busy career as a corporate attorney. They had sold all of their sophisticated city-slicker furniture and moved to the country, purchasing the items they needed to furnish the new home when they arrived. According to a major architectural magazine, their efforts at remodeling and redecorating the house had produced a rustic showplace.

Pulling in front of the house by way of the circular driveway, Denise marveled at the remarkable display of plants and flowers. The manure-enriched soil produced the largest red blooms she had ever seen on plants that accentuated the white-brick rambler perfectly. The chickens pecking in the side yard added character and authenticity to the farm setting.

As if waiting for them, Mrs. Martin appeared at the door holding a tray as Denise and Tom climbed the steps. Extending her hand, she suggested that they take tea on the front porch so that they might enjoy the perfect weather. Reluctant to sit inside on such a lovely day, Denise willingly agreed.

Taking the offered seat, Denise starting the interview by asking, "When was the last time you saw your sister?"

"Two weeks ago," Mrs. Martin answered as she thoughtfully stirred her tea. "My husband and I drove to Philadelphia to hear her play a guest performance with their orchestra. She was a wonderful violinist . . . one of the best. We'll miss her very much and so will the music world."

"Did she mention any concerns or fears she might have felt for her safety?" Denise inquired as she alternated between sketching Mrs. Martin and the surroundings and sipping the delicious tea.

Speaking without hesitation, Mrs. Martin replied, "No, she was very happy . . . content professionally and planning a trip to England at the end of this month. She had been invited to play a concert in London. My sister was not only the first chair in the orchestra, she was an accomplished soloist."

"How was her social life?" Tom asked as he shifted in the wicker chair in an attempt to find a comfortable spot. He was still uncomfortably full from lunch.

Shaking her head, Mrs. Martin stated, "Sylvia had been seeing a lovely man for many years, but the relationship ended when he died a few months ago. She was quite upset by the loss and threw herself into her work with more than the usual enthusiasm. She enjoyed her freedom too much to marry, but being with Mike was one of the highlights of her life. We all miss him. They often drove up for the weekend. Both of them loved the serenity of the farm although neither ever would have been content to live here. I just couldn't see my sister collecting eggs and feeding the chickens."

Studying Mrs. Martin's grieving face, Denise asked solemnly, "Can you think of anyone who would have wanted to hurt her? Any rival who would have wanted her out of the way?"

"As I told your secretary when she phoned to arrange our meeting, I can think of absolutely no one. If you drove all this distance thinking that I might be able to help in that way, you've wasted your time," Mrs. Martin replied confidently. "As proof, I'll show you the collection of cards and telegrams we've received since Sylvia's death. I've saved all of them for the scrapbook I've kept of her life since we were kids. I have clippings, announcements, and programs that follow her amateur career and highlight her professional one. I can think of no one who carried a grudge against my sister."

"Are you saying that none of her colleagues harbored even the slightest jealousy about her success?" Tom asked, placing his cup on the heavily laden tray.

"That's right, Detective," Mrs. Martin responded

firmly. "I'm not foolish enough to think that everyone loved my sister, but I can't think of anyone who disliked her to the point of murder. What would anyone have to gain . . . a chair in the orchestra? Sylvia had already submitted her resignation from the symphony and was planning a world tour as a soloist. Mike's death both hit her hard and liberated her. She was free to travel and tour. It's a hard life, but one that she wanted to try."

"While I was searching her apartment, I found a conductor's baton on the floor," Denise stated casually as she tried to ease the tension. Mrs. Martin very clearly resented any thought that someone might have disliked her sister. "Was Ms. Butler planning to conduct as well as play?"

"Goodness, yes!" Mrs. Martin exclaimed. "For a long time now, Sylvia has done both. She was a very multi-talented musician. She composed and often directed nationally recognized orchestras in playing her original pieces. That's why I said that the music world would miss her. Sylvia contributed so much to the genre. I'm hoping the similarity between Sylvia's death and that of the other musicians is only superficial. If not, I hope you'll find the murderer quickly, Detective. We need closure."

Denise realized that their interview had come to a close. Easing her sketchbook into her bag, she rose and looked at the cornfields. Turning to Mrs. Martin, Denise stated, "You have a lovely home. It must have been a drastic change from the city."

"It was, but a very welcome one," Mrs. Martin replied, as she accompanied them to their car. "See that man on the tractor? That's my city-slicker husband. His cholesterol and blood pressure have dropped considerably since we moved here. He's under so little pressure, and life is so much slower. It's the best decision we've ever made. Good luck, Detectives, and good-bye."

Mrs. Martin vanished into the house as they drove

down the driveway. Only the sound of Mr. Martin's tractor and the occasional dog barking broke the silence. Denise could easily understand the attraction of the countryside. Maybe one day, it would be the place for her, too.

"What do you think?" Denise asked Tom, as she maneuvered the car into the flow of traffic on the main street leading from the small town.

"I think you've got a difficult case here, Dory," Tom replied, as he watched the last of the town vanish into the countryside.

With a sigh, Denise replied, "I sure don't have much information. No motive unless it's greed. No murder weapon unless the FBI finds something on the batons. No clues to the suspect's identity unless the radio selections lead me to something. This might prove to be the most difficult case of my career."

"The FBI won't be of much help on this one," Tom added, as they zipped along the main highway leading back to the Washington area.

"Why do you say that?" Denise inquired with a quick glance in his direction.

"I phoned our contact before we left the restaurant," Tom disclosed slowly. "He says that the batons were clean. No residue of any of the known poisons or harmful chemicals. He even checked the more obscure ones, knowing that your cases often lead down paths seldom traveled by others. He found nothing."

"Then I'll have to hope for clues from the murderer. He's bound to offer something that I can use," Denise replied thoughtfully.

"Either that or he'll strike again," Tom commented, looking out the window.

"He already has," Denise stated dryly.

"What? How do you know?" Tom sputtered in confusion.

"I have a cell phone, too, you know," Denise replied with a lift of her eyebrows. "While I was in the restaurant bathroom, I phoned Ronda to see if anyone had called us. The chief had left a message that another musician, this time a local country western singer, had fallen at the hands of a murderer. I guess that's what the murderer meant when he said that I'd learn more tomorrow. I had thought that he meant that the interviews would provide information. His clue meant that another musician would join his list of victims."

"Who was it this time?" Tom asked with a shake of his head. Denise never failed to amaze him. She was always one step ahead of him.

"His name was Adam Fraser," Denise responded. "He's a local to the Washington area. He attended private schools all of his life, an Ivy League college, and a pricey conservatory. He's been a star in the country arena for a long time. His fiancée found him dead on the floor in his bedroom. Ronda says he lived in Old Towne, Kensington, in one of those old, but very expensive, condos formed from renovated warehouses. She mentioned that one of his most famous songs had something to do with bugs on a windshield. Ever hear of him?"

"Not really. Country's not exactly my thing," Tom grumbled with his usual disdain for any music outside his chosen preference.

"Mine either, but I've asked Ronda for a few of his CDs so that, when I interview his significant other tomorrow, I'll know something about him," Denise replied, studying the road sign at the fork.

"Go right," Tom interjected, knowing that Denise's sense of direction extended to arriving at a location but did not cover returning from it. As they merged with the traffic on the interstate, he asked, "Significant other?"

"Yeah. He lived alone but had a steady girlfriend of

many years who was also his music partner. This should make for an interesting interview," Denise stated with a bit of a smile.

"Girlfriend? You're using the term now, too, I see," Tom teased gruffly.

"I still don't like it, but there doesn't seem to be any other choice." Denise chuckled almost unwillingly.

"That's what I've been saying. No one has thought of the term for mature relationships. Everyone seems to think that love stops with high school graduation," Tom commented as he switched on the radio.

"When did you turn so sentimental on me?" Denise laughed as she followed the road that led homeward.

Huffing, Tom replied, "That's not being sentimental; it's stating a fact. Love gets better with age. I was a nervous, pimple-faced kid who could barely speak to the object of my first crush. Every time I saw her, I tried to hide. I nearly peed on myself more than once. She hardly noticed me anyway, so I don't know why I went to all the trouble."

"Why, Tom," Denise exclaimed teasingly, "this is the first time you've mentioned ever being vulnerable."

"Keep it up, Dory, and it'll be the last," Tom grumbled although his voice barely concealed a chuckle.

"Tell me more," Denise said encouragingly as she lightly patted his hand.

"There isn't much more to tell, and that's my point," Tom responded, tightening his grip on her free hand. "It's true that love's wasted on the young. It's so much better once you gain a little self-confidence."

"At our age, you mean?" Denise queried, appearing to fish for terms of endearment . . . or commitment.

"Sure," Tom growled with a nod. "Just look at us. We understand each other completely. We're not shy about discussing anything. We're a perfect team."

"I suppose love will only get better as we mature a bit more," Denise continued with a lightness in her voice.

"That's right," Tom concluded. "After we've been together for a few years, we'll be a real unit then. We'll be inseparable . . . two peas in one nice cozy little pod."

Pulling into the main street leading to Tom's apartment complex, Denise asked with a little tease in her voice, "What kind of togetherness do you have in mind? Are you talking about our professional team only getting better with age?"

"Dory, for a crack detective you can really be dense sometimes," Tom growled with his hand on the car door. "I'm talking about us, our personal relationship."

"Oh," Denise replied. "You're right. We'll be even better best friends after a few years."

Shaking his head at her apparent hopelessness, Tom replied, "I mean, Denise, that after we've been happily married for a while, we'll be a complete unit. Geez, woman, do I have to spell everything out for you?"

"Yes, when it comes to this topic you do," Denise stated, as she leaned over for a kiss.

"Get out of the car," Tom ordered, ignoring the inviting pucker of her lips and walking around to the driver's side.

Shutting off the ignition, Denise obeyed. As she stepped from the vehicle, Tom's strong arms pulled her toward him and enfolded her against his chest. His lips burned hungrily on hers as he expressed his feelings for her in a way that Denise could understand completely.

Looking into her eyes, Tom asked, "Do you understand me now, Dory? I love you and want us to get married one day."

"Do you have any particular day in mind?" Denise demanded, as she stepped away from him slightly. He knew her well enough to sense from the tensing of her face that Denise did not appreciate the hedging on this particular subject.

"Soon. Once we've gotten to know each other a little better," Tom replied with an uncertain half smile.

"Let me know when you think we know each other well enough to get married," Denise commented, as she slammed the car door. "Until then, I have work to do."

"Wait, Denise, you're taking that the wrong way!" Tom protested over the roar of the engine.

Putting the car in drive, Denise replied, "No, I'm not. I understood you perfectly. I'll let you know which day of which year is clear on my calendar, too. Maybe we can schedule a moment to visit the justice of the peace. See you at work on Monday."

"Dory, wait! Let me explain!" Tom shouted, as she pulled from the parking lot and into the flow of traffic.

Remembering their big argument in New York while on the designer murder case, Tom muttered in frustration to himself as he and Molly climbed the steps to his lonely apartment. Unlocking the door, he surveyed the silence that greeted him. If Denise had come in, she would have filled the room with laughter instead of the lingering smell of old carryout from two nights ago.

"When will I ever learn, Molly?" Tom asked, as he stroked the dog's head. "I step in it all the time. Every time I try to tell Dory how I feel about her, I mess it up. There goes the weekend. I even bought tickets to the symphony as a surprise. What a dope!"

Looking into his sad eyes, Molly seemed to understand. She licked his hand sympathetically and pressed her large, sturdy body against his. Thumping her heavy tail, Molly telegraphed her belief in him, as Tom stared helplessly out the window. He did not even remember that he had left his pie in her car.

Denise drove home without seeing any of the landscape that she usually enjoyed. She could not quite decide if she felt angry because Tom had not proposed or because he had not given her the chance to say that she needed time to think about it. He had not asked her and had given the reason that she might have expected. He had been too logical. Somehow, it did not seem fair that he had robbed her of the opportunity to ask for more time.

As she stepped into her apartment with the heavy cooler in her arms, the aroma of leftover coffee greeted her. Denise felt the warmth of a distant memory begin to wash over her, making her feel safe and comfortable. Only that morning, she had awakened to Tom's presence in her apartment. The previous night, they had shared a bed and their bodies. She would have to share her bed with Max, the cat, that night.

Kicking off her shoes, Denise walked into the kitchen, lugging the heavy cooler with her. Lifting the lid, she broke into gales of laughter at the sight of Tom's pie sitting abandoned at the bottom of her cooler. Barely able to compose herself, she transferred it to the refrigerator. It would keep until Monday.

Although she was not hungry, the pecan pie gave off a tempting aroma. Taking a plate from the cupboard, she cut a large slice and bit into it without waiting to find a fork. The pie melted in her mouth, as she padded toward the living room. Turning on the CD, Denise sank into the sofa and listened to the sound of three black tenors who sang everything from classical to gospel to jazz to show tunes. Max, her cat, joined her and sat on the back of the sofa.

Caught up in the music, Denise did not at first hear the telephone. Rising slowly, she walked to the kitchen on tired feet. Taking another bite of the pie, she answered the phone and waited.

"I'm sorry," Tom's voice said simply and without preamble.

"Don't worry about it," Denise replied around the

mouthful of pecan pie. "I feel the same way. You just didn't give me the chance to say it."

"We're still okay, then?" Tom asked hesitantly.

"Sure. Nothing can come between us. Just next time, give a girl a chance to turn you down or to ask for time to think it over," Denise stated gently.

"What's that you're eating?" Tom asked lightly, trying to match the tone of their conversation.

"Shoofly pie," Denise responded seriously.

"No, you're not. It's that pecan pie you bought," Tom replied with a chuckle.

"How'd you know that I bought one?" Denise demanded midchew.

Chuckling deeply, Tom replied, "I went back to the shop to buy one for you, but the clerk told me that you'd already beaten me to it."

"That just shows that we are a good couple. You want us to grow fat together." Denise laughed happily.

"Not fat but certainly old," Tom replied softly.

"I'll remember that when I step on the scale tomorrow morning," Denise commented and then added, "Good night."

"Good night, Dory," Tom replied and almost hung up the phone before remembering the tickets. "Dory, wait!"

"What?"

"I bought tickets for the symphony for tonight. Do you want to go?" Tom asked tentatively.

"That's sweet, Tom. I know how much the thought cost you. You'd prefer a root canal to the symphony." Denise melted, leaning against the counter. "I'm too tired, and it's too late for me to shower and dress. We'd miss too much of the music. I'd love to go with you. Exchange them for another night."

"Okay, I'll try for next week. See you tomorrow? Maybe we could ride bikes in the park," Tom offered happily.

"Sounds good to me," Denise replied with a stretch. "I'll meet you at the mill at noon. I'll be the one with the shoofly pie in the picnic hamper."

"Very funny, Dory. See you tomorrow. Good night," Tom concluded with a chuckle, as he hung up.

Denise smiled happily, as she turned her attention to the dirty plate. After washing the plate and setting it on the drain board to dry, she sank into the sofa again. Although tired from the day, she was not in the least bit sleepy. Selecting a book from the table beside the sofa, she began to read. Although she loved having Tom with her, she enjoyed the silence almost as much. Perhaps he was right; each of them needed to grow more before settling down together. Until then, a book, music, and Max provided ample company.

Six

Margaret Dell opened the door to Adam Fraser's apartment on the first ring of the bell. She had clearly been waiting for Denise to arrive. Motioning her inside with a sad smile, Margaret disappeared into the kitchen for sodas, allowing Denise to experience the loft-style apartment alone. However, she reappeared so quickly that Denise had only begun the effort.

The penthouse apartment was massive with ornate furnishings, watercolors and oils, priceless statues, and abundant numbers of plants. Peeking around pillars and potted plants, Denise saw that every table held an antique or a first-edition book. The atmosphere of the huge loft gave off a lived-in quality although the living room and dining room spaces did not look as if anyone had ever used them. The kitchen also sparkled as if new. The condo looked as if it were waiting for new inhabitants rather than welcoming old ones home. Accepting the soda, Denise allowed Ms. Dell to escort her around the apartment.

"How long had Mr. Fraser lived here, Ms. Dell?" Denise inquired, as she gazed out the window at the view of the park across the street.

"Since the building opened, I believe," Ms. Dell replied softly. "Adam was one of the first owners of these condos."

"Had he recently redecorated? Everything looks so

fresh," Denise commented, as she peered behind a painting in search of dust or telltale shadow on the wall.

With a melancholy chuckle, Ms. Dell responded, "Oh, yes, just last month. We were planning to be married soon and thought the place needed a little sprucing up before I moved in. He only returned the day before he died. I guess that was a waste of paint. He arranged for the decorator to change everything while he was on tour last month. It looks great, doesn't it? The furniture still smells new."

"I understand that you two were partners. Do you live near here?" Denise asked, as she followed Ms. Dell down the hall that led to the bedrooms, the only enclosed spaces in the condo.

Opening the last of the two guest room doors, Ms. Dell stated without emotion, "My condo is on the third floor. When I first moved in here, I couldn't afford a penthouse. I wasn't a celebrity like Adam. Thanks to our collaboration, I'm much more financially solvent now, although I don't plan to stay here. I'll move as soon as I can sell my condo and find another. Too many memories."

"How long were you partners?" Denise asked, as she took note of the tastefully furnished bedroom with its reading corner complete with wing chair and adjustable lighting.

"We've worked together for ten years," Ms. Dell replied without hesitation. "We've been romantically involved for about two years now. I guess both of those have ended now."

"I understand that it's often difficult to work with a romantic partner. Did the romance affect your professional life?" Denise asked, as she peered into the bedroom used as a television room. A massive entertainment center occupied the bulk of one wall while an incredibly inviting sectional welcomed visitors on the other.

"I wouldn't say that it has," Ms. Dell stated without

pausing to reflect. "I think our relationship was very comfortable. We had no feeling of competition. We were true collaborators. At first, Adam's reputation drew people to us, but, after a while, they started noticing that he was singing new material. That's when my work really began to take off. Many singers had recorded my lyrics, but I'd only made a comfortable living. Adam's voice, charisma, music, and ability to work an audience gave my lyrics a greater public acceptance. I couldn't have asked for more."

They continued the tour in silence as Denise reflected on the woman's rapid responses. She remembered that Ronda had said that the couple had recently been highlighted in all the magazines, both for the professional accomplishments and their successful personal life and upcoming marriage. Denise supposed that Ms. Dell had responded to so many questions for the articles that she was perfectly comfortable with more. Besides, the police had undoubtedly interviewed her the previous day as soon as she discovered Mr. Fraser's body.

The police tape glistened in the sunlight that streamed through the French doors as Denise stepped into the master bedroom. The report read that Ms. Dell had found Mr. Fraser's body after their lunchtime break. She had let herself into the condo as usual and gone directly to the music room. When Mr. Fraser did not appear shortly afterward, she went to check on him. Finding him lying on the floor, she had promptly phoned the police. He was pronounced dead on arrival at the hospital from unknown causes. According to the press, their manager had escorted a distraught Ms. Dell home whereupon her physician had prescribed medication for her nerves.

Walking around the tape silhouette, Denise opened the door to one of the two closets in the room. Tuxedos lined one side and kept company with business suits, sport jackets, and leisure clothing. Everything hung neatly while the shoes occupied shelves along the back. Mr. Fraser had arranged his shirts in order of formality with evening attire on one side and more casual wear on the other. No one had disturbed the order of the closet.

As Denise reached for the knob for the other closet, Ms. Dell stated flatly, "That one's empty. It was to hold my clothes."

Giving the knob a gentle pull, Denise opened the door. Ms. Dell gasped when she saw that women's clothing hung in the supposedly empty closet. Denise stepped aside and waited patiently for her to explain.

Looking completely shocked and much less bereaved, Ms. Dell stated indignantly, "That's not my stuff. I haven't moved anything into Adam's condo."

Stepping into the walk-in closet, Denise separated the clothing by carefully touching the hangers with her gloved hand. The red satin, size-ten evening gown with spaghetti straps hung next to a big white silk shirt that occupied the hanger next to the black leather slim-legged slacks. On the floor rested a pair of size-eight red satin dyed-to-match heels and a pair of fuzzy pink high-heel slippers. To Denise, it appeared either that Adam Fraser was a cross-dresser or he had a woman living with him who was not his fiancée and business partner. Considering that the autopsy report had indicated that he was a man of slightly above average size and certainly not a woman's size ten, she quickly put the transsexual angle from her mind.

Looking at Ms. Dell, Denise waited until the speechless woman could regain her composure. As if in response, tears trickled soundlessly down the young woman's face as the seeming reality of her relationship with Adam Fraser became clear. Much to Margaret Dell's anger and bewilderment, she was not the only partner whose company Adam Fraser enjoyed.

Sinking into the nearby chaise longue, Ms. Dell sputtered, as the tears washed tracks in her makeup, "I can't believe that Adam would do a thing like this. If he wanted someone else, we could have discussed the change in our relationship like mature people. I would have been heartbroken, but I would have stepped aside. He didn't have to let me find out this way, after he's dead. If he didn't love me anymore, he should have been man enough to say something."

Feeling very uncomfortable with the situation but needing to ask questions, Denise cleared her throat and inquired, "Is there any chance that there's another possibility? Could Mr. Fraser have used this outfit in his show? Might he have been storing the outfits for someone in his backup group?"

At first Ms. Dell only looked at Denise through miserably unhappy, tear-blurred eyes. She could only move her lips soundlessly. Then, suddenly, the grieving fiancée bust into uncontrollable laughter that shook her entire body. The tears of bewilderment mixed with those of hilarity as Denise watched the transformation and feared for the woman's sanity.

Reaching for yet another tissue from the box on the table next to the cream-colored chaise, Ms. Dell chortled, "That's too funny. Thank you, Detective. I needed that. You must not ever have attended any of our concerts. Adam only surrounded himself with young, thin, teenagers. No one in his backup group ever would have selected an outfit of that level of sophistication. Those girls are into belly button piercing and low-hung pants."

As Ms. Dell fell into convulsive laughter once again, Denise scanned the bedroom for photos of the couple. Finding none in the newly redecorated apartment, she stood patiently and waited for the obviously overcome young woman to compose herself. Gradually, the woman sat up and turned her attention to Denise.

Shaking her head sadly while she rolled the wet tissues into a tidy ball, Ms. Dell stated, "I'm sorry to have reacted that way, Detective, but Adam was definitely having an affair. He wasn't at all attracted to women with womanly shapes, or so I thought. He always watched every morsel of food that entered my mouth. Eating with him was like attending a diet seminar. The only time I enjoyed my food was while away from him and then I still couldn't eat with gusto. I was always afraid of putting on pounds. The monthly bloat was a real killer. No, Adam was cheating on me. I'm certain of it since I wear a size six. And to think that rat was cheating on me with a woman with boobs! Well, now I know that he liked his women with a less boyish shape. Too bad he didn't let me know sooner."

"I'm sorry, Ms. Dell," Denise consoled, feeling genuinely tender toward the woman who had lost the man she loved to death and another woman in a matter of days. "It was not my intent to inflict any more pain on you."

"Don't worry, Detective. I knew the moment you opened the closet and I saw those clothes that Adam was cheating on me. I think I've known for quite some time but was too blind or too busy for the reality to sink in. This find only proves it. You actually provided a moment of levity," Ms. Dell stated with a brave smile.

"Do you have any idea who the other woman might have been?" Denise asked, as she watched Ms. Dell rise and close the closet door as if wanting to cover Adam Fraser's unfaithfulness once more.

Leading the way to the living room, Ms. Dell replied sarcastically, "Sure, there were many women who wanted Adam and had the opportunity to have an affair with him. Any one of our female associates could have fallen to his considerable charms. I can think of a few female performers who definitely had the hots for him. He

seemed unimpressed by their attention. He always said
that they were too substantive for his tastes. Liar!"

"Do you think you could provide any names?" Denise
asked, as she sketched the woman's profile.

Straightening her spine and sitting more upright, Ms.
Dell replied, "No. The list would be too long. We have a
fairly long list of groupies who throw everything from
bouquets of flowers to hotel keys, panties, and bras with
phone numbers attached. Both of our telephone numbers are unlisted, but the fans always manage to discover
them. As soon as our engagement became public knowledge, I received threatening calls from jealous women
who wanted me out of Adam's life. I've changed my
number a few times to stop them. Adam has received
phone invitations to dinner, a mild call by the usual standards, to orgies, to marriage. You name it and amorous
fans have offered it. Any one of them might have se-
duced him or he could have wandered on his own.
There's no way of knowing."

"Is it possible that a business associate might have
stepped out of line and become involved with him?"
Denise inquired in what appeared to be a desperate attempt at finding a likely suspect.

"Sure," Ms. Dell replied with a crocked smile. "We
fired our publicist a few months ago because she became
too involved in Adam. She started taking him to dinner
without me, sending him theater tickets, and calling him
under the pretense of discussing business. She was totally taken by him, but I don't think she would have
killed him. I know those aren't her clothes in the closet.
She's really petite."

Hoping to elicit more information, Denise stated,
"Someone claiming to be the murderer has contacted
me at the precinct. His . . . or her . . . note said that I
would learn clues to his identity from a certain radio station's broadcast. So far, I've learned nothing. Do you

think that it's possible that Mr. Fraser's most recent recordings might contain a clue?"

"Not hardly, because I write all of the lyrics for his songs. Since we formed our partnership, I've been his exclusive lyricist. I even sing backup in his group when I'm not too busy writing, which happens less now that he's won a Grammy or two," Ms. Dell replied with confidence. Her expression quickly changed as she remembered something and added, "You might be on to something, Detective. On his last solo concert, Adam introduced a piece that he had written alone . . . music and lyrics."

"Do you have a copy handy?" Denise asked, as she grasped at one more unrelated piece of the puzzle.

"Sure do," Ms. Dell stated, as she rose and straightened her tall, thin figure. "I wasn't too pleased that Adam would go solo, but he claimed that he had written the words for me as an early wedding gift. I wonder if he really wrote this song for Miss Size Ten. Give me a minute, and I'll get it for you. It's in the file cabinet over there."

Denise watched as Ms. Dell opened the top file drawer and immediately found the song in question. She slipped something under her arm before stepping to the copier. Gazing out the window, she pressed the button and waited as the bright light flashed in her face, producing the copy. For an instant, Denise saw a glimmer of anger appear again on the woman's face. Ms. Dell appeared almost happy to assist Denise in learning the identity of Adam Fraser's lover and possible murderer.

Slipping the sheet of paper into an envelope, Ms. Dell returned to the sofa. Extending her hand, she said, "This is certainly a day for surprises. This wasn't Adam's either. Someone must have given it to him on this last trip, but I can't imagine who it would have been. People in our set don't use conductors' batons too often, hardly ever actually unless they're playing around. Wait a minute. I remember that Adam was a guest conductor of the National Symphony Orchestra once. They were performing a night of country music and invited him to join them. He really enjoyed it, if I remember correctly. I'd almost forgotten about it. He used Leonard Slatkin's baton that night. He didn't own one."

"Did he come home with one?" Denise asked, as she slipped on her gloves.

"Not that I remember. I think he returned it. I've never seen that one, but then, I hadn't seen the contents of that closet either," Ms. Dell added with a sad little twist of her mouth that might have passed for a smile.

Taking the baton in her gloved hand, Denise commented, as she dropped it into an evidence bag, "It carries the same mark as the others. I'll have the lab take a look at it. I've found similar ones at the other murder scenes. It looks as if someone wants me to see a connection."

"Keep it with my compliments. I don't want it back although I suppose that my fingerprints are all over it now. Oh, well, I'll gladly come to the precinct if you'd like to collect a full set," Ms. Dell responded quickly as she watched the careful detective.

"We'll call you if we need you, but I doubt that'll be necessary, Denise stated as they walked down the hall together.

"Good luck in solving this case and the others, too," Ms. Dell offered. "I'll continue to think about likely suspects, possible candidates for the title of Miss Size Ten. You'll never know how much your visit has helped me, Detective. I'm a woman on a mission now, not a grieving future widow. I'd like to know who killed him especially if it's the same person who was beating my time. Huh, sounds like a song title, doesn't it?"

"Thanks. Again, I'm very sorry for intruding and for the discovery," Denise replied as she took one last look around the freshly redecorated apartment that still possessed a slight smell of paint.

"Think nothing of it, Detective," Ms. Dell responded, as she locked the door and walked Denise to the elevator. "We might just have collaborated to help you solve a case and me to write new award-winning lyrics and to enjoy my meals more fully."

"What'll you do next?" Denise asked as the two women rode to the lobby entrance of the converted warehouse.

With a sad smile, Ms. Dell stated, "I might write a new song, find a new partner, or take a much-needed vacation. I might just take that honeymoon trip to Tahiti, minus the groom of course. I don't know. I have so many choices now that I'm not going to become Mrs. Adam Fraser. I wonder if I would have been the first in a series of wives for Adam. It's possible that Miss Size Ten wasn't Adam's first fling. I was blind to this one; I might have missed other signs, too. Since he had pretty much gotten away with this one, he might have been quite experienced at it or at least planning to try again."

"One thing's bothering me, Ms. Dell," Denise interjected as the elevator stopped on Ms. Dell's floor. "Why did he hang Miss Size Ten's clothes in your side of the closet? It doesn't make sense with you living downstairs and the date of your wedding coming so soon."

With outstretched hands, Ms. Dell replied, "He probably thought that I wouldn't find out. You see, I was supposed to be in Hollywood until the day before the wedding. I was working on an album with another of my regular collaborators while Adam was on his solo tour. I hadn't called to say that I was coming home since I wanted to surprise him. I arrived in time to brief him on my trip before breaking for lunch. Since I had so much unpacking to do, we didn't have an afternoon session or eat dinner together. I didn't see him again until the next morning when I discovered him dead.

"It was a surprise, all right . . . a surprise on me. If I hadn't finished my work early and returned a day ahead of schedule, Adam would have had time to clean out the closet. I never would have found out about her. I would have gone into marriage without ever knowing that the man I loved had cheated on me at least until one of my 'friends' felt it her duty to enlighten me. They always do, don't they? In a strange sort of way, your murderer did me a favor and saved me a lot of embarrassment and heartache."

"The police report stated that Mr. Fraser had been dead for at least eight hours before you found the body. Did anyone else have a key?" Denise inquired as she pressed the door-open button on the elevator door.

Shaking her head sadly, Ms. Dell replied with a touch of sadness returning to her face and voice, "I'm not the one to ask about that, Detective, since I didn't know that another woman existed in my fiancé's life. All kinds of people could have had keys. I thought that Adam, the super, and I were the only ones, but you never know. The only thing I know with any certainty at the moment is that the super always let the painter and the redecorators into the apartment himself."

"Well, thanks again. If you think of anything, give me a call," Denise commented as she handed Ms. Dell her card with one hand and released the elevator with another.

"I'll do that, Detective, and hope you'll do the same if you find out anything about Miss Size Ten," Ms. Dell replied with a wave as the doors closed.

The Old Towne Kensington neighborhood was bustling with cars and pedestrians as Denise stepped into the flow of humanity. Before going home, she wanted to visit a music store that she had spotted near the Torpedo Factory. Maybe the proprietor could shed a little light on music in general and the case in particular.

Although Old Towne was famous for its quaint atmosphere, Denise had not expected to step back in time simply by entering one of the many shops along its cobbled streets. However, as she entered Ye Olde Musik Shoppe, Denise felt as if she should don a hoop skirt and white lace cap. The shop with its dark-paneled walls, brass-arm chandeliers, and brass cash register looked like something from Dickens or at the very least Twain. The proprietor was appropriately dressed in billowing white shirt, waistcoat, buckle shoes, and cravat. Even if she learned nothing that would help her on the case, she would certainly enjoy spending time in the shop.

"May I help you? I am Joshua Smithe, the owner of this establishment, at your service," the proprietor said, peering over the pince-nez spectacles perched on the end of his nose and bowing at the waist.

From the amount of dust that had settled on them, Denise doubted that he needed them for vision. However, they were a nice touch to complete the period outfit. Besides, the man could not have been over twenty-five, standing tall and trim and ready to assist her.

"I'd like a quick lesson on conductors' batons," Denise replied as she pointed toward the cases of them that hung on the far wall.

"Gladly. I have very little opportunity to expound on their virtues these days since most of my clientele wants to purchase CDs and music videos," Joshua Smithe replied stiffly with all the formality of the period that he imitated so well, leading the way to the far cabinets. Turning toward her, he continued in more modern vernacular, "What'd ya like to know?"

"I'd like to know about their woods, their construction, and, I suppose, their use," Denise responded, stifling a laugh as she glanced quickly from the batons, to the file cabinets filled with sheet music, to the rows of tables holding CDs and music videos, and then back to the young man in the period costume.

"Wow!" Smithe exclaimed. "You've made my day. I haven't had anyone ask for specifics on these in at least six months. Most of the conductors who come in here already know the one they want to buy. As a matter of fact, I hadn't sold any until about six weeks ago. A guy came in here all dressed in black. He looked like a character from an old movie or *The Phantom of the Opera.* Anyway, he purchased a dozen of the basic model but didn't say why he wanted them. I didn't pry either . . . a sale's a sale."

Frowning slightly, Denise asked, "Can you show me the one he bought? And then I'd like to hear about the others."

"Sure," Smithe agreed with a grin. "That's easy. It's that little dark-wood-handled model on the end. I have tons of them. They're actually the most common model. Music students buy those from me, when I sell any. Like I said, I hadn't sold any for months until the Phantom bought those."

Taking the offered baton from his hand, Denise commented, "I'm a police detective doing a little investigative work for a case. This baton looks exactly like one left behind at a murder scene. As a matter of fact, it matches the one in my briefcase. If the customer returns, please give me a call."

"Sure, will do. I'm not surprised at the similarity," Smithe stated frankly. "We're the only shop in the area. That's what makes it so easy for me to remember strange-looking customers. The next closest one is in Baltimore or the Internet. Come to think of it, our business has fallen off since a few of the famous baton manufacturers started offering their product on-line."

Indicating the more pricey batons in the case, Denise inquired, "Can you think of any way to differentiate one of these from a model just like it?"

"No, not unless your lab can trace hand oils," Smithe replied with a shake of his head. "All of the models in the line that you're holding are exactly the same—same weight, same balance, same color. These others here have different woods for the handles, but they're balanced appropriately for their type, too. There's really nothing to differentiate any of them. It's not until you get to the custom-made jobbies that you get the individual attention."

Remembering the Hornblatt collection, Denise stated, "I just saw a fabulous collection of engraved, bejeweled batons. Probably handmade, right?"

"This industry isn't exactly what you'd think," Smithe began as he leaned against the magnificent wood of the cabinet. "That mass-market model you're holding was not handcrafted, but almost all of the others are. As a matter of fact, I can't think of any of the better ones that weren't handcrafted. Now, that doesn't mean that they were custom made. The ones you saw were probably good handcrafted batons that someone had personalized for a special occasion. I'd love to see them myself. I've never seen a jeweled baton. I would think that it would only be for show. The jewels in the handle would throw the balance out of whack."

"I don't follow this discussion at all," Denise commented with a puzzled expression on her face. "Do you think you could break it down a bit more for me?"

"Sure. Have a seat," Smithe replied as he brought two three-legged stools from a nearby corner. He waited until Denise had extracted her sketchbook before beginning.

"I'm ready," Denise stated as she balanced the book on her lap.

Apparently pleased to have the audience, Joshua Smithe began Denise's instruction. "First, good batons are handcrafted with special attention to the balance. The conductor wants to feel that the baton is an extension of his hand and arm, not a club that he's swinging at the orchestra. Second, a good baton has a handle made of domestic or exotic woods, ranging from cedar and cherry to bubinga and mahogany. Obviously, the more elaborate the wood, the more expensive the baton. Third, the handles come in many different shapes; they aren't all that teardrop shape. Some have a bulb shape or a slender handle, and some have a wide end that tapers toward the shaft. Fourth, the shaft isn't wood at all but often fiberglass. Actually, it's not even called a shaft but a wand or a stick. Am I going too fast for you?"

"No, I'm with you so far," Denise replied. "From what you've told me, I can see that you sell a little of every shape and wood."

"That's right," Smithe agreed. "Our clients demand a selection. Our inventory, unfortunately, stays rather high, but it's worth it, I guess. At least my dad thinks that it is."

"Your dad?"

"Yeah, he's the owner." Smithe nodded. "Actually, he's mostly retired now. Goes fishing as often as he can. He collects batons, too, and conducts a little now and then . . . local stuff. He sometimes conducts my group although we don't really need him. When he was younger, being a conductor was his dream. Then the reality of a wife and kids changed all that. He hardly ever comes in here anymore. He'll probably turn the shop over to me by the end of the year when he retires completely."

"Great! It's wonderful to have a business of your own," Denise stated with a smile.

The shop was lovely and tastefully decorated. The dark paneling definitely created the right environment for an old-time music shop. The old file cabinets along the wall were much more effective and in keeping with the shop's theme than metal ones would have been. The brass and milk-glass chandeliers and wall sconces provided ample light without being glaring and were delightfully reminiscent of gaslights. Although the elegant old gold-plated cash register was only for show, it brought to mind photos of old saloons. Window shades rather than blinds covered the windows, allowing the sunlight to reflect off the glass-front cabinets and shiny countertops. Joshua's father had obviously spent a great deal of time and money in creating the perfect ambience for the store.

Gazing toward the back of the store, Denise saw that someone had managed to make the section that housed modern music seem equally at home in Old Towne and in the shop. Rather than filling the space with rows of metal bins, Joshua's father, or perhaps Joshua himself, had used antique wooden cabinets to hold the plastic cases. The shiny wood floors united the two sections and made for a seamless journey between time periods with Joshua and his staff as the tour guides.

"It's a living," Joshua Smithe said with a shrug. "Actually, to tell the truth, I'm more interested in the modern music end of things. Despite this getup, I'm a New Age kind of guy. My group specializes in electrified classical music, sort of like that Greek guy. I've bored you enough with info about me. Back to the batons."

"You didn't bore me, but you're right. I'm keeping you away from your business as it is," Denise replied with a smile.

Smithe beamed. "The clerks have everything under control. I'm mostly the greeter here when I'm not stuck in the office. It's nice talking with someone for a change. But anyway, where was I?"

"You had just finished talking about the wand," Denise recapped.

Scratching his head and settling in to the manner of a professor again, Smithe continued, saying, "Oh, yeah, well, conductors who demand perfection have their batons made for them, taking into consideration the wood in the handle, the balance, and the length. From there, the craftsman weights at the point that the wand meets the handle so that it feels perfect on the fingertips. It's really quite a skill. Those elaborately decorated batons you saw probably wouldn't work well. The weight of the jewels would have made the handle too heavy."

"Are all wands made of fiberglass? Won't they break when the conductor taps the stand?" Denise asked as she continued to sketch not only the information but its source.

"No, not at all," Smithe replied with a little shake of his head. "One of the most famous baton makers uses not only fiberglass but hickory in either its natural or painted form. A baton reflects the personality of the conductor just as the performance of the orchestra represents his pulse. Batons can be of almost any material, length, taper, and color.

"The most important functional element is the balance. Again, the conductor doesn't want to feel as if he's waving a club at the orchestra. It's not only bad for morale, but it's tiring. Imagine swinging a baseball bat to four-four time for the length of a concert. The conductor's arm would give out.

"Now, back to your original question about the commercial-grade baton. It's as much like any other by that manufacturer as, to use a hackneyed expression, a pea in a pod. The only difference would be among manufacturers of basic batons, but, again, each manufacturer's product is equal in every way to the others in the line."

Closing her sketchbook, Denise smiled and stated, "You've been most helpful. I'll give this information to the lab. Since the baton in my bag appears to carry the same manufacturer's marks as the others that the murderer left behind, the lab should be able to conduct fairly conclusive tests on them."

Rising, Joshua Smithe replied with a broad smile, "I'm only too glad to help and to have the company. Come by again if you need any more information. You might like to hear one of my concerts, too. The group's name is the Workhouse. Apropos, isn't it?"

Smiling happily, Denise replied as she extended her hand, "Great idea! Thanks again."

Denise chuckled all the way to her car. She had completely enjoyed the session with Joshua Smithe, who was not only informative but entertaining. He had shed so much light on the construction of batons and made Mr. Hornblatt's collection all the more impressive for its uniqueness. Unfortunately, she still did not see the connection between the victims. They were all from different genres within the world of music. They were young, married, single, and more mature. She could not see a connection.

Driving back to the precinct, Denise turned the radio to the classical station. Remembering the need to gather clues, she slipped through the traffic without really seeing it. Her mind was busy sorting through the material that she had already gained. Perhaps the afternoon selections would help her connect the events with the batons.

The music, as always, was soothing as Denise steered her car through the heavy early rush-hour traffic. Studies showed that the traffic congestion in the area worsened every year, and, from the number of people on the road, Denise could believe the reports. It took her longer to travel from a murder scene to the precinct every year.

As she turned onto a shortcut through the park, Denise allowed the sweet smell of flowers and grasses to relax her troubled mind. She knew that the information that she needed lay within grasp of her fingers, but she just could not draw it to her. The murderer was deliberately leaving behind mass-produced orchestral batons as his calling cards, but she could not figure out the reason. The selection made sense since all of the victims were musicians, but that was the end of the similarity between them.

Suddenly, she became aware that the station had

changed from playing Salieri to a Broadway tune. Denise could only chuckle at the murderer's ability to influence the music station's selection. Never in all the years that she had been listening to that classical station had she known any of the DJs to play anything other than classical selections. For a moment, she wondered if the DJ might actually be the murderer. However, she thrust that thought from her mind. The station had not changed personnel in years. She could count on hearing the same names and voices every day.

Pulling into the nearest parking space in a picnic cove, Denise paid full attention. After all, the murderer had carefully selected the music for its ability to speak to her, to communicate his plans to her. So far, she had heard but not understood, and another musician had died. This time, she would listen more carefully. The murderer had not selected randomly; he deserved her full attention.

Leaning her head against the rest, Denise listened attentively to the violin's melody. Slowly, she began to hum the lyrics but the name of the piece would not come. The music was haunting and the title elusive, as the murderer continued to be.

"Come on, Dory, you can do it," Denise coaxed her memory in a whisper that grew almost into a shout. "You know that tune. You can see them dancing on the stage. Okay, it's a music number. He's bald, and she's wearing a hoop skirt. Here it comes! 'Shall we dance? And shall you be my new romance?'"

As the selection ended and the station returned to its usual classical theme, Denise edged into the traffic. She continued to hum the piece that had long been one of her favorites. She was amazed that she could have experienced any difficulty in recognizing it. Everyone knew the famous play about the unspoken love between an English woman and a king.

Yet, Denise did not know the connection between

the victims, the murderer, and the music. She had to work it out soon. If not, the lab would need to redo all of its tests. A clue to the connection between the murders and to the murderer's identity had to exist in the batons themselves somewhere. Denise decided that the music must only be a guide to the next victim.

Seven

The precinct parking lot was almost empty. Denise decided that everyone was either enjoying a late lunch or working cases. She hoped that Tom would still sit slumped over his caseload, pretending to work but, in truth, waiting for her to return.

Denise rushed to her desk without even pouring the customary cup of coffee. Molly wagged her tail and looked up with an accusatory expression on her face as if scolding Denise for making them late to lunch. Lumbering to her feet, Molly licked Tom's bare elbow to gain his attention. When he only patted her absently on the head, Molly signed and returned to her position on the floor beside him.

"You busy?" Denise asked over her shoulder as she sorted the contents of her briefcase into the appropriate slots in her desk organizer.

"No, I'm sitting here because my girlfriend stood me up for lunch, and I'm too weak to move," Tom snarled with an expression of disapproval on his face that matched Molly's.

"I didn't stand you up. I was working and couldn't get away. I was unavoidably detained," Denise rejoined as she pulled her chair to his desk.

"That's only semantics," Tom replied without looking up from the case that demanded only a small portion of his attention.

"What?"

"Let me explain," Tom began angrily, as he folded his massive brown hands on the desktop. "If I had been the one to arrive over an hour late for our usual lunchtime without phoning, you would have accused me of standing you up, being rude, and exhibiting typical male behavior. Since you're the tardy one, I'm supposed to accept it graciously. Does that sound like a double standard to you?"

Frowning and puzzled, Denise asked, "What's wrong with you? I know you didn't get out of the wrong side of the bed, so what's up? I haven't seen you this cranky in a long time."

"Nothing," Tom declared and then said, "It's just that this case has only begun, and it's already absorbing all of your time. You don't even remember to phone."

"Whoa! Where's this coming from? Has something happened?" Denise demanded, raising her hands in the sign of surrender.

"Yeah, something's happened," Tom growled more in pain and frustration than in anger. "While you were out hobknobbing with the rich and famous, I've been transferred."

"Don't kid me like that," Denise replied angrily. "I know you're mad at me for being late and not calling, but that's hitting below the belt."

"I'm not kidding," Tom stated with a crooked smile. "It seems that you're not the only famous one in this team. My work with Molly and the canine pilot has been so successful that I'm being transferred and promoted to head a unit. Today's my last day."

"Oh!" Denise exclaimed with a puff as if something had knocked all the wind from her body. "The promotion's great, but the transfer part really stinks. Congratulations, I guess, but this is awful."

Tossing a few of his personal items into a box that

Denise just noticed on his desk, Tom commented, "Tell me about it. I tried to talk the captain out of doing this to us, but he wouldn't listen. He said it was time I received recognition of my work, too."

"But you do . . . all the time. You're always appearing in the paper for your work with Molly," Denise objected as she sat watching him. She felt helpless to move even a finger.

"The captain doesn't think that's enough. I told him that I was happy with the status quo, but he wouldn't hear of it. I report tomorrow," Tom said in a manner more appropriate for a funeral than the announcement of a promotion.

"What'll I do without you? I know I'm being selfish, but who'll watch my back? I don't want a new partner. I want you," Denise cried as if her heart would break.

In one of their few public displays of affection, Tom rested his massive hand on Denise's small one and said, "I'm not leaving your life, Dory, I just won't be sitting behind you anymore. We'll see each other every evening for dinner and movies. Nothing can change that. I love you, Dory."

"You pick this moment to tell me," Denise replied as she wiped angrily at the stinging tears that trickled down her cheeks. "Your timing is dreadful. This can't be happening. We're a great team. Working together is part of our fiber, part of our relationship. I'll go to the captain and resign if he transfers you. He's not even giving us time for a promotion party."

"There's no point, Dory. It's done. The chief signed the transfer papers this morning. I report tomorrow. Besides, you know I wouldn't want a party. We'll have a private celebration," Tom said softly as he continued to caress Denise's cold fingers.

Sighing, Denise stated, "I'll never have another partner like you. We think alike. We're the same person. It takes too much time to build a relationship like that. I don't have the energy to do it. You're my partner for now and always. I love you, Tom, and want to spend every day with you."

Smiling broadly, Tom beamed, "I never thought you'd say it. So you love me, huh? Well, we'll just have to form another kind of partnership now that this one is over."

"Oh, come on!" Denise exclaimed, stepping back a little. "If you're talking about marriage, you know that neither of us is the marrying kind. We're too stubborn. That's why this relationship works so well. We're together all day but separate at night unless we choose otherwise. It's very convenient."

Barely able to hide his disappointment at having his informal proposal rejected, Tom stated, "You're one exasperating woman, Dory! Yes, you're right. We are too stubborn to think of making this a more conventional relationship. I guess I forgot in the emotion of the moment."

Smiling in an effort to ease the tension between them, Denise demanded without further reference to his request, "Tell me all the details of your new assignment. After you finish, I need help from you on the Music Man Murder case."

Pushing aside his wounded ego, Tom acknowledged that Denise had always been a tough one to read. Conversation that interested other women held her attention only for short bursts of time. He knew that she seldom thought of love while they were at work. He had long ago recognized that ability as both a strength and a weakness. Denise was completely capable of compartmentalizing her life and his so that their personal and professional lives hardly ever touched. He had misread her initial reaction to his promotion and transfer as being more than professional longing for the established partner. He would try again later to steer the conversation to marriage once they were alone in their bed.

"Well," Tom began, "the captain says that I'll head a group of ten detectives. They've all been involved in some level of canine work, but they haven't taken it to the depth that I have with Molly. Instead of working drug and bomb cases, we'll work homicide. It should be an interesting assignment."

"It sounds like a wonderful opportunity for you," Denise conceded. "The captain's right; it is about time that you receive the recognition you deserve. You're a great detective who, unfortunately, once had a few spots on his reputation. You deserve this break and all the others that come your way in the future. I'll miss you.

"No, you won't. Solving this case and breaking in a new partner will take all your energy. I know you, Dory. You won't think about me at all, but I'll miss working with you. You were the only one who was willing to give me a chance. You weren't afraid of my bark," Tom replied with sadness in his voice.

Brushing aside the comments and the memories of their first meeting, Denise responded, "Enough of this! I thought you were hungry. We can discuss the case over lunch. My treat in celebration of your promotion."

"Okay, and I'll pick the place," Tom agreed as he slipped into his jacket. "I want one of those delicious pizzas at Margo's. I want to leave here in style."

"You mean that you want to add to your cholesterol level. I guess one last time won't hurt you. But it's salad for dinner tonight," Denise stated as she grabbed her purse and chased Tom's retreating back. Inwardly, she hoped that her next partner would wait until she was ready before he bolted to the door.

Her next partner. Walking down the street, Denise could not push the thought from her mind. She had accepted Tom as a partner after no one else would take him. His reputation for a foul mouth and a quick temper had preceded him to their office, and no one wanted to work with him. Since she was in need of a partner, she accepted him, knowing his liabilities and his assets.

Tom had never disappointed her. Although, initially, he was not pleased with having to work with a woman partner, Denise and Tom quickly formed a partnership that surprised everyone in the precinct. They made decisions almost without speaking. They protected each other through the use of a finely developed sixth sense. They were completely compatible. Although their colleagues initially teased them about being the Mutt and Jeff of the department, Tom only laughed and continued to cast a protective shadow over Denise's smaller frame.

Now, the end of an era had arrived. They both knew that their partnership could not last forever. Denise's fame in law enforcement circles caused her name to appear at the top of headhunters' lists constantly. She turned down lucrative transfers to other police departments and even prestigious posts on government agency rosters. Denise was happy at the Montgomery County Police Department.

Denise had never thought that Tom would be the one to have a promotion that he could not refuse thrust upon him. She thought that he would be able to fend off that kind of attention and recognition. She never anticipated the possibility that fame would separate them. She knew that the canine pilot was bringing him great renown, but she had underestimated its internal appeal. Denise had read of the community's reaction to the special group, but she had not thought that the chief had ranked it as highly as the press. She had been wrong. Both of them had underestimated the chief's appreciation of Tom's work on the pilot.

Sopping the grease from the little pepperoni cups on her first slice of pizza with two of the restaurant's cheap paper napkins, Denise looked across the small table at the man who had protected her back so well. She had never worried about becoming a victim with Tom behind her. She could sleep at night because he had her back during the day. Now that security would end.

Reaching for another slice and absently performing the same degreasing procedure, Denise wondered about the impact the professional separation would have on their personal lives. Tom's promotion and departure would mark the first true separation in their association. His shyness and her devotion to work had made admitting their attachment difficult. They had teased each other from the very beginning of their relationship. Yet, when the joking had assumed a more personal tone, each of them had refused to acknowledge that a personal relationship had developed.

Now that they would not occupy desks next to each other and would not share almost every meal together, Denise wondered if the physical distance would produce an emotional one as well. Watching Tom wipe the spot of pizza sauce from his chin, she hoped it would not. She would miss him terribly if he were suddenly not in her life. He had fit perfectly as a partner as soon as they formed their working relationship. They had developed an uncanny sense of each other's needs that almost made verbal communication unnecessary.

Denise could hardly remember the moment at which she realized that she loved him. She simply knew. Perhaps it was the way he always fussed after burning his tongue on the overcooked coffee or the way he grumbled about the paper-clip chain that she left on his desk that caused him almost constant irritation. Maybe it was the way he rushed to the door at lunchtime but took his time about leaving her apartment in the evening that had won her heart. She remembered the cups of soda that would appear on her desk unbidden when she was thirsty and the feeling of total security as they worked cases together. Mostly, Denise could feel the warmth of his arms and chest as he enfolded her. She never wanted that closeness to end.

Tom was thinking along the same lines as he rolled the sides of a pizza slice and chomped away hungrily. The thought of leaving Denise alone on the streets frightened and worried him. She was often so involved in her work that she did not notice when she was in a hostile environment. She had a one-track mind, and, when she focused it on catching a perpetrator, she was like a horse wearing blinders that saw the task ahead and nothing else. Denise could also be stubborn. She would never ask him to rescue her from a tight situation. Instead, she would hint that she needed his help in putting the pieces of the case together. He worried that the next partner would take too long to learn that she really did need the support. Denise could be so involved that it was difficult to see that she was also human.

He also worried that a new partner's ego might not be able to withstand the pressure of being Denise's partner. She was regularly either in the newspaper or on television for having solved the mystery of one big case or the other. Tom had learned that it was not easy being her partner. His ego had suffered considerably until he learned that Denise did not seek the attention; it simply found her. She was extremely generous and helpful and an ideal partner.

He would miss the intimacy of their silence and the camaraderie of their chats. Tom loved watching her chew and enjoyed listening to Denise work out a sticky clue to a difficult case. He would miss the days spent in the office together and the little pranks she played on him. He had long suspected that she was the perpetrator of the paper-clip tangle but could never catch her in the act. Although their working relationship would change, he knew that he would do everything in his power to preserve their nights.

He would not allow her to get away from him. Nothing would ever separate them.

"What are you thinking?" Denise asked now that they had satisfied their initial need to feed their bodies.

"About us," Tom replied frankly.

"Me, too," Denise confessed.

"Ladies first," Tom stated as he enfolded her small hand in his.

"I was just wondering what'll happen to the personal us now that the professional us is over," Denise mused as the waiter deposited the check on the table at an equal distance between them.

"Nothing. I won't let it," Tom replied with confidence.

"It's happened before you know it," Denise stated as she placed cash on top of the check. They always ordered the same thing and took turns covering the tab. Lunch should have been on Tom, but she intended to treat today in celebration of his promotion.

"What has?" Tom asked as they headed toward the door.

"Professional separation often breaks up a romantic partnership," Denise replied as they almost sprinted back to the precinct.

"Says who?" Tom demanded without changing the brisk pace he had set for them as usual.

Trotting a little to keep up, Denise commented, "Remember Mary and Ben from burglary? As soon as she accepted the transfer to check fraud, they split up. He got a new sexy partner and, suddenly, the old one didn't appeal to him any longer."

"I don't remember them. Maybe their relationship was only professional. We're not like that," Tom stated as he opened the station door for Denise to enter.

"They were engaged! They were weeks away from getting married when he called it off. She had bought the gown and had it altered, ordered and mailed the invitations, and paid for the hall. It was a mess," Denise stated as she stowed her purse in the bottom desk drawer.

Looking around, she saw that everyone had returned from work. They all knew about Tom's promotion and transfer and had nodded at him as they walked to their seats. They seemed to anticipate the usual Denise and Tom afternoon show of witty bantering.

"I don't remember. Anyway, that won't happen to us. We won't let it," Tom declared as he turned his attention to closing out his cases. He had to write reports on all of them before he could leave at the end of the day. Denise's new partner would need to be able to take over all of them except those directly related to the canine pilot. The captain had indicated that his replacement would arrive the next day.

"What's to keep it from happening?" Denise asked as she waited for her computer to boot. Unlike Tom, who never turned his off, she never left it on when she would be away from the office. The little Internet-monitoring fiasco of the chief's had caused her to password-protect all of her files and her computer.

"We're deeply committed," Tom stated as he looked into her eyes, allowing his attention to rest on Denise and not his work.

"That could change. You might fall for someone else," Denise whispered so that the others in the squad room would not overhear the conversation.

"Not likely. To quote from one of your many favorite plays, 'I was serenely independent and content before we met. Looks like I could always be that way again, and, yet, I've grown accustomed to your face,'" Tom replied with a big smile and his version of a whisper.

"Okay, I know when the discussion's gone far enough." Denise beamed with pleasure that he would re-member the play that they had seen on their first date.

"Considering that I practically had to drag you to see *My Fair Lady,* I'm surprised that you remembered any of it."

"That was our first real date. Besides, I only pretended to sleep through most of the plays to get on your nerves." Tom laughed so loudly that the detectives at the coffeepot turned in their direction.

"Shh! Be quiet, Tom! 'Don't laugh at my jokes too much. People will say we're in love,' to quote *Carousel,*" Denise replied as a very becoming blush swept over her cheeks.

"Okay, you win! You're letting this Music Man case affect your wits. That's enough playing around for one day. Now let's get back to work, Dory. We'll continue this discussion at my place tonight," Tom ordered with feigned seriousness and a deep chuckle at their closeness.

"I thought it was your turn to stay at my place," Denise suggested as she involuntarily rearranged the overflowing pencil box on his desk.

"Maybe it is, but I want to try the steak house around the corner from my building. It just makes more sense for you to stay over. Okay?" Tom concluded as he removed the newly color coordinated box from her fingers before Denise could arrange the pencils and pens by height.

"Fine. I'm going for a cup of afternoon tar. Would you like one?" Denise asked as she blew the imaginary dust from her cup.

"Na, I've already consumed enough to keep me awake all night," Tom replied with a shake of his head. "While I was waiting for you to return, that's all I did."

"By the way, we haven't discussed my case, and I need your input on a few details," Denise stated, standing behind him on her way to the coffee machine.

"Let's do that tonight. Right now I have to finish the work on these cases," Tom responded without turning in her direction. His slumped posture told Denise that all conversation had ended until after work hours.

The other detectives barely looked up as Denise

walked past them on the way to the coffee machine. A familiar, almost sweet feeling of anticipation filled the air as Denise poured the afternoon sludge that passed for coffee into her cup. They were waiting for something to happen and soon.

Suddenly, the silence exploded as Tom shouted, "All right, you clowns! Who did it? Who strung all of my paper clips together? Damn it! I can't even go to lunch with my girl without someone messing with my stuff."

Tom suddenly looked incredibly embarrassed by the sudden proclamation of his relationship with Denise. Although everyone in the squad room was aware that their partnership extended past the workday, no one discussed it. The others broke into loud, happy laughter that instantly restored the mood of the squad room. Everything was right in the precinct. Tom would leave them at the end of their workday, but, for now, life would proceed as normal.

Eight

The steak house offered fabulous food, great ambience, and, surprisingly, a dance floor. She had been expecting a little hole-in-the-wall and was pleased to see white linen napkins and matching tablecloths, fancy china with the restaurant's golden E in the center, and crystal stemware. Fortunately, Tom had warned her to wear something simple but elegant for their last meal as partners. Otherwise, Denise would have been very embarrassed if she had appeared in jeans and a light sweater. Her conservatively cut long-sleeved black sheath dress and high-heel pumps proved perfect for the evening.

That night, gentle strains of the quartet wafted through the air. Looking closely, Denise recognized one of its members. Joshua Smithe smiled and nodded. Inclining his head in the direction of the man conducting the little group, he mouthed his father's name. Denise smiled at the sight of father and son producing enticing music together.

The wait staff eased through the room carrying gleaming trays as the diners chatted quietly. The carefully folded towel never seemed to slide from its position on their forearm. The sommeliers glided on patent-leather-covered feet from one table to the other, offering suggestions for the ideal wine to accompany the perfect entrée. The chandeliers sparkled off the mirror that graced the center of each table, reflecting not only the twinkling lights above but the mellow glow of the candle. Even the menus demanded careful consideration, being enclosed in burgundy leather trimmed in gold. Denise was impressed.

Tom looked especially handsome that evening. He had selected a deep gray suit with deeper gray pinstripes and a coordinated tie from among his somewhat unimaginative wardrobe. Even the tone-on-tone white shirt worked perfectly. He looked more handsome than Denise had ever seen him. His deep brown skin glowed with happiness at having selected such an unexpectedly delightful restaurant and pleasing her with his choice. Usually, Tom leaned toward hot dogs and pizza. The Emanuel was a complete change.

Watching the sparkle in his eyes, Denise sighed with the realization that it would be a shame to spoil the evening with shoptalk. However, at some point, she would have to mention the case. She needed Tom's help immediately. Starting the next day, she would not be able to turn to him for assistance. Tom would no longer occupy the desk behind hers. She would have to find a new lunch partner, too, since his office would be across town. She would only see him in the evening after work if their schedules would allow.

"This is gorgeous!" Denise proclaimed as she gestured at the splendor of the room.

"I thought you'd like it." Tom beamed with pleasure at having done something nice for the woman he loved.

"How did you now about it?" Denise asked as she sipped the aromatic wine that sparkled a deep pink in her glass.

"Believe it or not, I occasionally read the paper," Tom joked lightly. "The *Washington Post* food critic said that this is a restaurant that everyone should visit. I phoned for a reservation, and, voila, we're here. I'm glad you like it. As a matter of fact, it's even grander than I thought it would be."

"It's the perfect place for a celebration. Did you know about the promotion before today?" Denise inquired as a slight frown played across her forehead.

"The captain had sort of mentioned it," Tom confessed with a shrug. "I guess I was hoping that it would go away."

"Why didn't you tell me?" Denise asked as she tensed with the hurt and confusion of having been left out of the early discussions of their fate.

Placing his hand on hers, Tom replied, "I didn't say anything because I didn't want to upset you. I asked the captain to try to talk the chief out of this silly idea that I'm supervisory material. I'm just a cop. That's who I am and what I want to be."

"How long have you known?" Denise queried as she allowed the warmth of his hand to ease her unhappiness.

With a crooked smile, Tom confessed, "For about two weeks. It was hard keeping it to myself, but I wanted the idea to fade away. I convinced myself that, if I didn't think about it, neither would the chief. I had hoped that the captain would have some luck in getting her to change her mind, but you know the chief. Once she gets a thought in her head, there's no shaking her. The captain said that she wouldn't budge on this one."

Patting his hand, Denise conceded, "Too true. Most of the stuff she implements is good, but, occasionally, she comes up with some real winners."

"Like that the Internet-monitoring idea she implemented," Tom offered, able to smile now that Denise had relaxed a bit.

"Yeah, that and the map consoles for the squad cars. More cops were lost because they depended on that system than for any other reason. The driving directions were too indirect. No one needs to go three blocks out of the way to reach a destination. Nothing beats good old-fashioned landmarks for navigation." Denise laughed warmly at the shared memory.

Growing somber again, Denise added, "So, I guess it's final then. You'll start your new job tomorrow."

"Yep, and you'll start training a new partner," Tom responded in a mood that matched hers.

"I don't want one," Denise stated flatly. "I sent an e-mail to the captain today, stating that I wanted to go solo for a while. I don't want to break in a new partner."

Interrupting with a wave of his hand, Tom stated emphatically, "Forget it, Dory. You need someone to watch your back on stakeouts. You can't go it alone. I want you safe. Argumentative and opinionated, but safe. You understand?"

"That's what the captain said, too," Denise reluctantly agreed. "He left a voice-mail message while I was in the shower today. He said that I'll meet my new partner tomorrow at noon, like it or not. I won't like it, but I'll do it."

"Good. Now, how would you like your steak?" Tom inquired, as the waiter appeared to take their order.

As they munched escargot and clams Rockefeller, Tom leaned over toward Denise and asked, "Who's that guy in the quartet? He keeps looking over here."

"That's Joshua Smithe, the guy who owns or soon will own the music shop in Old Towne. Why? Are you jealous?" Denise explained, smiling into Tom's eyes.

"No, but I don't like him staring at you like that," Tom replied while looking past Denise at the young man in the musical group. Joshua slightly inclined his head when their eyes met.

"He's a nice guy . . . totally harmless," Denise stated with a playful grin.

"Well, he certainly has eyes for you. I'm surprised that he can keep up with the music the way he's watching you," Tom commented with a tinge of jealousy in his voice.

"Whatever," Denise replied, putting an end to that line of discussion. Tom had no choice but to return to his appetizer.

After they had dined on the best filet mignon she had ever tasted, Denise managed to steer Tom onto the dance floor. He was a skillful but reluctant dancer. His parents had insisted that he take dance lessons when he was twelve years old. Along with playing baseball, football, and basketball, he had learned to waltz, tango, and two-step. When his buddies had learned of his Saturday morning activities, they almost soiled their pants for laughing. However, years later when Tom was the escort of many beautiful black women at their cotillions, he had the last laugh.

Denise had been one of those young women who watched ballroom dancing on television and dreamed of doing the intricate steps with a dashing partner. Since she did not know any black people who competed in the national competitions, she set her heart on being the first. She was good at it, too, and won several local contests. However, once she entered college, her direction changed completely. Her desire to perform turned from the dance floor to the stack of books that covered her desk. She had danced at weddings and parties since then but had never thought of competing.

Gliding across the floor, Tom and Denise proved once again that they were a well-matched couple. She fit perfectly into his arms. When he dipped, she dipped. When he turned a sharp corner or performed an intricate step, she melted into his body, enabling them to turn as one. They danced the tango so well that the other diners stopped eating to watch the sultry display.

With each step, it became more apparent that Denise and Tom had much in common. Her leg wrapped around his as his hand found the base of her spine. Her lower body pressed against his as he bent her slowly backward until she lay perpendicular to the floor in his arms. His fingers ran slowly and tantalizingly from her chin to the soft flesh between her breasts in one graceful movement. His lips brushed the air above hers as he languidly pulled her to her feet only to push her away in a fast spin.

Then they reunited with only inches to spare. Her fingers played at the base of his neck and traveled to his wide shoulders. She gazed passionately into his eyes, seeing no one but him. Slowly her left hand eased down his back as she pressed toward him. Their eyes locked for a long moment. As if to punish her for wanting him, Tom released her, leaving her to fend for herself. Slowly they pranced around each other to a rhythm that seemed to originate in their souls. They hardly breathed and never looked away from each other.

Just as suddenly, they were in each other's arms again. Bodies melding into one, they locked cheeks and hands. Together, they glided across the floor, moving their hips to a sensuous, undulating current. When the music finally slowed, so did they. Denise's arms reached to the ceiling as Tom's hands ran the length of her body as he fiercely pulled her to him for the last time. Their lips parted and almost met. They stood frozen in the heat of their passion as the music stopped and the applause began.

Her cheeks red from the exertion of the dance and the passion that flowed through her body, Denise looked with sweet embarrassment at Tom. She always avoided being the center of attention, but now all eyes were on her. She wanted him to rescue her, and, yet, she desired the dance to begin again. She felt as if she could not get enough of the closeness, the energy, and the passion that was the tango.

Never had Tom danced the tango with such passion.

Lessons and cotillions had not prepared him for the feel of Denise in his arms on the dance floor. He had not anticipated that she would give herself so completely. He felt as if they had made love for everyone to see, and he wanted to do it again.

Tom's eyes flashed and his chest heaved from the closeness of her and the music. He slowly allowed the passion to wane and reality to return. Moistening his lips and smiling contentedly, he took Denise by the hand. They slowly walked from the dance floor to their table, nodding their heads in recognition of the applause.

"Dessert?" the waiter asked with a wicked smile.

Laughing, Tom replied, "We'll take the check, please."

Denise could only look down at the charger plate on the table in front of her. The dance and the closeness of Tom's body had shattered her usual composure and conservative demeanor. For the first time in her adult life, Denise knew the feeling of total abandonment. For the first time in her relationship with Tom, she had held back nothing. Their lovemaking had always been satisfying, but this dance showed that they had only just begun to explore each other's passion.

Smiling sweetly at the retreating waiter's back, Denise turned to Tom stated, "It's my treat, remember?"

"Which part? The meal or the dance?" Tom inquired in a voice still husky with passion.

"Both," Denise replied, gazing into his eyes fixedly.

Barely able to stand being so close to Denise while not being able to touch her, Tom breathed, "Let's walk home quickly."

"Sounds like a good idea to me," Denise purred seductively in a bustling dining room that seemed to hold only themselves and no one else.

"Wave good-bye to your friend," Tom instructed at the door.

Laying her hand gently on his, Denise replied, "Whatever."

For the moment, Denise did not care about Joshua's growing infatuation with her. She saw only Tom. Joshua Smithe would simply have to wonder about the nature of their relationship.

Later that evening Denise and Tom lay exhausted from the intimacy that had started on the dance floor and finished in the privacy of his bedroom. Snuggling deep into his strong chest, Denise sighed contentedly. Loving Tom and making love to him were extremely satisfying. She could push aside all cares and give herself to him in a way that had never happened in any other relationship. Not that she had enjoyed much social time, but, when she did find the time for relationships, something had been lacking in all of them. The men had been charming, attentive, attractive, and as devoted to their professions as Denise was to hers. However, they simply did not click. Their conversation was sufficiently witty and their company entertaining, but the energy was not right.

With Tom everything worked. Professionally, Denise could not have a better partner. Personally, she also had no complaints. The silence between them was as meaningful as the conversation, and the intellectual stimulation was on a par with the physical expression of their devotion. She was perfectly content. Even their little arguments amounted to nothing.

Resting her hand lightly on his moist chest, Denise muttered, "I hate to break the spell of the moment, but I really need to talk with you about the case."

Chuckling softly, Tom commented, "You're the only woman I've ever known who brings work to bed."

"That's what you get for loving a cop. You should have fallen in love with a teacher or an attorney. You know that cops can't leave work at the office. These cases get under my skin, and I can't get rid of them," Denise replied sleepily. "Now, will you help me?"

Slipping another pillow under his head, Tom adjusted his position as Denise leaned on one elbow to face him. They smiled gently into each other's eyes as Denise began her explanation of the intricacies of the case. The clock in the hall chimed midnight as Molly noisily settled in the doorway. The apartment was ready for sleep, but Denise was not.

Lacing her fingers in Tom's, Denise outlined the extent of her investigation, saying, "The perpetrator has murdered conductors, composers, and musicians from different genres. They've been male and female, black and white, and single, married, and involved. The only commonality that I can see is that they're all famous in their respective fields. The black female single violinist was as well respected as the engaged white male country composer. Nothing that I've found suggests they they knew each other. They probably would have known each other's music and reputations, but that's all. I haven't found anything that suggests that they ever entertained or collaborated on a project together. Each was famous in his or her own area."

Interjecting a question, Tom asked, "Have his clues been helpful?"

"No, not really, but that could have been my fault." Denise sighed loudly. "I missed the first one completely. I thought he meant that he'd send a more definitive clue the next day, but what he really meant was that he'd strike again. This most recent one is almost as obscure."

"You didn't tell me that he'd sent another radio message," Tom exclaimed, sitting up a bit higher on the pillows. "I wonder who he knows at the classical station. This guy worries me. He's too abstract . . . almost a character from one of your beloved plays."

He was completely awake now and concerned that the

perpetrator had contacted Denise again. Denise had a tendency toward attracting murderers who did not maintain a safe distance from her. The last one had succeeded in dancing on a Hawaiian stage with her.

"Probably no one. Anyone can make a request. Don't worry so much," Denise advised as she adjusted her position on the pillows to match his. They were both sitting upright and leaning against the headboard.

"How can I not worry? I'm leaving you in the hands of a rookie partner while you're in the middle of a murder investigation. Of course I'll worry. See these lines? You gave me all of them. My forehead was smooth before I partnered with you." Tom gesticulated wildly before pointing to the deep furrows on his brow.

Sighing at his protectiveness, Denise replied, "He hasn't made any effort to contact me personally. No music on my desk, no phone calls. He's playing it pretty straight, so far."

"Humph!"

"Anyway," Denise continued before Tom could wind up again, "he also leaves a baton at the murder scene. I've found one in each home. Even the victims who didn't use one professionally receive one from the killer. I can't figure it out."

"Is there anything special about the batons?" Tom asked with great composure although Denise could see the bulging vein in the side of his neck.

"Nothing," Denise replied with a shake of her head. "I stopped by a shop in Old Towne that sells them and had a pretty good conversation with the owner's grown son. He says that the perpetrator's batons are fairly ordinary and mass-produced. One of the victims, Mr. Hornblatt, had a wonderful collection of antique and jeweled batons that must be worth a fortune. However, the perpetrator only left simple, inexpensive ones with his victims."

"Did he bludgeon his victims with them?" Tom asked as he tried to be helpful.

"No, that's the strange part about this case," Denise replied. "The batons don't seem to factor in to the murders. They just seem to be items randomly left behind. They don't carry any markings that differentiate one from the other. I don't understand the logic behind leaving seemingly insignificant batons at the crime scene. The only unusual thing about them is the tiny holes in the handle. I've been meaning to ask Joshua about them but haven't gotten to it yet."

"Maybe he's a conductor. Maybe he feels that he's being overlooked and not receiving the press that the others do," Tom suggested, making a face of disgust at the mention of the infatuated young man.

"If he is, he hasn't left any other clues to his identity. I've asked the family of all the victims if they can think of anyone who'd harbor a grudge, but none of them could think of anyone," Denise replied with a big stretch.

"What's the murder weapon? Maybe there's some similarity that you've overlooked," Tom suggested as he pulled her against his shoulder again. The momentary physical separation had made him feel cold despite the comfortable warmth of the room.

"I haven't been able to find one yet," Denise lamented, moving slightly away so that she had room to gesture with her lovely hands and arms. "The coroner says that they've all died of natural causes. However, the chief says that she received a cryptic note from someone claiming responsibility long before she received the report. According to the note, one person of unidentified gender committed the murders and plans to strike again until we catch him. He specifically asked for me, as many of them do these days. The person claiming responsibility had carefully typed the note and mailed it from a location in Gaithersburg. Since then, except for the one note on my desk and the two radio station clues, there's been no contact. I don't know what to make of it."

"No enemies, no motive, no murder weapon," Tom summarized. "You don't have much of a case here, Dory."

"You're right," Denise agreed. "All I have is corpses."

"What's your next move?" Tom asked as he pulled her close again.

With a shrug of her shoulders, Denise replied, "I don't know. The last radio clue was from *The King and I*. Maybe I should see if there's a production in town or in New York. I wouldn't mind seeing a play on the department."

"I can arrange that," Tom said as he reached for his wallet on the nightstand.

Opening it, he extracted a small, white envelope. Handing it to Denise, he said, "I wanted to surprise you. The play's at the Olney Theater. I picked up tickets this afternoon. I ordered them after hearing the music on the radio this afternoon. You're not the only one who listens to that classical station these days."

"Tom, you never cease to amaze me!" Denise exclaimed as she fingered the tickets for orchestra seats for the next night.

"Good. I'd hate to think that I'm so dull that I can't surprise you anymore," Tom muttered as he accepted the happy kisses that she placed on his cheeks, chin, and, finally, lips.

"We'll have a wonderful evening, a real date for a change," Denise gushed happily. "You'll be able to tell me all the wonderful news about your new assignment."

"A real date! What do you call this? It felt pretty real to me," Tom joked as he ran his lips down Denise's cheeks and edged toward the tender spot on her throat.

Laughing, she held him tightly. "Yes, Tom, this is very real," she stated softly as his lips silenced any further conversation.

Thoughts of the case flew from her head as Tom's fingers explored all of the sensitive spots on her body. Denise sighed and melted into him. They were no longer simply lovers; they had become one person, seeking to express the full extent of devotion. Not even the thumping of Molly's tail as she dreamed of chasing a cat could disturb them.

Nine

Denise arrived in the squad room early. She was not at all curious about her new partner and would have slept late if Tom had not slept so restlessly. Although he did not confess it, she could tell that he was both excited and pleased with the promotion and the new responsibility. She, however, had not adjusted to the idea of having a new partner and doubted that she ever would.

The squad room was strangely quiet, and it smelled funny. Actually, it did not smell of anything in particular but a combination of aromas. The **massive room** contained the odor of people, printers, and copiers. Missing for the first time in years was the biting aroma of freshly brewed, too-strong coffee. As a matter of fact, no one had made coffee at all. All of the usual coffee drinkers stood looking at the machine, wondering at its operation. They did not even know where to find the instruction manual. Tom had always been the one to purchase the supplies and brew the coffee. They complained about its strength but downed cups of the thick almost black brew anyway. With his absence, there was no one to take on the job.

"Hey, Denise," Nick called as soon as she entered the room, "do you know how to use this thing?"

"Don't look at me. That was Tom's baby," Denise replied as she tossed her briefcase and purse into her desk drawer. She tried hard not to look at the empty desk behind her, but she could not keep her eyes from the scarred surface behind which Tom had sat for so long.

Before leaving the office, Tom had completely cleared his desk. He had left nothing, not even a paper clip. As was tradition in their office, Ronda would provide the newest member of the group with all the fixings for a well-equipped desk.

Denise ran her fingers over the scratches and remembered the origin of most of them. Tom had slammed down his stapler and made a gouge the day that he had leaned that the captain had assigned him to work the canine pilot. Once, while opening a box sent to her by a perpetrator, he had scratched a snakelike line into the desktop. Wet coffee cups had left circles upon circles like concentric rings. The perspiration from his muscular arms had bleached the finish from the spot on which he leaned every day to listen to her complaints and concerns. Her hands had left smaller prints in the varnish on her side of the desk. But now that would not happen again.

The captain had made it clear that he expected her to be in the office to welcome her new partner after he finished giving the new man the twenty-five-cent tour of the building. Knowing that they would not arrive until close to noon and needing to pass the time, Denise reviewed her sketches. She had to find the connection between the murders or she would not be able to stop the perpetrator from striking again.

Deciding that the batons must represent more than she initially assumed, Denise pulled them from their individual bags and spread them across her desk. Although the FBI lab had thoroughly examined them, she still took the precaution of donning gloves before inspecting them. Turning them over in the palm of her hand, she again saw that each one was just like the other. The handles showed no wear, and the wands remained straight and true. The murderer had definitely not used any of them as a weapon.

Pulling hard on the connection between the baton and the wand, Denise managed to separate the pieces. The wand was slightly flexible fiberglass that bent a little under the pressure of her fingers. The inside of the handle offered little more. It had been carefully finished and then stained. Repeating the process on the other batons, Denise saw that they all looked the same. There was nothing to differentiate one from the other, including the tiny holes in the handles.

Reattaching the pieces, Denise swung the baton to get a feel for its balance. Thanks to Mr. Smithe's instruction, she could appreciate the need for harmony between the pieces. Without it, the conductor would, indeed, feel as if he were swinging a bat at the orchestra. Unfortunately, she still could not see the connection that this simple musical accoutrement could possibly have to murder.

"Detective Dory, I didn't know that you had taken up conducting." The familiar voice broke the silence of her thoughts.

Placing the baton hastily on her desk, Denise turned her attention to the grinning face of the captain. Smiling, she replied, "No, sir. I haven't taken up a new profession. I'm just clue shopping."

"Very well then. If you can spare a minute, I'd like to introduce you to your new partner. Denise Dory, this is Craig Panns, recently from Germantown's homicide division. He's a sharpshooter and music lover," Captain Morton stated seriously. "Craig, meet Denise Dory, one of the best detectives I've ever known, or so she tells me constantly."

Extending her hand to her new partner, Denise sized up the man who might sit at Tom's desk but would never be able to replace him. Craig Panns was almost as tall as Tom but not quite. His shoulders in the well-tailored suit were almost as broad but missed by at least an inch. The hand that enveloped her was almost as strong but did not exude the same level of self-confidence. His gray eyes twinkled in a healthy beige complexion as he surveyed her face and figure but lacked the arrogance of Tom's gaze. His dimples, although incredibly deep, did not command the same attention as Tom's. Craig Panns was tall and handsome with just the right mixture of visible intelligence in his eyes and mischief at the corners of his mouth, but he was not Tom.

"Nice to meet you, Craig. Welcome to the squad room. I'm sure we'll make a good team." Denise stated the right words but without the appropriate sentiment.

"Thanks, Denise. I'll give it my best. You tell me what you want, and you'll have it," Craig stated as he gave her hand a manly shake.

Unable to control herself, Denise replied under her breath, "If I have to tell you, we're in trouble."

Captain Morton instantly intervened, realizing that Denise still needed more time to get used to the idea that Tom would no longer be her partner. Placing his hand on Craig Panns's shoulder, he steered the new member of his team toward the back of the room and the other detectives. The poor man would learn Denise's temper soon enough.

Returning to her work, Denise pushed the thought of the new partner from her mind. Picking up the baton once again, she studied the series of small holes on either side of the handle at the spot that it joined the wand. Looking at the others on her desk, she saw that the same almost imperceptible row of tiny holes seemed to follow the same random pattern. Taking a magnifying glass, she saw that they were not evenly spaced and did not appear to have been part of the construction process. They were all even in size, however, suggesting that the person had used a tiny drill bit to produce them.

Dialing the shop in Old Towne, she phoned Mr. Smithe, who answered on the first ring. "Hold on a second, Detective. Let me look at a few of the ones I have here," he stated as soon as she explained the discovery and her question.

Returning quickly, he said, "There's nothing on these. Someone must have deliberately created them on all of the batons you have. Do the holes go all the way through the handle?"

"They sure do," Denise replied. "What do you make of that?"

The voice on the other end sounded as confused as Denise as Mr. Smithe responded, "I can't imagine why anyone would want to drill holes in the handle. They wouldn't do much for the aerodynamics of the baton, that's for sure. Unless he wanted to fill it with a scented powder, I can't see the point. Even then, I don't understand why anyone would want to shower himself and others in the powder that would sprinkle out with every wave of the baton. People do funny things, don't they?"

"Often," Denise replied, "that's what keeps me employed."

"By the way, Detective, you certainly looked good on the dance floor," Smithe commented. "Nice tango. Not everyone can handle that dance. Looked good."

"We did our best. My partner and I were celebrating his promotion. The dancing was something extra." Denise chuckled warmly at the memory.

"Oh, he's your partner. Well, you certainly dance well together," Smithe concluded happily.

"We've worked together a long time. I guess we're in synch with each other's moves," Denise stated.

Thanking him for his help, she returned to the batons. The question loomed unanswered before her. She could not understand why anyone would want to spew powder on himself. Fingering the batons, she decided that the more appropriate question should revolve around the identity of the powder.

Grabbing her sketchbook and purse, Denise rushed from the squad room after jotting a quick note on her calendar in case anyone was looking for her. For the first time in ages, she did not turn to Tom's desk to let him know her destination. She did not even have to step carefully to avoid the big paws of his canine partner. She was alone, and she did not like it one bit. She missed Tom terribly. The squad room was no longer her second home. The camaraderie of it had left with him.

Jane Blues only barely looked up as Denise entered the morgue. She had been busily polishing her nails the last time Denise visited, and she was still occupied in applying the black polish. From the appearance of her desk, polishing her nails was the only task that Jane performed regularly.

"Do you think I might see Dr. Childs?" Denise inquired when no greeting came her way.

"Sure, she's not too busy at the moment. Go right in," Jane Blues directed with a tilt of her head. For a receptionist, she certainly did not receive the visitors to the morgue with any energy, making her a perfect match for the location.

The same was not the case for Dr. Childs, who leaped from her chair as if happy to see a living person. Obviously, Jane Blues's presence did not count. Motioning to a chair at a small round table in the corner, Dr. Childs greeted Denise as a welcome distraction from her work.

"What can I do for you, Detective Dory?" Dr. Childs asked as soon as she had settled into the seat beside Denise.

Dr. Childs was a smallish woman with vibrant eyes that appeared almost unnaturally bright. She wore tennis shoes and jeans over which she had thrown a lab coat that was much too large for her. Her gray-streaked hair sat in a neat bun on the back of her neck. The smile lines around her mouth showed that she had a good sense of humor.

"I need help on the Music Man Murder case and thought that you might be just the one to provide it," Denise replied as she accepted the ice cold soft drink that Dr. Childs produced from the small refrigerator beside the table.

"Okay, but I don't think I can shed much light. It's all in the report," Dr. Childs replied, sipping her soda through a flexible straw. She had offered one to Denise, but drinking soda through straws made her burp so she had declined.

"I have a hunch that there's more to the batons than meets the eye," Denise began. "I found tiny holes around the base of the handle in all of the ones that I found on the murder sites. I understand from the report you ran tests on them."

"Still sketching your interviews, I see, Denise. Well, I'm not a very interesting subject." Dr. Childs laughed as she touched the tiny tendrils of escaping hair. "Let's see, yes, we tested the batons and found nothing."

"Did you find anything that struck you as unusual about the bodies?" Denise probed.

"Not really," Dr. Childs commented. "As I've noted in the report, the victims appeared to have died of natural causes. There was no sign of foul play on any of them. The bodies were clean . . . no fingerprints, no sign of strangulation from ingesting a foreign substance, and no entry wounds of any kind. Nothing."

"What exactly in this case are natural causes?" Denise continued, unsatisfied to end the discussion with no more information than she had had before coming to see Dr. Childs.

Tapping her fingertips together, Dr. Childs stated, "In this case, to die of natural causes means that no one murdered them. They simply stopped breathing. One of them aspirated a little of the liquid she was drinking at the time, but it was not the cause of death. They simply died."

"But if they were healthy, there had to have been a cause," Denise persisted as she sketched Dr. Childs's expressive face. The high cheekbones and almond-shaped eyes made her, contrary to her own opinion, an ideal model.

"No, unfortunately, that's not true," Dr. Childs responded after a sip of soda. "Perfectly healthy people die all the time. We call it cardiac arrest or stroke, but the reality is that they did not die of any preexisting condition. They simply died. That's what happened to these people."

Growing frustrated at wondering down a blind alley, Denise stated, "Then you found nothing similar about their deaths. No commonality existed at all."

Reaching for a copy of the reports that Denise handed to her, Dr. Childs flipped the pages in silence for a few minutes. Finally satisfied with her review of the case, the chief medical examiner again turned her attention to Denise. The kindly doctor exuded confidence in her lab work and appeared genuinely sorry that she could not help Denise solve the case.

Shaking her head sadly, Dr. Childs responded, "Denise, the only thing that these people had in common was the presence of a dietary supplement that many people take these days even if they don't need it. The amount was small, hardly worth considering. It offers a high similar to that of excessive caffeine. With everyone running from one activity to the other, some people feel that a little extra something helps them make it through the day. Some scientists say that too much of the supplement can prove fatal, but the FDA hasn't concluded its studies yet. It's not regulated as a medicine since it's a dietary supplement. I made a brief note of it in my reports but didn't think much of it."

Stopping her sketching in midstroke, Denise stared at Dr. Childs in almost childlike disbelief. Here was the lead for which she had been searching. The victims' bodies contained traces of a dietary supplement known to cause death.

"What's the name of this supplement and where do people purchase it?" Denise asked as she sat poised with pencil in midair.

"It's called ephedra and is available at health food stores alone and as an additive in other supplements," Dr. Childs replied. "As a matter of fact, I saw it on the shelf in the store around the corner yesterday. I was almost tempted to buy some. Jane takes it, not that I see an increase in energy. I've warned her of the risks, but she won't stop. Vanity."

"What do you now about it?" Denise asked, resuming her sketching with appropriate notes in the margins.

"The FDA claims that ephedra alkaloids can cause reactions from nervousness and sleepless to hypertension, stroke, seizure, and heart attack in people who do not have other health risks," Dr. Childs stated and then added, "I see where you're going with this thought, Denise. I suppose I should have thought about it, too, but the victims lived in the fast lane. It's not unusual for people of that ilk to take uppers of all kinds. Besides, the dosage was relatively low compared to some of the other stuff I see."

"Don't worry about it. Ephedra might not have been responsible for their deaths at all. I just need to check every possibility, and, at this moment, this is the only lead I have," Denise responded, hoping to keep Dr. Childs from shutting down.

Getting comfortable in her chair once again, Dr. Childs began her minilecture, saying, "Like with any other upper, medical science doesn't exactly know all of the possible side effects. What exactly is too much? The manufacturer claims that ephedra is completely safe if taken as directed, but we all know that, if anyone takes an upper and feels better, the likelihood is good that the person will want even more energy. The secondary benefit for many people is weight loss, not that any of these victims was overweight. However, many obese people see it as the solution to their problem. The manufacturer takes advantage of that constant quest for thin and markets it to people's vanity."

"Does the public know about the potential dangers of this stuff?" Denise asked as she sipped the last of her soda.

"I don't think so," Dr. Childs replied with a grimace. "If they did, I don't think they'd take it. But then again, they take other uppers knowing the risk. The *New England Journal of Medicine* published an article a year or so ago that detailed the findings of a study conducted in California, but ephedra is still on the shelf. I could buy it today and feel energized by tomorrow and maybe be dead by the next day. The very least I'd experience would be permanent disability and death. I made a conscious decision not to reach for the attractive package in the store, but others don't."

Leaning forward as she listened intently, Denise asked, "Is it possible for a person taking ephedra to feel fine one minute and fall dead the next?"

Nodding emphatically, Dr. Childs responded, "Sure. Those people might not have known what hit them. The violinist is a prime example. If I remember correctly, she was drinking coffee in her kitchen at the time of death from coronary arrest. She never had a chance to call for help. She simply slumped over dead. The drug, for want of a better term since I don't see it as a dietary supplement, plays havoc with the central nervous system. People only have to take twelve to thirty-six milligrams per day to put themselves at risk even if they have no medical problems."

"How did the industry react to the study?" Denise

inquired, encouraging the coroner to continue offering the helpful information.

Smiling knowingly, Dr. Childs voiced her opinion pronouncedly. "Of course, it denied the validity of the report and criticized the journal for spreading information based on factual error. However, it's not easy to deny that deaths have occurred among people taking this supplement. Ephedra is bad news. Even without causal analysis, people should stay away from that stuff."

"Is this a naturally occurring substance?" Denise asked, needing more information that might lead to the source of the poison. In addition to the usual sources for murder weapons, Denise had pursued killers into botanical labs and jewelry centers in the hunt for clues. She wondered if the same were true of this killer.

"Yes, and an old one," Dr. Childs stated. "The Chinese have used it as a dietary supplement for thousands of years although it has always been known that high doses could lead to asphyxiation and heart failure. They call it *ma huang*. However, a synthetic form known as ephedrine hydrocloride is a common ingredient in cold medicines. Most state laws and industry standards prohibit the use of synthetic ephedrine in dietary supplements. Let's see what's on the Internet about these products. I've exhausted my memory bank of information."

Denise waited as Dr. Childs logged on to a server and searched for ephedra capsules. In a relatively short time, she had found many on-line companies touting the energizing capability of the herb and selling it in large dosages. One site called it the "world's strongest stimulant."

Looking over Dr. Childs's shoulder, Denise remarked, "The toxic red color of those capsules would put me off taking ephedra."

Dr. Childs agreed, saying, "Me, too, but for some, it's a come-on. Red means hot, sexy, busy, and active. Some people gravitate to that color and would select the product because of its packaging. Look at the dosages! No wonder people are dying from taking this compound. Dosages this large are foolish at best and basically suicidal. I'm sure they don't stop with taking only one. If one feels good, two or three would boost energy to the max."

Searching another Web page, Denise commented, "At least this one warns of possible hazards."

"True, but look at the wording," Dr. Childs said as she pointed to the computer screen. "It says 'generally' safe. I doubt that anyone looking for this energy punch would worry about being outside the norm. Besides, not many people consult their physicians before starting extreme diets or taking energy-boosting medications. Sad fact, but true."

"Look at that one. They won't sell to anyone who lives in Canada, Nebraska, or Sweden. They even state that ephedra's only for healthy people. Nine states have tried to regulate its availability," Denise added as she scanned the page.

Shaking her head, Dr. Childs commented, "It's a shame that people will abuse helpful products. For years, the Chinese used ephedra as a treatment for bronchitis and allergies. Now that people wanting that amphetamine have started abusing it, it's being monitored for its negative properties rather than praised for its positive ones."

Finishing the last of her notes, Denise said, "I guess that's human nature, unfortunately. I wonder why the victims used it. More than that, I'd like to know if the murderer forced it on them or if they were already consumers. They all lived extremely busy lives. Maybe they were willing to try a higher dosage without regard for their safety."

Returning her attention to the reports on her desk, Dr. Childs stated, "The reports show that each of them had consumed the substance. Unfortunately, I don't know the time or the method of consumption. They had eaten a few hours prior to death. More than that I can't tell you, Denise. Sorry."

"You've been a great help, Dr. Childs," Denise said as she rose from her seat at the little table. "I'll visit Adam Frazer's fiancée to see if she can shed any light on his use of ephedra. She might be a user, too, and needs to be warned about the possible consequences of abusing it. Ms. Dell mentioned that she's always careful about her intake of calories."

"I'll call you at the precinct if I think of anything else that might help you," Dr. Childs said as she led Denise to the outer office.

"Thanks, again, Dr. Childs," Denise replied. Turning to the receptionist, she asked, "By the way, Ms. Blues, do you know anyone who uses ephedra for weight loss or as an upper?"

"Yeah, one of my friends used to use it," Ms. Blues responded as she looked up from the letter she was typing. Her work was very slow because of the need to protect the polish on her very long nails.

"Why did she stop?" Denise asked as Dr. Childs stood at her side.

"She died," Ms. Blues stated frankly. "I guess she took too much. Her mom said that she had a heart attack."

"How did she consume it? Capsules?" Dr. Childs interjected.

"Usually capsules, but sometimes she'd brew this really strong tea with it," Ms. Blues said and then added. "I tried it a few times, but it made me too nervous. I couldn't get to sleep at night. I gave it up."

"Good," Dr. Childs commented. "You might have been next if you hadn't stopped using it."

"Yeah, I thought of that when Jeannie died. It could have been me," Ms. Blues remarked, shaking her head.

"I'll see you two later. I have to see a lady about her fiancé's habits," Denise said as she left the medical examiner and the receptionist engaged in conversation.

Denise did not bother with telling anyone of her change of location. Instead, she hopped into her car and quickly drove to Ms. Dell's apartment. She wanted to ask her in person about the ephedra usage. Denise had a feeling that she would deny the use of the drug over the phone but would admit it in person.

Ten

Ms. Dell seemed surprised to see Denise again so soon. She opened the door to her smaller and more humble apartment on the first ring. Instead of looking like the grieving fiancée, she appeared almost jovial. With a cigarette in one hand and a glass of scotch in the other, she motioned Denise into the room.

"Would you like a little light refreshment? A glass of scotch perhaps?" Ms. Dell asked in speech that sounded a little more than slightly slurred.

"No, thanks, it's a little early for me," Denise replied as she declined the opportunity to help herself from the well-stocked bar at the other end of the room.

"It's never too early. As a matter of fact, have a seat while I freshen my drink," Ms. Dell stated as she wove her way across the room.

Denise watched the very unsteady Ms. Dell bump off furniture on her way to the bar. She poured another stiff drink before joining Denise on the sofa, spilling large splashes on the apricot carpet as she staggered along. Draining half the contents of the Manhattan glass, she turned her watery attention to Denise and smiled crookedly.

"What can I do for you? What brings you back here so soon? Is it my charming personality? I'm not used to so much company. I've never been so popular. Adam was the one everyone, especially the women, wanted to see.

First, the police come to interview me, and then you, a special police person, come to see me, and then all those 'old friends' of Adam's who wanted to console the grieving partner and fiancée. The only one who hasn't come to see me is Miss Size Ten," Ms. Dell stated with a slow, sloppy sniff.

"Let's hope she doesn't," Denise commented softly in a very consoling manner.

"She's the last person I want to meet. Why are you here? Have you found out who killed Adam?" Ms. Dell asked, taking another large mouthful of her drink.

"I've learned a few things that I'd like to bounce off you, if you don't mind," Denise stated as a smile played at the corners of her mouth.

Ms. Dell made a lovely drunk. Her clothes were perfectly in order. Her hair looked as if she had just stepped from the page of a fashion magazine. In fact, she looked more put together now than the first time they had met. If she had not been so terribly drunk, she would have been stunning.

"Bounce away," Ms. Dell retorted, sipping her drink while holding the glass with both unsteady hands.

"Have you ever heard of the dietary supplement called ephedra?" Denise asked as she sketched the lovely and terribly drunk Ms. Dell.

"Sure, who hasn't?" Ms. Dell burped wetly. She appeared to be experiencing difficulty focusing her eyes. Denise decided that she had better ask her questions fast before the strength of the drinks interfered with Ms. Dell's thinking processes.

"What do you know about it?" Denise inquired, watching her carefully for any change in expression.

"Well, it's good for added energy and weight loss," Ms. Dell stated calmly. "I've used it."

"Are you still using it?" Denise asked quickly.

"No, I didn't think it worked. I didn't lose any weight."

Ms. Dell sniffed again. "It kept me awake, but I didn't feel energized, only nervous and cranky. I couldn't concentrate on my music. A composer who can't compose isn't much good to anyone."

"What did Mr. Fraser think about your use of it?" Denise asked, sketching the carefully made up face.

"Not much. Actually, he hated it. He said that anyone who used drugs needed to have his or, in my case, her head examined," Ms. Dell responded slowly. Her speech was becoming considerably more slurred by the minute.

"So you never knew him to use anything?" Denise repeated.

"He drank a little, but I never saw him use drugs of any kind. He hated taking medicine, even vitamins. Adam preferred to eat fresh vegetables rather than rely on pills. He was a real health food nut. He used to fuss at me all the time for eating so much chocolate. Claimed it wasn't good for me. He thought that a good sweat in a steam room would cure almost anything, including obesity. He went crazy every time he saw me pop those pills." Ms. Dell sniffed.

"Do you still have them?"

Running her shaking finger in the frost on her glass, Ms. Dell stated, "No, he made me flush them while he watched. Adam said that they had made me so grumpy that he couldn't stand me anymore. He threatened to end our business partnership if I didn't stop taking them. Funny, he said he'd rather I gained weight than stay a grouch. Now I understand why. He was probably having an affair with Miss Size Ten or someone like her even then. And to think I initially lost weight because he said that I was too heavy to be a member of his backup group. I started taking the pills to lose the weight fast. I needed to go from an eight to a size six in three months. It's not much weight, but, for a chocoholic, it seems like a ton."

Denise sat for a moment watching the drunken

composer. Ms. Dell had not flinched when asked the questions about the ephedra or denied using it. She appeared to have been open in both her use of the drug and Adam Fraser's aversion to it. Denise decided to venture a little further.

"The autopsy showed that Mr. Fraser had taken ephedra sometime the day he died. Do you have any idea how he might have gotten it?" Denise inquired, studying Ms. Dell's face for a change of expression.

At first, nothing happened, but then slowly, Ms. Dell began to respond. The alcohol had obviously dulled her wits and slowed her thought processes. Gradually, she stopped drawing on her glass and turned her unfocused eyes on Denise.

"What? That hypocrite was taking ephedra? After making me flush my stash, after lecturing me about the hazards of addiction, he used ephedra?" Ms. Dell sputtered wetly.

"I don't know if he regularly used it or if someone poisoned him with it. The other victims also had amounts of ephedra in their systems when they died," Denise explained calmly.

"Poisoned him? Who would do that? Who would hate him enough to do that? What would anyone gain?" Ms. Dell blurted the entire string of questions in one breath and then took a few long swigs on her drink. Finishing the glass, she staggered to the bar for a refill.

"You tell me. Who would have wanted him dead?" Denise shouted over the rattling of the ice cube in the glass.

"No one. No one would gain anything. I certainly wouldn't have. Everything we owned was in both names. I could have cleaned out the accounts and left town at any time," Ms. Dell responded as she fell into her chair.

When Denise did not answer, Ms. Dell focused on her with watery eyes. As she stared, Denise could almost hear the slow, deliberate workings of the woman's sodden mind. She had come to the logical conclusion that she was now a suspect.

"I didn't kill Adam!" Ms. Dell almost shouted. "I loved him."

"I didn't accuse you, Ms. Dell," Denise replied softly.

"No, but you're thinking it. Everyone else probably does, too. Now I understand why people kept asking me when I'll move to the penthouse." Ms. Dell sobbed drunkenly.

"Are you planning to move?" Denise asked gently.

"Yes, but I don't have any choice," Ms. Dell blubbered. "We sold my apartment. I went to the settlement this morning. The movers are coming tomorrow."

Denise felt sorry for the woman whose life had been so completely turned upside down. She sat quietly for a long time, watching Ms. Dell sob uncontrollably into her hands. The poor woman rocked herself childlike, searching for comfort that would not come. Denise involuntarily wondered if she herself would react the same way if something fatal happened to Tom. She had been desperately worried about him when he had ingested the contaminated dinner rolls and had fallen ill to ergot poisoning. If he had not recovered, she would have found herself in the place of the lonely Ms. Dell.

"Ms. Dell, I know this is difficult, but can you think hard for a few minutes? Who might have visited Mr. Fraser while you were at lunch the day of his death?" Denise asked gently.

As the rocking and sobbing slowed, Ms. Dell uncovered her face and responded between gushes of tears, "I don't know. Adam didn't mention anyone. He hadn't mentioned having an appointment that day. He certainly wouldn't have had one at lunchtime. He's always too tired after our morning work sessions to do anything except eat and, perhaps, take a little nap. He doesn't even exercise until after we finish work for the day."

"Did he order anything from a carryout for lunch?"

"No, I made his usual lunch of tuna salad on a huge bed of lettuce before I left. I always take half of it home for myself," Ms. Dell replied and then added, "It's looking worse for me all the time. Do I need to phone my attorney?"

"No, you're not a suspect, Ms. Dell, at least not yet," Denise responded. "Someone killed Mr. Fraser and the others with an excess of ephedra to make it look like a heart attack. That someone had access to all of them. I need to find out who it was so that I can solve this case."

"I can't think of anyone who would have done it," Ms. Dell moaned, clutching her stomach and rushing from the room.

As Denise waited, she wandered around the living room and looked at the paintings on Ms. Dell's walls. The art was so different from Mr. Fraser's penthouse, more intimate and less famous. Ms. Dell appeared to be a supporter of new artists rather than a collector of recognized greats.

"I'm sorry," Ms. Dell stated as she returned. "I obviously drank too much. I'm not feeling very well. Is there anything else you want to ask me?"

"Yes," Denise answered quickly. "Take me up to the penthouse. I want to look around a bit."

"Okay, but I can't imagine what you'll find there," Ms. Dell replied as she took the key from the desk drawer.

"Neither can I," Denise stated frankly.

Denise and Ms. Dell took the elevator ride in silence. Ms. Dell was feeling none too steady and appeared a bit green around the edges. She leaned heavily against the paneled walls and looked ready to fall asleep at any minute.

Opening the door, Ms. Dell said, "I'll lie down on the sofa. Let me know when you're ready to leave."

Pleased to be on her own to search the apartment, Denise watched as Ms. Dell lay on the sofa and immediately fell asleep. The anger, grief, and worry coupled with the excessive booze to put her into a quick sleep. Ms. Dell looked almost pretty again as the green tinge began to recede from her complexion.

Immediately, Denise walked into the kitchen section of the loft penthouse. Opening the cabinets, she searched for any sign of the ominous red capsules. She pulled out dishes and searched in the cabinet corners. Finding nothing, she turned her attention to the pantry.

The pantry was very well stocked with every imaginable shape and size of pasta, variety of cereal, and kind of grain. Mr. Fraser definitely took his health seriously, quite an irony for someone who had died from an overdose of an herbal food supplement. Even the canned foods had been processed naturally without the addition of chemical preservatives. All of the foods remained in their sealed boxes. No one had poisoned the items in the pantry.

Denise's next stop was the bathroom. Again, she found nothing suspicious. The medicine cabinet contained only a toothbrush and toothpaste, shaving cream and razor, and an unopened box of generic aspirin. The safely seal was still in place.

Ms. Dell snored lightly as Denise again walked through the living room on her return to the kitchen. As she scanned the almost empty counters, her eyes fell on the stainless steel canister set. Remembering the Internet information about Mormon and Native American use of the dietary supplement, she opened the tea canister. Inside, she found oversize bags of tea with names that she did not recognize. On close examination, she saw that the bags contained not only the tea leaves but a powder that resembled the cornstarch often used to keep items from sticking together in processing. Opening an evidence bag,

Denise poured the contents of the canister inside. She did the same with the flour and sugar.

Picking up one of the bags in her gloved hand, Denise studied its bulging sides. The tea itself was more finely ground than the usual commercial teas with which she was accustomed and its fragrance was considerably stronger and fresher. The paper of the bag was not the commercial white either. Denise concluded that Adam Fraser drank organically grown and processed tea in addition to eating organic foods.

Studying the bag more closely, Denise saw that someone had carefully opened the little staple at the top of the bag and then resealed it with a slightly larger one. She could see the location of the original staple. She guessed that the murderer had carefully added the ephedra to the tea so that Adam Fraser would not notice. The perpetrator must have known Mr. Fraser's routine well in order to have the time to tamper with the bags and to know that Fraser would not question the bag's slightly dusty appearance.

Leaning against the counter, Denise allowed her mind to play with the possibilities. It was possible that the murderer had entered the apartment while Mr. Fraser was away on his last road trip and substituted the altered tea bags for the uncontaminated ones. If the bags usually contained a dusting of powder for freshness, Mr. Fraser would not have noticed the difference in the appearance of the product. Further, it was also possible that someone he knew had made the switch while he was in the apartment. Mr. Fraser could have left the perpetrator alone in the kitchen, making the switch possible.

However, the second possibility was less likely since the opportunity for being discovered increased significantly with Mr. Fraser in the apartment. If someone he knew had made the switch and he had discovered the person in the act, Mr. Fraser would have become suspicious about the motive. He would have phoned the police unless the person regularly had free access to the apartment. Perhaps Ms. Dell had made the switch. However, with all of the finances in both names, Ms. Dell had nothing to gain. Her only motive would have been the revenge for Mr. Fitzgerald's infidelity if she had known about Ms. Size Ten prior to Denise's discovery of the clothing in the closet, which was not likely from her reaction.

Focusing on someone other than Ms. Dell, Denise reflected on their recent conversation. Ms. Dell had said that they had completely restocked the apartment in preparation for the upcoming marriage and change in living arrangements. They had returned none of the old produce to the shelves after the remodeling process. Mr. Fraser had wanted to avoid any possibility of paint and dust contamination. Ms. Dell had said that the grocer had delivered all new items to fill the freshly refinished cabinets.

Returning to the living room, Denise slowly awakened the sleeping Ms. Dell. The nap had done her good. Her complexion had returned to normal and her eyes, once completely open, focused with greater ease.

"Did you find anything?" Ms. Dell asked, rubbing the sleep from her eyes.

"Maybe," Denise answered, avoiding the question directly. "What do you know about Mr. Fraser's choice of tea? The fragrance is much stronger than grocery store varieties."

Swinging her feet to the floor, Ms. Dell replied, "I told you that Adam was a health food nut. Well, he only drank organically grown teas that the specialty grocery stores carry."

"Did he completely restock the tea after the remodeling?" Denise inquired, watching the other woman adjust her clothing and hair. The transformation was miraculous from bed-head to beauty in a matter of seconds.

Stretching, Ms. Dell explained, "We threw out everything before he left on his last tour and I headed for California. Actually, we carried a big bag of stuff to the local shelter the night before we left. We didn't leave anything in the cupboards. There really wasn't much to toss since he had allowed supplies to dwindle in preparation for the remodeling. Adam wasn't one to waste money by throwing out good food if he could help it."

"Did he have someone restock the apartment while he was away?" Denise asked.

"Oh, no, not Adam. He did that himself. He always had the store deliver his groceries but the restocking was his job. He was such a perfectionist. Besides, he wanted all of the paint smell to subside before he added any new food. He probably did that the day he returned. I wish I had been with him. Maybe I could have prevented this from happening," Ms. Dell replied with sadness at the memories that flooded her heart and mind.

"You mentioned on our first visit that you arrived in time for a brief reunion. Refresh my memory, did you prepare lunch that day?" Denise asked as they walked toward the door.

"Yes, I always did. I divided our portions and left. I wish now that I could have seen him later, but we both had so much to do. Do you think that someone tampered with Adam's food?" Ms. Dell answered with an expression of shock on her face as she carefully secured the apartment's lock.

"It's possible. Did you notice anything different about the contents of the kitchen? Did anything look out of place?"

"No, nothing. Adam had completely set up the apartment. I only made lunch and left. Everything looked as it always did, only fresh and new with a very slight paint and new-furniture smell. Do you think that someone poisoned the tea?" Ms. Dell asked unsteadily as she leaned against the wall for the trip to her floor.

"It's possible," Denise stated matter-of-factly. She saw no reason not to be honest with Ms. Dell. If she were the perpetrator, Denise would put the pieces together soon enough.

"Oh, no! Who would do something like that?" Ms. Dell lamented more to herself than to Denise as she pulled her key from her pocket.

"What's the name of the tea Mr. Fraser drank?" Denise asked, standing at the open elevator door.

"Franklin's. You can buy it at the specialty food store on the corner," Ms. Dell answered without hesitation.

"Does it have a dusty appearance?" Denise asked.

"A little, I guess. They package it in something to keep the bags from sticking together in humid weather. Except for that, it looks like any other tea only the bags haven't been bleached and the flakes are smaller," Ms. Dell replied, motioning Denise inside.

Declining the invitation, Denise stated, "I'll buy a box on the way back to the precinct. Thanks for all your help, Ms. Dell."

"Any time, Detective. Please let me know what you find out. I guess I should throw out the flour and sugar when I move into the apartment as a precaution," Ms. Dell mused. Her body had begun to emit the stale smell of liquor, and her eyes had become very bloodshot.

"I already did. See you later. Thanks again for the help," Denise replied and stepped back into the waiting elevator.

Driving back to the precinct, Denise switched on the radio. She had stayed at Ms. Dell's for so long that it was almost time for her afternoon program. She listened carefully as the music changed from classical to show tunes. The selection was a repeat; the murderer had not given another clue to his identity. The answer lay somewhere in the play that she and Tom would watch that night. Somewhere in the lyrics of a song from *The King and I* Denise would find the next piece of the puzzle that led to the murderer's identity. Before she could change for her evening at the theater with Tom, Denise needed to give the lab a sample of the tea bags.

Pulling into the precinct lot, she hurried to her desk without having to step over Molly's outstretched legs. It seemed strange to find Tom's desk vacant so early in the afternoon and so tidy. Tom never left the squad room before the rush-hour traffic died down and often later if she did not drag him away.

Writing the necessary instructions for the lab, Denise decided that she would have to get used to the changes. In time, she would not notice the vacant, organized desk and the missing smell of overcooked coffee. It would not be easy, but she would try. However, she would never be able to accept Craig Panns as Tom's replacement. He might prove to be a respectable, reliable partner, but he would never replace Tom.

An important message from the ARABESQUE Editor

Dear Arabesque Reader,

Because you've chosen to read one of our Arabesque romance novels, we'd like to say "thank you"! And, as a special way to thank you, we've selected four more of the books you love so well to send you for FREE!

Please enjoy them with our compliments, and thank you for continuing to enjoy Arabesque...the soul of romance.

Karen Thomas
Senior Editor,
Arabesque Romance Novels

Check out our website at
www.arabesquebooks.com

SPECIAL OFFER!
4 FREE BOOKS

ARABESQUE ®

A PRODUCT OF

BET BOOKS™

3 QUICK STEPS
TO RECEIVE YOUR "THANK YOU" GIFT
FROM THE EDITOR

Send this card back and you'll receive 4 FREE Arabesque
novels! The introductory shipment of 4 Arabesque novels – a
$23.96 value – is yours absolutely FREE!

There's no catch. You're under no obligation to buy anything.
You'll receive your introductory shipment of 4 Arabesque
novels absolutely FREE (plus $1.99 to offset the costs of
shipping & handling). And you don't have to make any
minimum number of purchases—not even one!

We hope that after receiving your books you'll want to
remain an Arabesque subscriber. But the choice is yours to
continue or cancel, anytime at all! So why not take us up on
our invitation to receive 4 Arabesque Romance Novels, with
no risk of any kind. You'll be glad you did!

Call us
TOLL-FREE
at 1-800-770-1963

THE EDITOR'S "THANK YOU" GIFT INCLUDES:

- 4 books absolutely FREE (plus $1.99 for shipping and handling)
- A FREE newsletter, *Arabesque Romance News*, filled with author interviews, book previews, special offers, and more!
- No risks or obligations. You're free to cancel whenever you wish... with no questions asked.

BOOK CERTIFICATE

Yes! Please send me 4 FREE Arabesque novels (plus $1.99 for shipping & handling). I understand I am under no obligation to purchase any books, as explained on the back of this card.

Name _____

Address _____ Apt. _____

City _____ State _____ Zip _____

Telephone ( ) _____

Signature _____

Offer limited to one per household and not valid to current subscribers. All orders subject to approval. Terms, offer, & price subject to change. Offer valid only in the U.S.

Thank you!

AN033A

Accepting the four introductory books for FREE (plus $1.99 to offset the cost of shipping & handling) places you under no obligation to buy anything. You may keep the books and return the shipping statement marked "cancelled". If you do not cancel, about a month later we will send 4 additional Arabesque novels, and you will be billed the preferred subscriber's price of just $4.00 per title. That's $16.00 for all 4 books for a savings of 33% off the cover price (Plus $1.99 for shipping and handling). You may cancel at any time, but if you choose to continue, every month we'll send you 4 more books, which you may either purchase at the preferred discount price. . . or return to us and cancel your subscription.

THE ARABESQUE ROMANCE CLUB: HERE'S HOW IT WORKS

ARABESQUE ROMANCE BOOK CLUB
P.O. Box 5214
Clifton NJ 07015-5214

PLACE
STAMP
HERE

Eleven

Denise dressed with special care for the evening with Tom. As she applied quick-dry to the topcoat of polish on her toe- and fingernails, she wondered at her need to go to so much trouble for her old partner and lover. He was still Tom and she was the same old Denise. The only difference was that they had not spent the day sitting near each other. Nothing else had changed, except that, in a funny kind of way, everything had. Not seeing Tom all day added a new dimension to their relationship. They were no longer coworkers who happened to be lovers and sharing an evening of musical theater. For the first time in their relationship, they were lovers who were going on a date.

Plucking the few stray hairs in her eyebrows, she examined her complexion and decided that a few minutes with a cleansing mask would brighten the skin a bit. As her skin began to shrink under the mud-colored compound, she selected the honey-gold sheath with matching embroidered jacket and shoes that she would wear for the evening at the theater.

Washing off the dried mud, Denise inspected the change and splashed on a little toner. She carefully applied her makeup and gave her hair a quick brushing. Chuckling at herself, she massaged a concentrated emollient cream into her freshly showered body, paying special attention to her knuckles. A splash of her best perfume

completed the process. Max, the cat, sat on the toilet lid
and watched the preparations that usually only happened
on Sunday as part of her weekly beauty regimen.

"Don't look at me like that, Max. I don't know why I'm
doing all this for Tom. I can't help myself. I haven't seen
him since early this morning. I want to knock his socks
off when he arrives. I want him to . . . Oh, I don't know
what I want. Yes, I do. I want him to have missed me as
much as I've missed him," Denise remarked to the cat
that had been watching her with great interest.

Max meowed understandingly and followed Denise
into the bedroom. He watched as she slipped into a gold
satin bra and panty set. He patted at the toe of her panty
hose as she eased the shimmering gold fabric over her
feet and up her thighs. He stared as she performed the
little panty hose dance and wiggled her hips into the
nude panty part of the contraption. As she slipped her
feet into the thin-strapped slides, he lost interest and left
the room for his usual seat on the living room sofa.

"Some friend you are," Denise called after the vanishing
cat. "You didn't even give your final approval."

Stepping into the dress, Denise slipped the soft material onto her shoulders. She looked into the mirror,
adjusted the hips, and smiled. She was pleased with the
result and hoped Tom would be also. Reaching for her
purse, Denise flipped off the light. Show time!

They had arranged to meet at the Olney Theater. He
had been concerned that the demands of his new job
might delay his arrival. At least this way, one of them
would see the play's opening numbers.

Standing under the twinkling chandelier, Tom scanned
the faces, looking for Denise. He, too, had rushed home
and changed into his best black-on-black suit with a white-
on-white shirt. He had even made sure that, for once, he
was not wearing any of Molly's fur. He had put on his
fancy-dress black-tassel shoes and gold cuff links. After

showering and shaving for the second time that day, he had splashed on his favorite cologne. Now, waiting for Denise, he discreetly checked his appearance. Finding that he cast the desired image, he turned his attention, once again, to the crowd in the lobby.

Feeling strangely jittery almost as if he were a teenager again, Tom, who had been waiting for thirty minutes for fear of being late, could hardly wait until Denise arrived. He, too, had anticipated the change in their relationship since the morning. He had thought about her almost constantly, comparing his new group with their old comfortable partnership. His new canine corps associates seemed like nice people, but they did not have Denise's wit and enthusiasm for life. They seemed very focused on their work and dogs rather than being able to see the total relationship of all the parts. However, he realized that Denise was no longer a part of his working world. He would have to learn to communicate day-to-day events with her the same way he would with any other woman. The comfort level of being professional partners had ended.

He did not have long to wait. Magically, the crowd appeared to thin as Denise stepped into view. Tom smiled broadly at the sight of this beautiful, poised woman who had chosen to love him. He had always known that she was a knockout, but seeing her walk toward him with her head high and her hips swaying only confirmed it. Denise was the most beautiful woman he had ever seen and not just because he loved her. The other men in the Olney Theater hall watched her with hungry eyes as she glided past. The smile that played on their lips spoke volumes.

"Have you been waiting long?" Denise asked as she planted a sweet kiss on his lips. Her heart pounded with pleasure at the sight of her handsome lover.

Taking a quick glance at the hall, Tom could see the other men turn green with envy. His chest felt tight with the love and pride he felt for Denise. Not only was she one of the top detectives and criminal investigators in the country, she was breathtaking in the gold that seemed to glisten on her skin like water. The shimmering effect caused a double take from the men and women in the hall.

His eyes fell on a familiar face. Joshua Smithe and his dad appeared to have enjoyed the sight of Denise in that gown as much as the other men. They nodded in recognition and returned their conversation.

"No," Tom sputtered, so taken with her beauty that he could hardly speak. He added, "I mean yes. I arrived early so that I wouldn't be late."

"Are you okay?" Denise demanded as she studied the bewildered expression on his handsome face. She had been too overwhelmed by Tom's handsome appearance to notice the smiles of appreciation of the people in the hall.

"I'm fine. I just . . . You look great! I missed you," Tom replied, pulling her toward him and kissing her soundly. For a few seconds, no one existed in the great hall of the Olney Theater except the two of them. His slight irritation at the sight of Joshua Smithe and his father quickly subsided.

As he released her, neither could speak. The fears that both had felt about the dissolution of their relationship because of Tom's promotion and transfer proved to be unjustified as they stared into each other's eyes. From that kiss, they both knew that the impact to their professional separation would only be positive for their personal life.

The bong of a distant chime broke the spell as the other theatergoers began moving toward the stairs leading to the theater. Slipping her arm through his, Denise allowed Tom to escort her from the majesty of the red-carpeted hall to the grandeur of the mezzanine. The theater, illuminated only by the dim light of the stunning chandelier, the plush upholstery on the seats, the thick carpet underfoot, and the curtained stage welcomed them to a delightful evening.

The usher smiled, handed each of them a playbill, and escorted them to their seats. Sinking into the comfortable seat, Denise scanned the theater for signs of anything unusual. Instead of possible warnings from the perpetrator, she saw only a stage waiting to receive the cast who would enthrall the audience with its ability to bring music and drama to life.

Scanning the playbill, Denise searched for anything that might indicate the potential for foul play. She had only read the first page when the lights flickered and the orchestra began to play the overture. Smiling at Tom in the dimming light, Denise slipped her hand in his and settled back to enjoy the play.

As the lights went dim, Denise whispered, "Did you recognize someone in the hall a while ago?"

Putting his lips close to her ear, Tom replied, "Yeah, your shopkeeper, Joshua Smithe, and his dad are here, too."

"Oh, that's nice. It's good to see father and son doing things together," Denise mused softly.

"Young Smithe was watching you more than he was paying attention to his father," Tom muttered with a tinge of jealously in his voice.

"You're exaggerating," Denise replied with a chuckle.

"No, I know what I saw. He was looking at you the way Molly looks at a steak bone," Tom stated in a deep whisper.

"Whatever," Denise whispered, thrilled with the attention.

With perfect timing, an announcer's voice filled the space between the overture and the opening of the curtain. Denise listened as the man's mellow tones informed them that the understudy would play the lead of the king of Siam. No one seemed to mind, knowing that the fabulous music would not suffer from the change.

The play was as wonderful now as the past two times that Denise had seen it. Looking at Tom in the darkness, she saw that he seemed to be enjoying the story also. She could not imagine anyone not liking the bewitching music and lyrics. The time passed so quickly that Denise did not even feel the need to stretch.

Intermission was much too short to allow for anything but a quick trip to one of the many ladies' rooms and a handful of chocolate candies from the bag that Tom had bought. Resuming her seat, Denise decided to check the credits of the understudy, who was doing a wonderful job in the role of the king. Reading his bio, she discovered that he was a television regular. Although he had appeared on many soap operas, Denise did not remember either his name or face.

Curious about the regular star of the show, Denise scanned his biography also. According to the playbill, Timothy Morton had made his debut as the king on Broadway following a successful run of *How to Succeed in Business*. He was married to an actress whose name Denise remembered from *A Doll's House*, an Ibsen play that she had seen last summer with several of her women friends since Tom had refused to accompany her.

Reaching the last sentence, Denise froze. Timothy Morton was not only an accomplished thespian and occasional television personality. He had also conducted the National Symphony Orchestra, the Baltimore Symphony Orchestra, the Boston Pops, and the Philadelphia Philharmonic. Critics had voiced great approval and welcomed him to the world of the orchestral conductor.

"Tom," Denise whispered as the lights flickered to announce the imminent opening of the curtain, "look at this."

"What is it?" Tom asked as he strained in the dimming light to read the paragraph at which she pointed.

"It's Timothy Morton's bio. Not only is he the star of the show, but he's a conductor," Denise explained, placing her lips close to his ear as the curtain rose and the applause filled the theater.

"So?"

"He's sick and couldn't play the lead today," Denise explained.

"Okay. People get sick all the time, even actors," Tom retorted without a sign of comprehension.

"All of the victims are conductors. Timothy Morton is a conductor. The clue drew me to this play. Don't you understand?" Denise exclaimed sotto voce.

"I understand that you're determined that I won't see the second act of this play. Let's go," Tom instructed as they rose from their third-row center-aisle seats that had cost him a small fortune.

The great hall was empty as they ventured into the light. For a moment, Denise was not sure of the next move. Then she spotted one of the ushers, who directed them to the production office down a small corridor away from the view of visitors to the theater and memorial to a fallen president.

Knocking on the door bearing the title of production manager and the name of Bill Fitzgerald, Denise stated as she flashed her ever-present badge in the face of the man with rolled-up sleeves, "I'm Detective Dory of the Montgomery County Police Department and this is Detective . . . er . . . Lieutenant Phyfer. Might I ask you a few questions?"

"Sure. About what?" Mr. Fitzgerald asked as he motioned them inside.

Stepping into the bright, cluttered room she said, "I understand that Timothy Morton is ill tonight. Would you happen to have more information? I'm investigating a case and might find what you have to say useful."

"I'm afraid that any information you might want about Timothy Morton you'll have to get from the public relations office. They're preparing a statement for the press at this moment," Mr. Fitzgerald replied with an expression of sorrow on his face.

"Why?" Tom inquired, choosing to ignore the direction to seek help elsewhere.

Looking from Denise to Tom, Mr. Fitzgerald replied, "I guess there's no harm in my telling you. But remember, you didn't hear it from me."

"Tell us what?" Denise urged, growing impatient with the man's need to follow protocol.

"He's dead," Mr. Fitzgerald stated. "Timothy Morton died in his hotel room this evening."

"How?" Denise demanded.

"We don't know," Mr. Fitzgerald replied, growing more comfortable with the attention. "When he didn't appear for makeup, we phoned his hotel suite. He didn't answer so we called in the understudy just in case he wouldn't arrive in time. I'm glad we did."

"How do you know he's dead? Who found the body?" Denise asked in gentle interrogation.

"I did. I know a dead man when I see one," Mr. Fitzgerald stated firmly. "He was slumped over the room service cart. Dead."

"What did you do after that?" Tom inquired.

"I phoned the police department and stood in the hall until they arrived. I didn't want to be in the room with a corpse," Mr. Fitzgerald explained, sitting heavily in his chair.

"Did you see anything unusual in the room, like maybe a conductor's baton?" Denise asked as she studied the man's stricken face. She wished she had her sketchbook rather than having to rely on memory.

As if reading her mind, Tom pulled a sheet of paper from the printer on the man's desk and a pencil from the desk. Mr. Fitzgerald did not appear to notice. He continued to stare into space.

Looking up with bewilderment on his face, Mr. Fitzgerald replied, "As a matter of fact, a baton lay on the floor beside him. I don't know why he would have needed one. We have a conductor for the orchestra. There's no way Timothy Morton, as good as he is . . . was . . . could have directed and acted at the same time."

"Do you know what happened to the baton?" Denise inquired.

Nodding his head in the affirmative, Mr. Fitzgerald said, "Yeah, sure do. The police have it. I saw one of the investigators put it into an evidence bag. I didn't see much else because I left almost as soon as they arrived."

"You've been most helpful. We'll let you get back to work," Denise remarked almost absently as she cut a quick look at Tom.

"Work!" Mr. Fitzgerald exclaimed. "I haven't been able to work at all since I found Timothy Morton's body. He was a wonderful man and a great talent. He seemed to have been in great shape. How could he possibly be dead? We'll have to use the understudy until the producer makes a decision about the show. I'm just devastated."

"Perhaps you should go home," Denise offered.

"Maybe, but I'd only have to return tomorrow to the same mess," Mr. Fitzgerald replied, motioning to his desk. "I'm waiting for a call from the producer now. What a mess! Personally and professionally, I've never seen anything like it. I know you see dead people all the time, but it's a shock to me. How do you get used to it?"

"We don't," Tom remarked gently, "but it's part of the job."

With that, they left Mr. Fitzgerald to sort out the the-atrical mess that Timothy Morton's death had made while trying to deal with the grief of someone he knew. Closing the door behind them, they returned through the winding halls until they stood in the great hall once more. Deciding simultaneously without words to skip the rest of the play, Denise and Tom headed to the garage and, eventually, the police.

The precinct was bustling as could be expected in an urban city. Prostitutes in their scanty outfits and their pimps in elaborate clothing argued with the arresting officers that time spent in the police station meant money lost from working the street. Battered wives and husbands tried to convince the officers that they would never do it again although they were regular visitors to the precinct. People posting signs on the precinct bulletin board about missing animals looked bewildered by the level of humanity and anxious to leave the station.

After waiting in line for almost an hour, Denise and Tom finally had a chance to speak with the desk sergeant. He did not seem to notice Denise's attire, being too overworked to care. Showing their badges and introducing themselves, they explained the reason for their visit. The officer barely grunted as he directed them to Lieutenant Grange's office through the door and down the hall to the left.

The door was open and a short, stocky man sat typing and fussing. He barely looked up as they approached. Motioning to the well-worn chairs beside the badly cluttered desk, he finished the report before turning his attention to Denise and Tom.

"So? What can I do for you?" Lieutenant Grange demanded as he sat back in his chair. A momentary twinkle lighted his tired eyes as he looked at Denise in the stunning gown.

Showing their badges, Denise explained, "I'm working on a murder case in which the perpetrator leaves a conductor's baton beside the victim. We were in the Olney

Theater tonight and learned that Timothy Morton had been found dead in his hotel room. We understand from the man who found him that a baton was next to him. I'd like to examine it if I might."

"You're right on all counts," Lieutenant Grange responded as he pulled a big brown envelope from the pile on his desk. "I was just finishing the report on the case. I'm sending the baton to the FBI along with the other items we found in the room, but you can take a look at it."

"Thanks," Denise replied as she slipped on the gloves he handed her along with the envelope.

Inside a plastic bag, Denise found the baton. Holding it under the strong light on Lieutenant Grange's desk, she examined it for markings that would make it a match to the others found at the murder scenes. The shape and color of the handle were exactly the same. The wand fit into the handle at exactly the same position.

Pointing to the tiny holes at the juncture of the wand and the handle, Denise stated, "See these? They're the same as on the other batons.

"They look like pinholes to me," Lieutenant Grange remarked.

Nodding, Denise replied, "They are, but they aren't part of the original construction of the batons. Someone drilled these tiny holes into the hollow handle for a purpose. If I'm right, the murderer placed a lethal dosage of ephedra into each baton in addition to the amount that he slipped into the victim's food."

"Why would anyone want to kill an actor? I don't understand," Lieutenant Grange said as he sat back in his chair.

"That part I don't know. When I do, I'll be able to stop any further murders," Denise responded. "However, Timothy Morton wasn't only an actor. He had also conducted very prestigious orchestras. All of the other victims were also conductors as well as composers, violinists, and performers. Now we have an actor/conductor victim."

"What's this ephedra you mentioned?" Lieutenant Grange asked and then added, "I suppose I should mention it in my report and cross-reference the other murder cases, too. The coroner might need to know about it."

"Ephedra is a dietary supplement that, if taken in excess, can cause death that imitates coronary arrest. I'd like to know if the coroner finds any in the victim's stomach or on his hands," Denise commented as she returned the bagged baton to the lieutenant.

Writing her case numbers on the back of her business card, Denise waited for the lieutenant to speak. He appeared to be deep in thought until he snored. Denise then realized that he had fallen asleep with his eyes open.

Tom practically startled the man from his chair when he asked, "Do you think we could visit the coroner and see the body?"

Shaking himself, Lieutenant Grange apologized and said, "I've been awake for three nights straight. New baby. Sure, I'll make the call, but it'll be okay. Take the report with you, if you don't mind. He'll need it and so will the forensics department next door. He'll take care of sending it to them for me."

They thanked him and left with the report securely under Tom's arm. The desk sergeant barely acknowledged them as they pressed through the crowd that still stood in front of his desk. Waving their thanks, Denise and Tom left the throng behind them and headed to a quieter place.

The morgue was not as busy as the one in Rockville. The coroner greeted them at the locked door when they arrived and led them back to his office near the autopsy room. His white lab coat, although sparkling white, was very wrinkled and his name tag hung crooked on the pocket. Like all morgues, this one smelled of a combination of fluids. The coroner's expressive eyes twinkled as they took in Denise's appearance and Tom's stature.

Extending his hands for the envelope and a handshake, the coroner introduced himself, saying, "Thanks for bringing this to me. I'm Calvin Otis. Lieutenant Grange said something about a possible connection between this death and a case you're working."

"Dr. Otis, we're Detective Dory and Lieutenant Phyfer of the Montgomery County Police Department. Yes, I think a connection might exist," Denise stated as they shook hands all around.

"Have a seat. Tell me about it," Dr. Otis directed as he almost flopped into his chair from the fatigue that lined his face and created dark circles under his eyes.

"We've had a series of murders in the Maryland suburb involving members of the music community," Denise began as Tom settled into the seat beside her. "I think this one might be related."

"In what way?" Dr. Otis asked with genuine interest.

"All of the victims have been found with conductors' batons near them. However, they haven't all been primarily conductors. With the exception of one of them, each had another primary field of interest with conducting as simply an extra activity. For instance, Timothy Morton, the deceased, was an actor who happened to have conducted several prestigious orchestras. Another victim was a violinist who accepted a guest conductorship as the result of her reputation as a first-chair violinist and soloist. Another was a cross-over country singer and performer who happened to do a little conducting. Mr. Hornblatt was the only conductor by profession and he was originally a composer."

Dr. Otis smiled and agreed, saying, "You might have a valid theory there, Detective Dory. What's this about ephedra being involved? It's a very old dietary sup-

plement. I know that the FDA has started monitoring it
and warning about its use. How is it connected to this
case? Lieutenant Grange was very sketchy about that one.
It's surprising the man could remember anything considering the hours he's keeping. New dad, you know."

"So he said," Tom injected.

"Our coroner found ephedra in the stomach of all the
victims," Denise explained. "At first it didn't mean anything to me when I read the reports or to her either, but
now it does. It might just be our murder weapon. I also
found tea bags in one of the victims' kitchen. I've sent
them to my FBI contact since I think they were laced
with ephedra."

"Okay, I'll examine the stomach contents for ephedra.
Anything else I should know?" Dr. Otis asked as he took
notes.

"You might want to test the baton, too," Tom interjected. "Detective Dory thinks that the perpetrator
drilled holes into the hollow handle and filled it with
ephedra."

"Really? Why?" Dr. Otis asked with genuine interest.

Explaining, Denise stated, "Again, this is only a theory,
but I think the murderer poisoned the food that the victim consumed with ephedra. However, just in case the
victim didn't eat, he laced the handle with enough
ephedra to kill the victim. He probably thought that the
victim would pick up the baton and wave it around without thinking much about it."

Finishing her thought, Tom concluded, "The victim
would breathe in sufficient ephedra to cause bronchial
dilation and apparent heart attack."

"Nice theory," Dr. Otis conceded as he finished his
notes. "Now, who did it? Who would want to kill these
musicians?"

Handing him her business card, Denise replied,
"That's the part for which I don't have a theory. It might

be someone with a grudge against conductors, but I can't figure out the motive. The killer wants me to find him, however. He leaves clues to his next strike on the classical radio station."

"What?" Dr. Otis asked incredulously as he escorted Denise and Tom to the door.

"That's right," Denise explained. "I didn't understand the first one from the musical *Annie*. He arranged for the DJ to play 'Tomorrow.' The next day, he struck again. This time, the DJ played 'Shall We Dance?' from *The King and I*. I understood that he'd strike in relationship to this play. I couldn't identify the victim, but I knew the connection to the play was real. At first, I thought it would be the conductor, but when he appeared tonight, the murderer confused me. Now I know to look for an expert in his or her field of music who has done some conducting but who isn't necessarily a conductor."

Smiling his agreement, Dr. Otis said, "That certainly gives you a wide range of possibilities. I'll work on this tonight and give you a call at your office tomorrow. If you're right about the ephedra, you'll have two pieces of the puzzle."

"Thanks, Dr. Otis. I'll be waiting to hear from you," Denise concluded as they shook hands again.

Denise and Tom took deep breaths of the night air as they walked toward her car. The cloying smell of the morgue still stuck to their clothing as they drove back to the Olney Theater to pick up Tom's car for the separate drive to his apartment. The lot was practically deserted with the crush of people who had long returned home. Although the evening had not gone as either of them had anticipated, it had been very productive. They had found answers to many of their questions.

"I never know what to expect from an evening with you," Tom stated as they pulled into the space beside his car. "I take my girlfriend on a date to the theater and wind up getting involved in a murder case. You come here dressed to kill in that slinky gold number and end up following a killer's trail. I just don't know what to make of you, Dory."

"You like this little dress?" Denise asked as she gently laid her hand on his arm.

"What man wouldn't?" Tom growled in appreciation.

"I was a little worried about this date," Denise confided softly.

"Me, too," Tom confessed as he brought the warm, little hand to his lips.

"I guess we're still okay, huh?" Denise stated with a question in her voice.

"More than okay," Tom replied as he pulled her into his arms. Even the steering wheel could not interfere in the moment as he whispered, "You knock me off my feet with your beauty and your brains. I'm a lucky guy."

Snuggling against his shoulder, Denise responded, "And here I thought that I was the lucky one. I guess we've both been blessed."

Chuckling, Tom said, "Let's go home and enjoy a little more of that blessing."

"My thoughts exactly," Denise agreed with a laugh.

Denise watched as Tom slid from the seat and closed the door. He walked like a proud tiger or a conquering hero. His broad shoulders rocked gently with each step. He had never looked more handsome or sturdy. No longer did she worry about the effects of professional separation on their personal lives. The expression on his face when he had greeted her in the Olney Theater's grand hall and the warmth of his lips on hers had erased all doubt. Nothing could come between them.

Tom led the way although Denise could navigate the turns in her sleep. His mind was more on the incredibly impressive woman in the car than on his driving. After many years of searching, he had found his ideal woman, his soul mate, and his partner. One day, he hoped that she would be his forever.

The evening had offered even more than they had anticipated. It had been an evening of surprises and affirmations that had lived up to their expectations and surpassed it. The night had been perfect for love . . . and murder.

Twelve

Denise's new partner already sat at Tom's desk when she arrived in the morning, clearly making himself comfortable in his new surroundings. He had that bright, confident expression of a man who thinks the world belongs to him and dares anyone to disagree. He had purchased a fast-food breakfast and coffee on his way to the office and sat contentedly munching as she unpacked her briefcase.

"Good morning," Craig Panns greeted Denise as she joined him in their section of the squad room.

"Morning," Denise muttered, not wanting to spoil the memory of the weekend with Tom by conducting a conversation with Craig.

"Here, I bought you a cup," Craig stated as he handed a steaming cup of coffee to Denise.

"Thanks," Denise managed to reply. He was trying to make friends. However, she was determined that the effort would come to nothing.

"No problem. I thought you might like a cup since no one around here seems to know how to operate the coffeemaker," Craig stated with a big smile that lit up his handsome face.

"Tom, my partner . . . er . . . former partner, made it every morning," Denise said, sipping the delicious commercial black, but not overcooked, coffee. "I don't know where he put the instruction manual."

"No one else does either. I've searched everywhere," Craig stated with a tone of voice that made it clear that he would soon take steps to rectify the problem. "No problem, I'll buy another one."

"Oh, good," Denise said with a raised eyebrow.

She did not like Craig Panns. He was new to the squad room and their partnership, but he did not act new. He had an attitude of authority that put her teeth on edge. He was almost too handsome, too confident, and too well dressed. He wore his jacket in the office rather than wearing rolled-up shirtsleeves as Tom and the others always did. He smelled of expensive cologne and looked fresh from a men's fashion magazine. She simply did not like him.

Turning her attention to unpacking her briefcase, Denise tired to analyze her dislike for Craig Panns. She decided that her instincts were usually correct about people and that something did not sit right about him. She acknowledged to herself that the bulk of her dislike for him could have been in the fact that he had the thankless task of replacing Tom as her partner. However, when her sixth sense shouted an objection as it was doing now, she usually listened. She simply did not like Craig Panns.

Setting aside the coffee with its slightly waxy taste absorbed from the cup, Denise concentrated on her in-box. Not finding a phone call slip either from the FBI or the police department, she started a to-do list with the names of her contacts in both places at the top of the list. She needed to speak with the coroner to learn the results of the autopsy on the deceased actor, Timothy Morton, and the FBI's work on the dusty tea bags. She also needed to phone Tom. She had left an earring at his apartment and wanted him to put it in a safe place away from Molly's teeth.

The ringing of her phone stopped her in midlist.

A vaguely familiar voice on the other end explained, "Detective Dory, I've finished the autopsy, and you were right. Timothy Morton's stomach contents contained ephedra. I wouldn't have thought anything of it if you hadn't mentioned it. It's a fairly common dietary supplement that people abuse these days not only for weight loss but for increased energy."

"That's good news, Dr. Otis," Denise agreed, jotting down the information that connected Timothy Morton's death with that of the others and added to the victims in the Music Man Murder case.

"By the way, I've sent samples to the FBI so that they can search for other related incidents of ephedra-caused deaths. We might just have a nationwide serial killer on our hands," Dr. Otis commented.

"Possibly, but I think he's working in the Baltimore-Washington area exclusively. Unfortunately, I still don't know the reason. Thanks for the call, Dr. Otis. I'll keep you informed of any developments."

"Thanks," Dr. Otis stated and added, "Out of curiosity, I'd like to know about those tea bags, too."

"Sure thing. I'll phone as soon as I hear something," Denise agreed as she hung up the phone.

Normally, she would have turned around, placed her arms on Tom's desk, and shared the news with him. However, now that he was no longer sitting behind her, Denise kept the news to herself and stored it in a mental file of things to share with Tom when they met for dinner later that evening. Taking a quick glance over her shoulder, she decided that she would not allow Craig Panns into her confidence as yet until she no longer had that uneasy feeling about him. Once he grew on her, she would use him as a sounding board to test her theories just as she did with Tom.

Not waiting for her overworked contact at the FBI to phone her, Denise listened as the familiar tired voice answered on the third ring. Realizing that he was very busy, she came right to the point. They both had too much work to bother with formalities.

"Good morning, Joe, Denise Dory, MCPD, calling. Any news on those tea bags I sent you?" Denise asked.

"Hey, Denise. Right here. The lab just sent the report to me. I'm in the process of e-mailing it to you right now, but it confirms your suspicions. Those tea bags were full to the brim with ephedra," Joe replied as he completed the address and pressed the send button.

"Great!" Denise replied gratefully. "At least now I have the method. If I could only find the motive, I'd be able to apprehend this guy."

Remembering a bit of information, Joe added, "Well, I can't help you there. By the way, the lab took another look at the residue the chemist scraped from the inside of the batons and found ephedra in all of them, too. Your killer wanted to energize all of them to death, it seems."

"Thanks for the help. That's a good connection, Joe, since they all died of cardiac arrest," Denise stated as she scribbled the latest bits of information into the margin of her sketch of the batons.

"Be careful, Denise. You're getting close. With you, that always means trouble. I heard about Tom's promotion. Now that Tom's not your partner anymore, you have to take care of yourself," Joe advised with a tired yawn.

"Don't worry about me, Joe," Denise said with a chuckle. "If I remember correctly, it's always Tom who gets into trouble on my cases. I'll be okay."

"You're right about that." Joe laughed as he returned to his overflowing desk, leaving Denise to print off the report that would become a part of the permanent file on the murder case.

Reflecting on the bits and pieces of the case, Denise mused that the connection had to lie under her nose. Something she had missed must connect the murders.

She knew that all of the victims had dabbled in conducting although it was not their primary profession. They were all celebrated in their chosen line of work, having won critical and financial status. She decided to pay Joshua Smithe a visit. Being in the music business and the local supplier of batons, he might just know of something that would unit the cases. She could have phoned him, but she needed to leave the office and her partner.

"How's the case going?" Craig's voice interrupted her thoughts, something that Tom never would have done.

If there was one thing that Denise hated, it was having someone ask for details about her work. She was the kind of person who would share information willingly, but who disliked being asked about it. She would have to tell him about her little quirks before he bothered her again.

"Fine," Denise retorted shortly. "It's going fine. By the way, Craig, I really would appreciate it if you didn't ask about my work. I'll share when I'm ready but questioning rubs me the wrong way. Okay?"

"Hey, I was just being friendly," Craig replied as he raised his hands in a symbol of surrender.

"No harm done." Denise smiled as she slipped her sketchbook into her briefcase. "It's just one of those idiosyncrasies that you'll need to know. See you later."

"You're not going to finish your coffee after I went to all that trouble of bringing it to you?" Craig whined playfully, trying to lighten the tension between them.

Looking first at the cup of coffee cooling on her desk and then at her new and annoying partner, Denise replied with a forced smile, "I'll drink it later with a little crushed ice. It'll make great iced coffee as an afternoon treat. Bye."

"Bye, Denise," Craig called after her.

Denise could hardly leave the squad room fast enough. She jumped into her car and almost burned rubber leaving the lot. Craig had gotten on her nerves just being in the room, sitting in Tom's chair, and using Tom's desk. Asking about her work pushed her over the edge.

The drive to Old Towne helped to calm her nerves. Denise allowed the smells of the park to wash away her irritation with Craig. Putting him from her mind, she thought only of her meeting with Joshua Smithe. If he could not help her, she would have to wait for the afternoon clue from the perpetrator. Now that she had figured out the musical relationship between the victims and the weapon, maybe he would give her a clue as to his motive or his next strike.

Joshua Smithe met her at the door of his shop with a broad smile and a wave of welcome. As during her first visit to the store, he was wearing period clothing to match the shop's decor. With the exception of the addition of a red open vest, everything looked unchanged.

"What brings you here, Detective Dory? You need more information on batons?" Joshua Smithe asked as he ushered her inside and closed the door.

"No, but I thought I might pick your brain for a few minutes," Denise replied, accepting the offered can of soda.

"Sure, ask away," Joshua Smithe said with a big smile. "It's not every day that a big-shot detective comes to my shop."

"Big shot?" Denise asked with a frown. "What makes you say that?"

"You haven't seen the paper today, have you? Here, take a look," Joshua Smithe stated as he handed Denise the front page of the *Washington Post*. Pointing to an article at the bottom right of the front page.

Scanning the article, Denise saw that the chief had struck again. In an interview about the murders, the chief had mentioned that she had assigned Denise to the series of murders that had originate in suburban Maryland. The inquisitive reporter had researched Denise's past cases and made reference to them. He had even included a file photo of her on the grounds of the U.S. Capitol after solving that case.

With a sigh, Denise returned the paper and said, "Purely public relations hype. I'm just a working stiff like everyone else. Now, what might connect these victims? Is there some kind of competition or award for conducting?"

"Sure is. As a matter of fact, the National Symphony Orchestra will host one tonight at the Olney Theater. That's the poster on the counter. I was just about to add it to the stuff in the window when I saw you getting out of your car," Smithe stated as he reached for the poster that had been lying facedown on the counter.

Studying it, Denise asked, "Is this only for students or amateurs?"

"No, it's really for professionals. The purpose is to attract people to the concerts," Smithe explained. "I went last year. A lot of big-name celebrities took their turn conducting the NSO. It's a lot of fun and not very serious for the movie stars. They draw folks who would never usually attend a symphony. I saw Meryl Streep, Ted Kennedy, Bette Midler, Dustin Hoffman, and Al Pacino take up the baton last year. They didn't know what they were doing, but, with an orchestra the caliber of the NSO, they didn't need to know. The NSO played while the actors pretended to direct. Oh, yeah, Will Smith conducted, too, and he was really funny. He clowned the entire time. The funniest conductor was Robin Williams. Even the orchestra members cracked up working, or trying to work, with him. Everyone had a ball. The NSO gained a lot of new friends that way."

"Then it's not really a competition at all," Denise stated for clarification.

Shaking his hands, Smithe stressed, "No, it's a competition for the people who enter as serious contestants.

People like my father and music teachers do it just for fun. The celebrities appear as special guest stars interspersed between the serious competitors to keep the tone light and the audience interested. The NSO wouldn't be able to draw a large, diverse crowd if it invited only serious competitors."

"Is this a well-known event in the music world?" Denise asked, jotting down the information in her sketchbook.

"Sure is. The competitors have been planning for this event for a long time and so have the sponsors. They all want that forty-five thousand-dollar prize money and the guest conductor spots with the NSO and other orchestras. The competition's a great boost for their career," Smithe said. "I've known about it since last year and not just after attending the competition either. People in the musicians union receive early information about events like this. Schools do, too. Everyone who's really involved in music from DJs to small-time drummers would have heard about it. The poster's only to invite the spectators to a good show."

Thinking aloud, Denise muttered under her breath, "Then the murderer, if a member of the music set, could also be involved."

"Talking to yourself, Detective?" Smithe asked as he collected their empty cans and walked toward the storeroom.

"Yeah, comes with the job. That newspaper article didn't mention that hazard," Denise replied with a chuckle.

Returning to his seat, Smithe stated with an expression of admiration on his face, "If I can get someone to cover for me, I'll try to attend the competition. That's our night to stay open late. I'd hate to miss it. I heard great music, saw celebrities having a good time, and enjoyed truly good conducting last year. You should go, and not just for the job."

"I think I will," Denise replied, gathering her briefcase and sketchbook and heading toward the door. "It sounds like a great way to hear wonderful music."

"You won't be sorry," Smithe called, as he walked toward the customer in the R&B section of the shop.

Turning her car toward the Maryland suburbs, Denise decided that she would not miss the concert. Thinking about Joshua Smithe's information about the contest, Denise decided that, if the perpetrator had not struck again before the weekend, it would be the perfect time for him to make his move. With or without Tom, she would go to the concert.

Fortunately, Craig Panns was not in the office when Denise returned. She could not stand the idea of having him breathing down her neck about the case. Even if he heeded her instructions and refrained from asking questions, his presence would nag at her, knowing that he wanted to ply her with questions.

In the silence of the almost empty squad room, Denise ate the Caesar salad that she had purchased from the deli on the corner on her way inside the building. As always, it needed a little something, but it was edible, which was all she asked of the quick meals that satisfied her hunger during the day but little else. She would prepare something exciting for dinner with Tom that evening. She had a taste for primavera with roasted chicken strips and cold peach soup. Tom did not especially enjoy the soup, saying that dessert should come after the meal, but he loved the primavera. She would leave a little early to prepare the meal before going to the Olney Theater.

Rising from her chair, Denise carried the cup of cold coffee to the squad room's tiny kitchen. Opening the freezer door, she pulled out several ice cubes and threw them along with a little sugar, some milk, and the coffee into the blender that someone had donated for their use. Finding a relatively clean tall mug in the cabinet, she scrubbed it and then heaped the mixture inside. Carrying it back to her desk, she tasted it and judged it palatable. The sugar and milk had disguised the waxy taste from the melting cup.

Denise had just settled down to read her e-mails and drink her coffee when she heard a familiar sound. Placing her mug on the desk, she turned toward the door in time to brace herself for an affectionate greeting as Molly planted a wet, sloppy kiss on her cheek. Following the happy dog was her equally happy human partner.

"I thought we'd bring this to you. I found it under the sofa cushion after you left," Tom stated with a broad smile that lighted up his entire face. In his outstretched hand, he held Denise's gold hoop earring.

Standing and slipping sensuously into his arms, Denise purred, "You didn't have to do that. I could have waited until tonight."

"Maybe you could've, but I couldn't," Tom replied between kisses that he lingeringly placed on her lips. "I had to see you."

Smiling happily, Tom held Denise until Molly broke into the space between them. Laughing, they separated and patted the head of the dog that wanted to be a part of the group hug. As they smiled into each other's eyes, Tom eased into the chair beside Denise's desk.

"It seems strange to be sitting here," Tom said, as he drained half of Denise's iced coffee. "How's the partner working out?"

"He'll do," Denise answered with a sigh. "He's too into my business, too determined to make this work, too . . . put together. He never removes his jacket like the rest of the guys. I've never seen his bare arms."

Laughing, Tom exclaimed, "Give the man a break, Dory! He's just got a different style, that's all."

"Whatever," Denise replied, rolling her eyes and reaching for the more than half empty coffee mug.

As Denise raised the mug to her lips, Molly decided that she wanted a taste of the liquid, also. Standing on her hind legs, she leaned against Denise's arms and dislodged the cup from her hand. The sticky iced coffee cascaded down the front of Denise's deep-rose suit until it formed a puddle in her lap.

Barely able to hold back the laughter, Tom studied the startled expression on Denise's face. Her eyes narrowed and glinted angrily at the contrite dog. Molly barely breathed. Her ears lay flat, and her tail hung limply behind her. She was afraid of Denise's temper, too.

Looking from the dog to Tom and then at her damaged suit, Denise broke into gales of laughter. Ordinarily, she would have been furious, but she was so glad to see Tom that she would not allow a wet suit to spoil the visit. Wagging her finger at the contrite dog, she gave her e-mails a quick review, gathered her things, and prepared to leave.

"You're not angry?" Tom asked as he chuckled along with Denise.

"No. I wouldn't say that I'm thrilled, but I'm not angry. Besides, you owe me one for the mess your dog made of my suit," Denise stated with a grin and a peck to his cheek.

"No problem. I'll pay for the cleaning bill or buy you a new suit," Tom offered, happy that he and Molly were not in the doghouse.

"I know," Denise said with a wicked smile. "And I know exactly how you'll do it, too. You'll go to the symphony with me tonight."

Rising, Tom sputtered, "What! I said I'd pay the cleaning bill. Isn't that enough?"

Seeing his unsteady stance, Denise asked, "What's wrong?"

"I don't know," Tom replied as he steadied himself with a hand on his former desk. "I guess I'm getting old, probably overcome by your beauty . . . or the thought of going to the symphony. You know I can't stand that stuff."

Seeing that his balance had returned, Denise said, "I'm going to a conducting competition tonight, and I'd like for you to accompany me. It should be fun. Don't look at me like that!"

"Is there any other way for me to look?" Tom demanded as he grabbed Molly's lease. Because of his canine partner, he was stuck going to hear a bunch of budding conductors try to impress a group of judges.

"You'll enjoy it. Joshua Smithe, the proprietor of the music shop in Old Towne, says that celebrities participate to entertain the audience and draw a crowd. The poster in his store showed that James Earle Jones, Bill Cosby, and Patti LaBelle will perform there tonight. You enjoyed the play the other night. You'll enjoy this, too."

"What I saw of it, I liked. If I remember correctly, we threw away approximately eighty-five bucks that night, following a lead in your case. Do you think the captain would reimburse me?" Tom complained good-naturedly as they walked from the building.

"Probably not. I'll fix pasta primavera tonight for dinner if you'll come with me," Denise stated as she opened the door to her car. Turning to Tom, she added, "Are you sure you're feeling okay?"

"Yeah, I'm fine. Just a little tired. I'll do it for the price of the suit and the wasted theater tickets. I think we're even now," Tom agreed with a triumphant nod of his head.

"Okay. I'll see you at six. Be there on time. Pasta is very unforgiving," Denise ordered as she gave him a lingering kiss.

"What's for dessert?" Tom asked with a grin.

"We'll see . . ." Denise replied and drove away.

Smiling despite the sweet stickiness on her suit, Denise switched on the radio. The DJ on her favorite classical station introduced a Mozart piece. Listening contentedly, Denise allowed the music to sweep over her as she headed home. Mentally outlining her plans for the evening, she decided on the sequence of events, including her choice of outfit for the evening. The black pantsuit with the black and white lace camisole would look just perfect . . . not too dressy and definitely not too casual. The outfit would set the tone for the evening since it was one of Tom's favorites. Strange, now that they were no longer partners, she spent more time thinking about her appearance than she had when they worked together.

As the music changed to the anticipated show tune, Denise shook herself from the pleasant thoughts. Listening carefully, Denise strained to recognize the melody. Slowly, the tune began to take shape in her mind. Tapping her fingers on the steering wheel, she allowed the notes to wash over her until she was singing along with the music.

The first time, she had missed the clue, not understanding the perpetrator's mind. The second time, she had misidentified the victim, thinking that the murderer would strike a conductor, not an actor. This time, she understood that the killer meant to strike that night; the lyrics from *West Side Story* had confirmed it. Each one of the competitors could be in danger. "Tonight, tonight, we're going to rumble tonight."

Thirteen

Max the cat welcomed Denise with a long, lazy meow. He had not been standing at the door awaiting her return. She had managed to surprise him and hoped that she would be able to do the same to the killer.

Petting the fat cat on his head, Denise commented, "Caught you sleeping, didn't I, old man? I like to keep you on your toes whenever possible."

Carrying him to the bedroom, Denise quickly discarded her soiled suit on the bedside chair along with the cat. Donning into her robe and slippers, she padded to the bathroom and assessed the day's damage. Turning on the shower, she stepped inside and began to scrub away the grime of the city as she sang the lyrics from the juxtaposed song from *West Side Story*. In one, the lovers sang of seeing each other again and, in the other, the opposing gangs spoke of the pending fight. For Denise, both made sense, knowing that she would see Tom and that she and the perpetrator would go head-on into battle against each other. For the first time since she had bagun this case, Denise knew that she would soon meet the murderer. She was close, perhaps too close.

The telephone was ringing as she stepped from the shower. Wrapping her towel around her, Denise rushed to the nightstand. She had a feeling that Tom was calling to renege on their arrangements.

"Dory, it's me," Tom's voice stated weakly. "I'm not feeling well. I won't be able to go with you to the competition."

"Is this for real, Tom, or are you simply trying to avoid listening to the symphony?" Denise asked skeptically. "I told you that you'd enjoy seeing the celebrities involved in the show."

"No, Denise, I'm really sick. My heart's pounding, and I'm having trouble breathing. I think I'll go to the emergency room," Tom replied.

"Call an ambulance. I'll meet you there," Denise stated as she quickly toweled her hair.

"Okay, but don't take too long, Dory. I'm scared. It's not like last time. That struck slowly like a bad hot dog. This is coming on fast," Tom said as he hung up the phone.

Forgetting about the perfect outfit for the perfect evening, Denise slipped on a T-shirt and a pair of jeans. Pressing her feet into mules, she grabbed her purse and keys and was out the door so fast that Max did not have time to complain about the omitted head scratch. She would not allow the tears that burned behind her eyes to fall. She did not have time for anything that would delay her arrival.

Rushing to Holy Cross Hospital, Denise prayed that Tom would be okay. He was so healthy that she never thought of anything really bad happening to him. Even when he ate the poisoned rolls and the ergot poison made him sick, he made a speedy recovery. This time, however, he sounded really weak and vulnerable. She had to get to him as quickly as possible. For once, the late afternoon traffic cooperated. She would have abandoned the car rather than sit in a backup. The brisk run to the hospital would have helped remove some of the anxiety and worry.

Pulling into the first parking spot she could find,

Denise sprinted to the emergency room door. Stepping inside, she immediately checked to see if Tom had arrived. She was afraid that he might have passed out before phoning the ambulance. Following the woman's directions to curtain twelve, she took a deep breath, tried to compose herself, and walked as calmly as she could into the emergency room examining area.

As a beat police officer, Denise had visited the emergency room many times looking for perpetrators and interviewing victims of assault and car accidents. Until Tom's illness last year, she had not entered a hospital except to visit the maternity room. Within twelve months, she was making a second appearance into the bowels of the hospital in which specially trained professionals handled life-and-death emergency situations. For the second time, Tom was one of their patients in peril.

Stepping to the gurney on which Tom lay, Denise knew immediately that he was a very sick man. His breathing was erratic, and his chest rose and fell at alarming intervals. His coloring was florid and clammy. Yet, despite the severity of his sickness, Tom focused on Denise and managed a weak smile.

Taking heart, Denise teased through unshed tears that clogged her throat, "You'll do anything to miss the symphony."

"Almost," Tom replied in barely a whisper.

"Detective Dory?" the young physician asked with a shy smile. "I recognized you from the newspaper. Mr. Phyfer said that you were coming."

"How is he?" Denise asked as she ignored the reference to her renown. At the moment, she was only a very frightened girlfriend.

"He's very sick. Do you have any idea what might have caused this onset? Mr. Phyfer says that he's only eaten toast, cereal, two eggs, and orange juice this morning with you and pizza for lunch with his group. I've phoned them and no one is ill. I've ruled out food poisoning. Do you have any other suggestion before I start treating him for the usual CDC-recommended poisons?"

Poison. The word echoed through Denise's mind, bringing back thoughts of the rolls and ergot poisoning. The CDC procedures had not worked then and would not work now unless she could think of something more specific that the doctor could target. Looking at Tom's face, she suddenly knew the answer.

"Test him for ephedra overdose," Denise stated in a voice that sounded too stern for her own ears.

"Ephedra? That's a dietary supplement that people use to lose weight. Lieutenant Phyfer doesn't need to use that," the ER doctor explained.

"I know, but I think he drank a concoction intended for me," Denise replied firmly.

"I don't understand, but I'll do it. In the meantime, we'll begin the antidotes and increase hydration to flood his system and remove the toxins," the doctor stated, looking skeptically at Denise's trim figure.

Tom looked at Denise with the same unbelieving expression on his face that the doctor had worn. As he tried to form the words, the breathing difficulty proved too great. Able only to stare, Tom tried to communicate with his eyes.

"Don't worry. You'll be okay now. That's what you get for drinking my iced coffee," Denise commented with a shake of her head. "I had a bad feeling about Craig Panns, and now I know why. I bet he's not really a cop either."

Tom furrowed his brow in response.

Reading the expression, Denise explained, "My new partner brought me that coffee this morning. I can't stand him so I only tasted it to be polite. It had a waxy taste anyway, so I didn't especially want to drink it. I told him I'd drink it later and left for Old Towne. Anyway, when I returned, I made the iced coffee that you drank and Molly spilled on my suit. He had poisoned it with ephedra."

This time, Tom raised his eyebrows, requesting more information.

Drawing up the stool to his bedside, Denise held Tom's hand and continued, "Ephedra causes rapid heartbeats, central nervous system stimulation, elevation of blood pressure, bronchodilation, and cardiac arrest if taken in massive doses. You're lucky to be very healthy. If you'd had any health problems, it would have killed you."

Tom whispered weakly, "You mean that I did it again. My stomach got me into trouble."

Smiling at his rapid improvement, Denise said, "That's right. Only this time, rather than eating a few rolls intended for a competitor, you drank poisoned coffee meant for me. Considering the difference in our sizes and your reaction to the dosage, I'd say that Craig intended to kill me."

"Does he know that you didn't drink it?" Tom asked in a voice still shaky from the experience.

"I don't know. He wasn't in the office when I returned," Denise conceded. "Come to think of it, he really didn't push me to drink it. He only made one feeble attempt at guilt-tripping me into it."

"Just wait until I get my hands on him," Tom seethed.

Patting him on the hand, Denise continued, "By the way, I heard the most recent clue on the radio today on the way home. I wasn't surprised to hear it, either. According to the perpetrator's earlier note, he had arranged well in advance for the DJ to play them."

"He'll be surprised when he sees you at the competition tonight," Tom stated as the strength began to return to his body and his breathing became less labored.

"Maybe. It all depends on his confidence in my consuming the coffee today. Anyway, he'll see me, but I doubt that I'll see him. I would imagine that, if he catches a glimpse of me, he'd abandon the plan. He wouldn't possibly go forward with it, knowing that I'd apprehend him on the spot. Now that I can identify him, he would have to rethink his activities. He'd be a fool not to change course," Denise said, considering the possibilities open to the perpetrator.

"I'd better get out of this bed and go with you," Tom said, making a weak attempt to rise.

Pressing Tom firmly into the gurney, Denise exclaimed, "Are you kidding? You almost died, you silly man! You're staying here until the doctor dismisses you and then you're going home to bed. I can take care of myself."

"You need cover. What if he decides that a gun would be more productive, and you get in the way? You need someone to watch your back," Tom stated as he gave up the fight against the pressure of Denise's hand.

"I don't think he will. It doesn't fit his pattern. Besides, I'm not sure that the person I know as Craig Panns and the perpetrator in the Music Man Murders are the same person," Denise said as she settled into the stool beside the gurney.

Looking at Denise as if she should be lying on the gurney, Tom exploded, "What? Why would you think that? He tried to kill you. Isn't that proof that he's the same guy who has killed the musicians? You've gotten too close and spooked him into taking drastic action."

Leaning forward, Denise demanded, "Where's the baton? And remember, I can't sing a note or play any musical instruments. You and Max have a fit when I sing in the shower. Even Molly howls at the sound of my voice."

"You've lost me, Dory," Tom stated as he studied her face more closely. "Either you've lost your touch or you're playing down the situation to keep me in bed. You're not making sense."

"I'm making perfectly good sense," Denise retorted.

"Listen. The murderer leaves behind a baton at each murder scene. He didn't leave one either in the squad room or my mailbox at home. There's nothing in my car either. Further, he poisons food with the ephedra, but he's never on the scene when the victim consumes it. In my case, if I had drunk the coffee this morning, Craig would have been sitting behind me when the ephedra took effect. I don't think he's the perpetrator."

"Okay, Sherlock, then who is he? You have to do better than that. That doesn't keep me from putting on my shoes and getting out of here," Tom demanded, not buying Denise's explanation and needing more proof.

Holding Tom down again, Denise replied, "I've had this uneasy feeling about him since our first meeting. At first, I thought I just didn't like him because the captain forced the change on me. You know, I like to make my own decisions and pick my partners myself. Anyway, Craig is too polished, too perfect. He doesn't give off the aura of a cop. Something's just not right about him. I don't care if he does come to the department with all the best credentials. I didn't like him before, and I certainly don't trust him now."

"Have you told the captain about your feelings?" Tom asked, resting from the effort of trying to sit up. He had improved considerably but was still very weak.

Shaking her head, Denise replied, "No, I haven't had time. Plus, complaining would have sounded as if I were only griping and not a 'team player.' If you'll behave yourself, I'll step outside and phone him now. He needs to hear about the poisoned coffee and issue an arrest warrant for Craig anyway. I have this hunch that something has happened to the real Craig and that this guy is a ringer."

"A ringer cop? How could that happen?" Tom asked incredulously.

"Easy," Denise responded. "If no one checked his

credentials and only went on the assumption that the real Craig Panns had arrived that day, a substitute could easily penetrate the squad room. How many times has a new person arrived with a box of stuff from the old job and we simply welcomed him aboard? It could have happened this time, too."

"I guess anything's possible these days. I still say that guy will pay when I get out of here," Tom agreed angrily.

"I see that you're feeling better." Denise laughed and planted a kiss gently on Tom's lips.

"I'm not that sick! You call that a kiss? Give me a real good one, woman. I'm in need of some true healing," Tom declared as he wrapped his arms around Denise and pulled her toward him.

As the unshed tears trickled down her cheeks and splashed onto his, Denise kissed Tom in a way that spoke of her love, her fear at losing him, and her joy at having him back. She had been terrified that Tom would not survive the ephedra poisoning. She had held back the flood of tears, talked of work, and tried to keep him calm while her insides had churned and heaved. Her heart had pounded with every beat of his, and her breathing had labored from the unreleased agony that threatened to rip her into two dysfunctional pieces. Now that Tom appeared to be out of danger, Denise could relax and let the tears flow.

Looking into her face, Tom murmured gently, "You won't get rid of me that easily, Dory. It takes more than poisoned rolls and coffee to kill me. You're stuck with me."

"I'm not complaining," Denise whispered into the depth of his neck.

Reluctantly, Denise separated from Tom's forceful grip. Smiling into his happy face, she said, "You seem to be feeling better. I'll go make my call."

"Don't stay away long. I'm feeling much better, and

the nurses here are really hot," Tom growled as he slowly released her.

"Just stay on the gurney, mister. I'll be right back." Denise laughed as she headed for the exit.

Outside, Denise took a deep breath to clear her lungs of the hospital smell. Now that Tom was recovering, she could think about the rest of the evening. After placing the call to the captain, she would need to attend the competition. She feared that the real killer would strike again.

"Captain, it's Denise. Yes, I'm aware that I'm phoning you at home, but you need to hear this. I suspect that the man who is now my partner might not be the real Craig Panns." Denise spoke into the phone as she scanned the parking lot for anyone who might be watching her. She needed to be wary after Tom's close call.

"You just don't like him, and you haven't given him a chance to prove himself," Captain Morton grumbled on the other end. He hated to be interrupted by work when he was relaxing with his family.

"I admit that I was being unfair at first, sir, but that's not it anymore. He tried to poison me," Denise replied with confidence.

"What?"

Nodding, Denise stated, "That's right, sir. He poisoned a cup of coffee that he gave me this morning. I'm at the hospital now because Tom drank it when he came to see me this afternoon. Craig, or whoever he is, probably doesn't know that I survived. He had left the office by the time I returned after following up on this case."

"Is he all right? I'll send someone to his house right now," Captain Morton growled, angry that one of his former men would be in danger.

"He's fine," Denise responded. "Tom's a strong man although he did have me worried for a while. Oh, and, Captain, don't be surprised if Craig's not there. At least, this guy won't be there. The real Craig Panns might be in serious trouble."

"I'll take care of it, Denise. You take care of Tom. See you tomorrow," the captain said as he turned his attention to finding the real identity of Craig Panns.

Returning to Tom's side, Denise relayed the result of her conversation with Captain Morton. The doctor had just left, and Tom was feeling much improved. However, as a precaution, the doctor had admitted him for further observation. Much to Tom's dislike, he would spend the night in the hospital.

"I'll check on Molly before I go to the competition," Denise said as she walked behind the gurney taking Tom to his room.

"You don't have to do that. She's okay. I fed her before calling you. I was afraid that I'd sleep through feeding her if I didn't take care of her right away. You just go get that guy," Tom commented in a very foul mood. He hated the smell of the hospital and wanted to go home.

"All right," Denise agreed as she straightened the sheet and smoothed his pillow. "You follow the nurse's orders. I'll phone when I get home tonight."

"You'd better or you ll find me on your doorstep at midnight. Be careful," Tom growled as he drew her into his arms for one more kiss.

"Don't worry about me. Get some rest," Denise replied as she eased toward the door.

Tom was snoring before she could step into the hall. The ephedra had taken its toll, and he was weaker than he cared to admit. Trembling uncontrollably, Denise discovered that she was considerably shaken by the closeness of the killer's actions. For the second time in a year, Tom had fallen ill as a result of indirect contact with a killer. She had almost lost him again and did not like the feeling one bit.

Fourteen

Denise drove home quickly on reasonably quiet streets. She would miss some of the celebrity portion of the competition but not the actual competitive conducting. Arriving late might prove helpful. The perpetrator would be too busy with the purpose of his appearance at the competition to pay attention to her.

Slipping into a black pantsuit, Denise fed the cat, checked messages, phoned on Tom, grabbed a banana, and left. Speeding up the interstate and taking all the back streets she knew, she arrived at the Olney Theater in record time. Finding a spot in the full lot, she hurried upstairs to the symphony hall and the home of the NSO.

Not needing a ticket for the free competition, Denise slipped into the back of the concert hall. A few years ago, she had heard Johnny Mathis sing in that hall, but it looked so different now. That evening, people in evening attire had filled the room to hear the master crooner, the man who had sung his way into their hearts and served as the background music for many a make-out session. Even though the evening was not a black-tie affair, they had donned their fancy duds in tribute to Johnny Mathis, who always worked a tux while performing. To do less would have meant insulting his craft. They knew that he would sing all the old favorites that made their hearts swell with memories of loves long gone. He deserved evening dresses and tuxes.

Denise's soon-to-be-ex boyfriend had refused to accompany her to hear what he considered sappy
music. Therefore, she had asked her father, who had
readily agreed. For her date with him, Denise had worn
a spaghetti-strapped slinky black gown with matching
silk shawl. Her father had brushed off the tux he had
purchased for her sister's wedding, thinking that he
would save money by purchasing rather than renting
since Denise's wedding would soon follow. When it did
not, Mr. Dory had covered it with an old sheet and
pushed the tux to the back of his closet. Years later, he
was thrilled to find that it still fit.

She had entered that night on the arm of a man who
adored her and had for so long been the center of her
universe. Her father had beamed brightly as he escorted
her to their third-row center section aisle seats. He had
noticed the way the men looked at Denise and smiled
even with wives or dates on their arms. Her father was
proud of the smart beauty who was his daughter. After
all, she had been conceived to the gentle melody of
"Chances Are" and "The Twelfth of Never." He felt lucky
to be the man escorting her to a Johnny Mathis concert,
especially since men of his age thought that Denise was
the younger woman in his life.

However, this night was different. Although Denise
turned a number of heads in her black suit, she was not
only without a date but in need of anonymity. She very
much wanted to see but not be seen. It was her night to be
vigilant and to respond quickly if something happened.

Scanning the crowd, Denise saw no one who even
vaguely resembled Craig Panns. She had phoned the captain as she rode from the garage to the main floor on the
elevator but had only reached the answering machine.
Leaving a request for feedback on the search for her new
partner, she had turned her attention to the assembled
throng of people.

Instead of tuxedos and evening gowns, the competition had drawn a combination of jeans and T-shirts on thin, obviously struggling musicians cradling portfolios and patrons of the arts in business suits, looking very smug and sure of themselves. Music teachers with clusters of would-be conductors and performers and symphony lovers expecting nothing short of wonderful entertainment mingled, exchanged glances, and barely acknowledged each other. Senior citizens looking for an inexpensive evening on the town flipped through the program and whispered softly about the splendor of the great hall.

Slipping into a seat in the back row on the aisle, Denise studied the crowd, yet she saw nothing suspicious. She nodded at Joshua Smithe, who sat in an aisle seat and appeared to be alone for a change. Perhaps his father was a competitor or maybe he had agreed to keep the store open while the son attended the competition. Watching someone she knew take the baton would add additional dimension to the evening.

Looking toward the stage at the other end of the hall, Denise saw that an unknown conducting student was now in control of the NSO. He handed them copies of the sheet music that they would play, allowed them a few minutes to become acquainted with it, and then raised his arms and baton in anticipation of the first note and all those that would follow. The result was not bad, but it lacked the energy of Bernstein and the insight of Zuckerman.

Watching the young man pump his arms to the time of the music, Denise thought of Tom and was glad that he had not accompanied her. He would have been bored and grumbling by now, and Denise felt that there was nothing worse than Tom in a bad mood. He would barely conceal his disgust, loudly sigh his resentment, and tap his fingers in frustration. Although she missed him, she was glad that he did not sit beside her.

A vaguely familiar figure took the stage after the lack-luster young man. Denise worked hard to connect the middle-aged-face with the one that wandered through her memory. If Tom were there, he would be able to help her. However, she was on her own and plagued with a nameless face.

Suddenly, the name came to her and, with it, the realization that the man might be in danger if he was the murderer's target. Richard Brymer, the actor who played Tony in the film version of *West Side Story,* had accepted the baton from the first-chair violinist and turned to the audience to take a bow. From the slow increase in intensity of the applause, Denise surmised that everyone had not recognized him initially. Then, as they began to recognize the face of the man who had so poignantly proclaimed his love for a woman from a rival gang, the sound intensified. Many of them gave him a standing ovation even before he could direct the NSO in a single note.

Quickly reading his biographical sketch in the program, Denise sighed with relief. Mr. Brymer was not a musician. He had not even sung the words to "Maria" but lip-synched them instead. He was simply in the hall to add celebrity presence to the evening.

Although hearing the familiar music brought back old memories, Denise had work to do. Easing from her seat, she made her way through the corridors to the back of the hall. Flashing her badge for the seventh time, she followed the signs to the competition manager's office. The strains of "Maria" filled the dingy behind-the-scenes halls of the majestic Olney Theater.

The man looked up impatiently. With so many hopefuls gathered in one place, he did not need the distraction of a police detective, beautiful though she was, that night. He reluctantly put down his pencil, pulled off his glasses, and rubbed his eyes before speaking to her.

"Well?" ask Mr. Fitzgerald impatiently.

"I'd like to ask a few questions, Mr. Fitzgerald, if I might," Denise replied, flashing her badge again.

Cleaning his glasses with a handkerchief of dubious cleanliness, Mr. Fitzgerald replied, "I remember you, Detective. Shoot but don't take too long. I've got to keep on top of this competition or else everyone will become completely disorganized."

Getting right to the point, Denise asked, "Have any of the celebrities not arrived or phoned in sick?"

Mr. Fitzgerald responded as he positioned the glasses on his fatigue-lined face, "Only one, and unexpectedly too. He's always here. Maybe that's why he decided not to attend today. He doesn't need another accolade. Probably decided to withdraw at the last minute and leave the competition to the young people. I wish he had told me. Kinda messed up the roster, but no harm done."

"Who was it?" Denise asked as she fought off the nervousness that started in the pit of her stomach.

"Oliver Smith," Mr. Fitzgerald replied. "He was the first to conduct a road show of *West Side Story*. Like I said, he didn't need the acclaim. After that, he conducted major orchestras everywhere and composed music for numerous movies and television shows."

Knowing that the killer had struck again, Denise asked, "Does he live in this area?"

Mr. Fitzgerald said absently as he turned to the evening's schedule, "No, he was only staying here for the competition. He booked a room at the Hilltop. He said he'd prefer to commute than live around this noise. That's all the time I can give you now, Detective. Enjoy the competition."

Thanking him, Denise searched for an isolated corner from which to call Mr. Smith. Receiving no response, she phoned the officer on duty that night and asked that he send someone to the hotel to search his room. She would remain at the Olney Theater. She had to find the killer, Craig Panns, or both.

Finding the hall completely filled, Denise headed to a space in the shadow at the back of the hall. From there, she waited and watched. She did not know what she would see exactly. She was confident that the killer had already struck. However, if he believed that she was dead from the ephedra poisoning, he might do something to call attention to himself.

Absorbed in the competition, Denise watched as the last competitor dressed as the Phantom of the Opera took the stage. With authority, he raised the baton and brought the orchestra to attention. With the gentle movement of his hands, he coaxed magnificent music from them.

Feeling more than seeing, Denise noticed an intruder in her little corner. She turned toward him just as the figure in black moved away. Darting after him, she stumbled and twisted her ankle as he blended with the other standing-room-only spectators. Landing on the floor hard, she softly cursed herself for not having asked for backup when Tom fell ill.

"Are you all right? I was hoping I'd see you here but not this way," a familiar voice whispered, pulling her to her feet.

"Yeah, thanks," Denise answered as she looked into the anxious face of Joshua Smithe.

"Did he hurt you?"

"No, but I twisted my ankle," Denise replied, a bit embarrassed that a lump in the carpet could down a veteran police officer.

With Smithe's help, Denise returned to the dark corner. Dropping to her knees and flipping on the little flashlight she always carried on her key ring, she felt the carpet for the source of the lump. Her fingers lightly touched the object that had tripped her. Slipping it inside her pocket, she allowed Smithe to help her hobble into the lobby.

"What tripped you?" Joshua asked, stepping closer for a better look.

"This. The guy who ran away must have dropped it," Denise replied, holding out her gloved hand in which rested a gift-wrapped box. Gingerly, she untied the gold ribbon and lifted the lid. Inside, lying on a bed of satin fabric, was a gold baton broach.

"I've only seen these in catalogues. They're too expensive for our little shop. Who sent it? Did he leave anything else?" Joshua inquired while holding Denise by one hand and examining the tiny baton with the other. Rather than being dressed like Dickens, he was wearing a somewhat wrinkled white shirt and faded jeans. He looked much younger without the costume.

"I don't think so. I shined the light well and used my fingers to examine under seats and in corners. I think this is all he dropped," Denise replied as she tested her weight on the sore left ankle. Finding it sturdy, she limped carefully toward the exit as the audience began to flow through the doors. The competition had ended.

"What does the card say?" Joshua asked as he pointed to the little card protruding from the corner of the satin.

Holding it in the light, Denise read, "Wear it with my best wishes."

"He didn't sign it," Joshua stated, as he looked over Denise's shoulder.

Smiling sarcastically, Denise replied, "Most killers don't sign their notes, Joshua. They don't want anyone to be able to find them. It would remove the element of the hunt."

"Where are you going?" Joshua demanded as he watched Denise pick her way down the steps.

"Home for an ice pack. Thanks again for the help," Denise replied as she turned and smiled at him.

Walking beside her, Joshua asked, "Would you like to go for a drink? I'll have to tell some friends where I'm going, but I'll only take a minute."

Seeing the signs of infatuation in Joshua's eyes, Denise replied as she continued to hobble along, "Some other time. I wouldn't be much company tonight. The perpetrator tried to kill me tonight and almost got my partner. I've twisted my ankle and feel as if I'm carrying a bowling ball at the end of my leg. My knee's starting to hurt from the impact of the fall. I haven't eaten since lunch. The banana I brought for a snack smashed when I landed on it and has filled my pocket with a baby-food-consistency mess. It's starting to smell and leak. You wouldn't want to have a drink with me tonight."

"Maybe some other time, then, huh? Or maybe you'd come to hear my group play?" Joshua asked hopefully.

"Maybe." Denise smiled as she reached the elevator that would transport her to the garage level. Turning to the very attentive she added, "Who won the competition?"

Shrugging a shoulder, Joshua replied, "A skinny guy dressed in black and looking like the Phantom of the Opera, complete with hat and half mask. He wouldn't give his real name. Just said we'd all find out in due time. He did a good job and should have won the competition. He seems to think that the world has dealt him a bad hand."

Muttering to herself as the door closed, Denise said, "I'm not surprised."

Putting the car in drive, Denise had never been so happy that she had traded the stick shift of her college days for an automatic. Her ankle throbbed. She should have gone straight to the hospital, but, instead, she took a detour to the Hilltop.

Each turn in the familiar park caused pain to shoot through her ankle. If only Tom were with her, he would drive. She knew that she needed medical attention, but she had to find out if the murderer had left a baton on the crime scene first.

The Hilltop was quiet that time of night. Tourists, too afraid to venture out at night, had settled down to sleep. The usually busy parking lot looked like a graveyard for Chevrolets, Fords, Mercedeses, and BMWs. The darkness equalized them into silent shadows.

Parking her little car, she hobbled to the front desk. Her ankle felt better when she was using it. Taking pity on the injured police detective, the night manager provided Denise with a wheelchair and a bellhop to push it.

Arriving on the tenth floor, Denise found the door sealed with police tape. Pulling off enough to ease under, she unlocked the door and wheeled herself inside, leaving the bellhop to wait outside for her. She did not want him to destroy the police scene by accident. She would have to explain the presence of wheelchair tire tracks in a follow-up report.

Wheeling through the suite, Denise passed the living room and moved to the bedroom in the back. Police chalk outlined the location of the body on the heavy spread. Easing to her knees, Denise looked under the bed just in case the victim had kicked it as he fell.

Standing beside the wheelchair, Denise surveyed the room. She knew the baton had to be in the room. It usually landed somewhere within reach of the victim's hands. Examining the perimeter, she continued to come up empty-handed. Finally, Denise decided to search the suite's bathroom, a massive room large enough to accommodate a small party. It was possible that the victim had taken the baton with him, yet collapsed later on the bed.

The bathroom was the best stocked she had ever seen in any upscale hotel. In addition to the usual soaps, shampoos, and bathrobes, Denise found courtesy razors, soft gold slippers, and samples of makeup. Oliver Smith had opened none of them. All of the packages were still sealed and the robe folded. He had also not dropped the baton in the bathroom.

Picking her way carefully while favoring her sore ankle, Denise returned to the bed. She ran her hand inside the carefully prepared fold that separated the pillows from the rest of the bed. She noticed that the pillows were still plump. Oliver Smith had collapsed across the bed with his arms at his side and had not disturbed them.

Lifting the pillows slightly, her fingers touched something hard. Bringing it forward, Denise held the baton gingerly between her fingers. Slipping it carefully into an evidence bag, she rearranged the pillows and stood up. Stripping off her gloves, she knotted them together and tossed them into the trash can before returning to the waiting wheelchair.

Before leaving the suite, Denise used her cell phone to call the captain, who answered on the first ring as if expecting her call. Without much preamble, she stated, "I've found the baton. It's definitely the same murderer."

"Good work, detective. By the way, the lab found ephedra in the victim's stomach, but no one can find Craig Panns," Captain Morton volunteered.

"Do you mean the real one or my new partner?" Denise inquired with a wry chuckle.

"Your new partner," the captain replied. "The guy who has spent the last day and a half in the squad room was not Panns. The real Craig Panns's wife said that he went fishing with his brother a week ago and is expected back this weekend. He doesn't even know about his promotion and transfer to our unit. Someone has used his identity to penetrate the squad room and get close to you. Be careful, Denise. Remember that you're out there alone."

"I'll be careful," Denise conceded.

"How's Tom?" the captain inquired.

"When I left him at the hospital, he was feeling better a little better. The doctor expects to release him tomorrow. Not much can keep Tom down," Denise replied with pride in her voice at her partner's stamina.

"Glad to hear it. Just remember, Dory, that he's out to get you," Captain Morton stated and then added, "You're no good to me as a statistic."

"Or to warn me, play with my head a little, make the big-time detective sweat and work for her money," Denise stated with a wry chuckle.

"Take care of yourself, Dory," Captain Morton instructed with affection.

"I will," Denise agreed as she snapped the lid on the phone.

The bellhop had waited patiently while she searched the room. He stood in the hall picking at his cuticles and pulling lint from his uniform. He smiled and wheeled the wheelchair toward the elevator.

On the ride down, Denise thought of Tom's brush with death, her fall in the concert hall, the closeness of the killer, and his brazen proclamation after winning the competition. She wondered if his black costume meant anything symbolic. He had promised through the use of the lyrics from *West Side Story* that they would rumble and they did. He had engaged her in combat, and she had fallen, literally. Instead of apprehending the murderer, she had hurt her ankle and gained a broach.

The perpetrator was trying to play games with her. She had to find him before he struck again. Tom's illness had made it personal.

Fifteen

For the first time in years, Denise phoned in sick and worked from home. She sat on the sofa with her badly sprained ankle resting on a pillow. Max the cat occupied the position on her left and Tom snoozed on her right. Her laptop and telephone were within easy reach. Despite the pain and Molly's slumbering presence, Denise felt happy.

The doctor had released Tom early that morning. As soon as he had learned that Denise had hurt her ankle at the Olney Theater, he had taken a cab home, picked up Molly's and Denise's favorite blueberry bagels, and rushed to her apartment. Together, they had eaten breakfast and read the morning paper. Now, like two married people, they sat on the sofa and did nothing.

Actually, until the perpetrator contacted Denise again, there was nothing she could do. She knew the murder weapon was ephedra and suspected that professional jealousy was the motive. Although she had stood within inches of him in the darkened corner of the concert hall, she would not have been able to recognize him in a lineup. As for the new partner, Denise had a gut feeling that he was not really the perpetrator. He might have worked for the killer, but his build did not match Joshua Smithe's description of the man on the Olney Theater stage dressed in Phantom of the Opera attire.

As Tom snored, Denise reflected on the pieces of the

case that she could fit together. From what Joshua Smith told her of the Phantom's acceptance speech at the Olney Theater, the perpetrator felt that the world had not acknowledged his conducting genius. From that, Denise surmised that the perpetrator was jealous of the accomplishments of all the people he had murdered. They were well established in their professions and respected in the world of symphony conducting. He was crafty and capable of entering the homes and hotel rooms of his victims. He used ephedra to poison their food, resulting in a quick death that resembled cardiac arrest. He left behind a baton in which he had drilled holes and added extra ephedra for good measure.

"Tom, wake up," Denise ordered as she jabbed him in the ribs.

"What? Can't a man get any rest around here? Someone was always poking me with something in the hospital, and now you're doing it," Tom growled sleepily.

"Stop complaining. I need your help," Denise stated, placing a kiss on his forehead.

"Well, if that's to be my payment, what can I do for you?" Tom asked, pulling her into his arms.

"I'm serious. This is important," Denise protested half-heartedly as she melted against him.

"So is this," Tom replied as he pressed his lips against hers in a kiss that left no doubt as to the seriousness of the matter.

Denise allowed the warmth of his embrace to sweep over her. Her body went limp and any interest in the case flowed away as Tom's hands caressed her body. Even the soreness of her ankle did not matter while she was in his arms. Time with Tom was perfect and unmarred by the realities of life outside her apartment door.

Resting her head on his shoulder, Denise murmured, "Aren't you the man who almost bought the ranch last night? You don't kiss like a sick man."

"Good loving is the best antidote for anything that ails a man," Tom commented as he pulled her even closer. "Besides, I had to get well in a hurry. You can't take care of yourself without my help."

"Me! What about you? You're the one who drank the poisoned coffee." Denise laughed softly without moving from the comfortable spot on his shoulder.

"But you're the one who fell over a box in the Olney Theater," Tom teased as he gently played with her earring.

"I guess we both need someone to take care of us," Denise concluded, looking into Tom's eyes.

Taking her face in his hands, Tom stated, "I've been trying to tell you that for a long time, woman."

"Well, it has only now starting to sink in," Denise replied as she tilted her face a little more for the anticipated kiss.

"What makes you think I want to kiss you?" Tom teased as he held back.

"The expression on your face gives you away every time." Denise chuckled, reaching for the kiss that Tom so generously delivered.

"What expression?" Tom demanded as he settled her against him once more.

"The hungry 'if you don't feed me, I'll die' expression," Denise joked, looking into his face and imitating his expression.

"Oh, that one. I'll have to remember to wear my poker face around you from now on," Tom said as he cleared all expression from his face.

"You can't hide the look in your eyes, big boy," Denise chided playfully as she leaned closer to study her reflection in his dark eyes.

"I'll wear dark glasses," Tom stated and nodded his head for emphasis.

Kissing the corners of his mouth playfully, Denise concluded, "No, you wouldn't. If you did, you'd miss all those kisses I give you simply because I can read the love in your eyes. You would really be hungry then."

"All right, woman, you win," Tom conceded with a groan. "Let's finish that serious discussion of yours so that we can have some play time."

"Oh, that, I'd forgotten." Denise sighed as she righted herself and returned her attention to the case.

"It's good to know that I still have that power over women," Tom joked as he picked up the little box that contained the gold baton. Suddenly serious, he added, "Did you have this checked for ephedra?"

"Sure did. Not a trace," Denise stated as she skimmed her notes.

"It's pretty . . . very delicate," Tom volunteered. "Too bad it came from a murderer."

"I know. Sort of removes some of the sparkle, doesn't it? Dulls the gold a bit," Denise commented, looking at the tiny baton.

Stretching, Tom asked, "Did you wake me just to show me this?"

"No, I need your help with the case," Denise stated and then added, "I know for certain that the person who poisoned the coffee is not the murderer."

"Really? How?"

"First, the murderer only strikes musically talented people, and I can't sing or play anything. Second, he always leaves a baton at the scene. Third, he's never at the scene of the murder at the time of death. The guy who poisoned the coffee stayed in the squad room until lunchtime and left no baton," Denise said, counting with her fingers for emphasis.

"Maybe he thought you wouldn't drink the coffee," Tom speculated.

"Perhaps, but he still would have left the baton," Denise explained. "That's been the whole point of them all along. He leaves a baton to ensure that the victim at

least inhales the ephedra. He knows that no one can resist pretending to conduct with one of those, especially
a musician. The baton's his insurance that the targeted
person will die."

"If that's true, then why did you find the last one
under the pillow? Why wasn't it in the victim's hand?"
Tom asked as he returned the box to the coffee table.

"The batons are really light. I would imagine that the
victim dropped it as he fell. The weight of the falling
body caused the pillows to lift momentarily and propelled the baton under them. When they settled again,
the pillows covered the baton," Denise concluded.

"I guess that could be possible," Tom conceded. "Now,
if the guy impersonating Craig Panns isn't the Music
Man Murderer, then why did he poison your coffee?"

"Remember that I told you he looked familiar?"
Denise continued. "I'm terrible with names, but I never
forget a face. I've been trying to remember where I've
seen him. It came to me last night. I remember a guy
from the police academy who would never remove his
jacket or roll up his sleeves regardless of the heat in the
room. A group of us decided that he either had mis-
shapen arms, not likely for a cop, or a tattoo of a naked
woman that he was ashamed to show in mixed company.
Anyway, I think that he's the guy who impersonated
Craig Panns."

"Why? Professional jealousy?" Tom asked as he studied
Denise's face. If his assumption was correct, she was in
grave danger from a renegade cop.

"That's right," Denise stated emphatically. "We graduated from the academy on the same day, but I've risen a
lot faster. I'm always, unfortunately, in the newspaper,
and he isn't. Everyone knows my name and face, but no
one would recognize him."

Agreeing angrily, Tom stated, "And he would have had

access to information, thanks to the chief's on-line system."

"Right," Denise said. "First, he would have known about your transfer since the captain would have advertised the vacancy. Second, he would have been able to determine the qualifications for your replacement via the promotions/transfers board. Third, the captain called the wife of the real Panns and learned that he was on vacation. If the captain could do it without any trouble, so could anyone else. His wife was very accommodating. Fourth, knowing that Panns was on vacation, this guy probably pretended to be Panns and confirmed his meeting with the captain, another of those standard practices. Then, he arrived on the appropriate date and time. No one would have been the wiser. The captain wouldn't have remembered the guy's face because he talks with so many people during the course of the day."

"He simply waltzed into the squad room, took over my desk, and prepared to off my girlfriend." Tom fumed at the ease with which a murder could happen in the squad room.

Shrugging, Denise continued, "He would have known that I'm working on a case involving ephedra and conducting batons. Thanks to the efficiency of the local press, that information is in all the papers. Ephedra's easy to find; it's in many of the health food stores. He wouldn't have needed to work hard to make it happen. He noticed that no one was making coffee and decided to bring a cup for me. I remember that it tasted waxy so I didn't drink it."

"He laced a cup of coffee with ephedra, handed it to you as cool as can be, and waited for you to drink it and die," Tom offered with flames of anger billowing around him.

Continuing with her assumptions, Denise said, "When I wouldn't drink it until later, he thought better of sitting there. After all, he had no intention of doing any work. He had only one purpose in being there. He saw that his little plan was too risky and certain to get him arrested. He left while I was out of the office and hasn't returned since. He has probably read every section of the *Post* this morning, looking for an article about my death or, at the very least, my obit."

"You've told Captain Morton all of this?" Tom demanded.

"I phoned him again this morning with my thoughts," Denise stated. "They're searching for the guy now. He might have left town, but he won't be hard to find as soon as we have his name. The captain is having someone search archives for academy graduations. He'll e-mail them to me as soon as he has them."

"I never should have let the captain push me into this new job," Tom lamented. "If I hadn't left, this guy never would have gotten to you."

"Oh, yes, he would," Denise disagreed. "My graduating class is holding a reunion next month, sort of a 'what are we doing now? let's catch up on the years' kind of thing. He would have found a way to strike then if not now. The list of attendees is on the Internet. You know, it's a great source of information, but it is capable of providing too much information to the wrong kind of people."

"I'd like to get my hands on him," Tom fumed with eyes that were frightening to see.

"So would I," Denise agreed. "Don't worry. He'll get his. There's no way short of moving to another country that he can escape the manhunt. He's definitely a marked man. No one tries to kill a fellow officer without paying the consequences."

Tom got up and started pacing the room. He was no longer able to contain the energy that the anger had caused. Futile fury filled him and made him practically jog around the apartment while Denise watched. She had seen him in all types of furies, from mild at having someone tangle his paper clips to profound at eating the ergot-tainted rolls. However, she had never seen his this livid. He had accidentally eaten the poisoned rolls meant for someone he did not know as the result of a quarrel in the fashion industry. Now, however, he had consumed the poisoned coffee intended for the woman he loved. Tom's anger was almost beyond reason.

"Tom, remember that you were near death yesterday. Don't overdo it," Denise advised, knowing that she was only talking to herself.

"Someone had better catch that guy and fast before he finds out that you're very much alive," Tom said. "You're not out of danger yet, Dory."

Nodding, Denise said, "I know. He could be lurking almost anywhere. However, I'll know him when I see him. He won't get close this time. He won't be able to make an attack on me look as if it were perpetrated by the Music Man killer."

"If this guy isn't the killer you've been tracking, who is?" Tom asked as he stopped his pacing long enough to look at Denise as she sat on the sofa.

"I don't know for sure, but I have a hunch," Denise confessed. "I'll let you know once it develops a bit more fully."

Taking Denise into his arms, Tom stated sincerely, "Regardless of who it is, I'm going to tell the captain that I want my old job back. I don't care about the money or the prestige of command, I only want to be where I can take care of you."

"Oh, no, you're not!" Denise exclaimed. "You're going to stay where you belong as the head of that unit. I wasn't in favor of your leaving, being a basically selfish person. But now, you have to stay. It's you due. I won't have you throwing everything away because of some jerk who has carried a beef with me all these years."

"But, Denise—" Tom began until Denise stopped him with a wave of her hand.

"No buts," Denise stated, shaking her head. "You're keeping that job and promotion. It's what you deserve for a job well done. Besides, you never know when you'll need to support a wife and children."

Sinking to the sofa beside her, Tom exclaimed, "What? Are you proposing to me, Denise?"

"Not exactly," Denise hedged. "I'm just saying that the day might come that I'll want to swap all of this excitement for rice, flowers, the picket fence, and diapers."

"Do you feel the urge for a change coming on yet?" Tom asked, looking a bit dejected that the lifestyle for which he yearned was still not within his grasp.

Taking his big hands in her small ones, Denise said, "Not yet, but you never can tell when the desire for a change will surface. I'm not getting any younger, and neither are you. It's about time for us to think about settling down. Two close calls in one year are too many for me. Because of the dangers of my work, I could have lost you."

Kissing her gently on the nose, Tom stated, "Just say the word and you'll make me the happiest man on earth."

Laughing, Denise kissed him and said, "Soon, but not yet. I still have things I need to do. But believe me, I'm thinking about it in a way I never did before."

"I guess I'll have to settle for that," Tom conceded as he pulled her onto his lap.

As they snuggled, the radio played Denise's favorite classical station in the background. The phone rang as they had just begun to enjoy the sweetness of their shared kisses. Reluctantly sliding from his arms, Denise reached for the offending instrument and answered it curtly. As expected, the captain's voice spoke on the other end.

"Denise, we found him. His name is Daniel White. He sat next to you for the academy graduation photo," Captain Morton announced.

"I don't understand. No one has sent me the photographs yet," Denise stated with confusion.

"He saved us the trouble," the captain explained. "It appears that White wanted to make sure that his plan had worked. He decided to pay us a visit at lunchtime, thinking that no one would be in the squad room. To his surprise, I had David Cox stay behind. I wanted someone on the scene in case he appeared. Cox apprehended him without a fight. he confessed after his attorney arrived."

"Did he give a reason for wanting to kill me?" Denise asked as she placed the phone so that Tom could listen also.

"Yeah, he said that he wanted to be the one to bring you down. He wanted his time in the limelight and figured that killing a famous detective like you would give him his minute of glory. Sick," Captain Morton replied with venom in his voice.

Shaking her head, Denise commented, "Well, he's got it. Only thing, it won't do him much good in prison. He'll be in a cell with a guy he helped to convict."

"I hope he doesn't drop his soap," the captain stated with a chuckle and clicked off.

Pulling Denise into his arms again, Tom said, "Now that he's behind bars, let's concentrate on us."

"I couldn't agree more," Denise replied as she slipped her arms around his neck and covered his face in kisses.

For the rest of the day, Denise rarely thought of her ankle and Tom forgot about the poisoned coffee. They were not police officers but lovers in need of the warmth and closeness that their lips and bodies could provide. They allowed their hands to say the words that their lips were too busy to utter. Not even the repeat e-mail reminders could make them abandon their need to possess each other.

The day passed into evening. Finally feeling hungry for more than kisses, they showered and ventured from Denise's apartment. With a happy Molly leading the way, they walked the few blocks to the closest Italian restaurant. Denise hardly limped and only rested lightly on Tom's arm for support. Depositing the dog in the office, they sat in a quiet booth in the back from which they could not be seen.

Just as the pizza arrived, Manny the owner motioned to the television over the bar, saying, "You've made the news again, Denise. Take a look. It's been on television since noon."

"Oh, no!" Denise groaned, picking up a slice of pepperoni pizza oozing with oils.

Gazing upward, they saw the photo of Daniel White on the left and Denise on the right. The reporter said that White was a veteran of the force who was now on administrative leave, pending trial.

Looking at Tom, Denise said, "At least, he gets his moment in the spotlight now."

"Yeah, but he has to share it with you," Tom replied, enjoying the irony of White's situation.

They ate in silence, each deep in thought. Denise allowed her mind to process the information she had gathered on the case, hoping to apprehend the murderer soon. She knew so much and still could not trap him. She had missed the radio clue that afternoon but had been able to listen to it on the Internet. However, the clue from *Annie Get Your Gun* only confused her. She wondered if the perpetrator was growing tired of the game and trying to tell her that he was throwing in the towel by selecting a song with lyrics that said "anything you can do." It was also possible that he was signaling an even bigger battle since the play was about lovers in conflict and denial of their relationship as both refused to give up their competitive natures. She would have to wait until the opening night of the show to find out.

For his part, Tom wondered if Denise would be able to step away from the excitement of her work. He knew that she did not seek the media attention and actually hated it. However, she loved the challenge of assembling the puzzle pieces until she finally understood the murderer's mind. This case was especially challenging. Even now, warm from bed and holding hands while sharing a meal, her mind was not on him.

Walking home, they stopped in the drugstore for a copy of the evening paper. The front-page article about White would make an interesting addition to Denise's scrapbook. One day, they might have children and grandchildren who would enjoy reading about her crime-fighting exploits. For the moment, however, they were both tired from the afternoon and the tension. Progenies were not on their minds as they headed for a good night's sleep and work the next day.

Sixteen

Uncharacteristically, the squad room was packed with detectives the next morning when Denise arrived. She usually had the place to herself, surrounded by almost perfect silence. However, that was not the case as she opened the door and stepped into the noisy chatter. She even sniffed the undeniable aroma of coffee. Someone must have found the instruction manual or bought a new coffeemaker. From the crowd gathered at her desk, she wondered if she should have stayed at home.

"Hey, break it up! Can't a woman get to her desk anymore?" Denise shouted over the noise as she used her arms and briefcase to part the crowd.

"You do work on the damnedest cases," Franklin remarked as Denise pushed past him.

"What are you babbling about, Franklin? I would have thought that you'd be off your caffeine high by now," Denise joked as she almost fell over the many feet that blocked the access to her desk.

"You'll see," Franklin replied as he bit into a fat jelly donut.

"Your partners are boomerangs, too," Leonard said, laughing, as he sipped the coffee that blackened the interior of his double-sized mug.

"I don't understand a thing you're saying. You guys need to get a life and get out of mine." Denise laughed, giving one last shove that propelled her to her desk.

Denise fairly fell into her chair and landed none too gracefully into the aged cloth seat. The men standing beside her almost spilled their coffee for laughing. Rescuing her sunglasses as they tumbled from the top of her head onto her lap, Denise stared openmouthed at the pillar of paper clip boxes complete with cascading strings of clips that almost covered the top of her desk. Other than at an office supply store, she had never seen so many of the shiny little links.

"Who did this?" Denise demanded as she searched for any sign of the sender.

"Guess," growled the voice from behind her.

Turning around, Denise almost leaped into his arms as the laughing human barrier parted. To her delight, Tom sat smiling like the Cheshire Cat. Although they had only parted company at the diner after eating an uncustomary workday breakfast, he had not mentioned that he intended to visit the office. She would have thought that he would enjoy about as much of the squad room as he could take, considering his last visit almost cost him his life. However, Tom looked totally at home. Even his coffee cup sat in its traditional ring on the desk.

"What are you doing here! You didn't tell me you were going to visit," Denise said as she clung to his neck, unmindful of the winks that passed between her colleagues.

"I'm not visiting. I work here," Tom stated solemnly as he kissed her gently on the lips.

"What? Did the poison do something to your memory?" Denise inquired with concern in her voice as she righted herself and straightened her skirt. They were, after all, in a workplace. She had never allowed her emotions to get that out of hand.

"No, I work here," Tom restated, taking a sip of his coffee.

With real concern wrinkling her brow, Denise said gently and slowly as if speaking to an invalid, "No you don't, Tom, you were promoted and transferred. Remember?"

"I haven't lost my wits, Dory." Tom chuckled as he held her hand to his lips.

"Between the paper clips on my desk and you sitting here as if it's natural, I'm confused," Denise stated, sinking into her chair. If Tom was not suffering aftereffects from the poisoning, then she had lost her mind from overwork and tension.

"I phoned Captain Morton from the hospital yesterday and made the arrangements. I didn't tell you because I thought you'd overreact or get angry. You were so determined that I keep my new assignment. I knew you needed a partner, so I asked the captain to take me back," Tom explained as the others patted him on the back and returned to their desks.

"But your promotion? The new group?" Denise sputtered, relieved that the stress of the case had not snapped her mind.

Shrugging, Tom replied, "Someone else will head the group. The captain said that I can keep the promotion. Actually, he said that he should have given it to me a long time ago. I'm back, Dory. Like it or not, you need me as your partner. I'm the only one who can watch your back."

"Why didn't you tell me this morning?" Denise asked with a broad, happy smile on her face.

"I wanted it to be a surprise," Tom replied in his usual matter-of-fact manner. "You are pleasantly surprised, aren't you?"

"I'm ecstatic!" Denise gushed as tears of happiness filled her eyes. "I couldn't be happier. There's no one I'd rather work with than you."

"Missed my coffee a bit?" Tom teased as he leaned comfortably into his usual position on the desk. The discolored spots in the surface fit his forearms perfectly.

"I missed your coffee, your grumbling, your strength,

your smile. I missed you, Tom," Denise admitted with a warmth that she hardly ever allowed herself to show in the squad room.

"Good, then I did the right thing. I was a little nervous at first. You were so set on my keeping the new position," Tom admitted with a big smile.

"It's not possible for me to become accustomed to being without you. This short time with that Craig Panns imposture was so lonely and horrible. I could hardly wait for the day to end so that I could see you," Denise stated as she laid her hand gently on his sweetly familiar bare, brown arm.

"You never told me," Tom said, studying her face.

Sighing, Denise spoke gently. "I was afraid that you'd abandon something so good for you professionally to be with me. I couldn't expect that of you."

"This is what's right for me. Being here with you, being your partner, that's what's right for me. Nothing else matters," Tom replied in the softest growl Denise had ever heard.

Tears burned behind her lids as Denise looked lovingly into Tom's face. Everything in her life was perfect again. Tom was beside her in work and love. No case would be too difficult with him at her side. She no longer had to separate her two lives. She could allow them to melt together as fate had meant that they would. Now she would be able to put all of her energy into solving the Music Man case. At least, she could once she removed the hill of paper clips from her desk.

Breaking the spell of the moment, Captain Morton joined them and asked with a chuckle, "Are you planning to make a suit of armor?"

Turning toward him, Denise stared over the mound and said, "No, sir, it's just a little joke from partner here."

"We almost didn't get them all piled up before you came. Ronda had one hell of a time getting them to balance and flow just right. She wanted the river-of-steel look. If you'd left that restaurant a few minutes earlier, you would have caught us in the act," the captain said, laughing.

"You were in on it? That's not like you, Captain." Denise joined in the laughter.

"I had to do something to help the man get back at you for all those paper clip chains. Now get back to work. The police department isn't paying you to sit around laughing," Captain Morton commanded with a broad grin. Turning toward Tom, he added, "Welcome back. The partnership's complete again."

"Not quite," Ronda stated as she rounded the corner with Molly trotted merrily at her side. "I think this belongs to you."

They watched as Molly took her usual spot on the floor between their desks. The assembled detectives, who had returned with the captain's appearance, slowly began to dismantle the paper-clip pile and clear Denise's desk. In a matter of minutes, the squad room looked and smelled like the old days.

Settling into her seat, Denise could feel delicious warmth. Tom was once again sitting behind her, grumbling about the condition of his cases. The station smelled of burned coffee, and Molly dozed on the floor. She was ready to work.

Turning on her computer, Denise checked her e-mail as she did every morning. The usual collection of memos and reminders appeared first. Ronda had been very busy sending messages and making paper-clip mountains while she was eating a leisurely breakfast.

Clicking off all the ones that she had read, Denise came to two with an unknown address. Opening one, she discovered that Joshua Smithe had e-mailed her an invitation to listen to his group perform that night at a local bar. He stated that he had a surprise for her.

Making sure that he understood that she would bring a date, Denise responded in the affirmative. He was a likable sort and had been very helpful at the Olney Theater the night she stumbled over the box. The least she could do was listen to his group as long as the attention did not feed his infatuation.

Thinking of the Olney Theater reminded her of the tiny gold baton broach that sat in the box in her briefcase. In all the confusion of Tom's return and the paper-clip mountain, she had forgotten to remove it. She placed the box in her bottom right desk drawer with the perfumes and the charm bracelet from other cases.

Denise then returned her attention to the second e-mail from Joshua. This one had just arrived and welcomed Tom's presence at the performance in the bar. She smiled, knowing that the company if not the music would make the evening worthwhile.

Remembering Joshua's comment about the value of the gold baton the perpetrator had given her, Denise decided to pay his shop a little visit. He had mentioned not stocking the little pin because of their cost although he had seen them in a catalogue. Not being able to find them on the Internet, Denise wanted to take a look for herself.

Denise followed familiar roads on the trip to Old Towne. She parked on the usual residential street and followed a well-worn path through the park to the main street. She was not surprised to see Joshua standing at the door, dressed in his period clothing as usual. Nor was she taken aback that his greeting was anything but warm.

"Well, Detective, what brings you here?" Joshua asked frostily. "I received your e-mail and didn't expect to see you until the little performance."

"I thought that you might be able to show me the catalogue with the little gold batons," Denise stated as she sank into the offered seat.

"Sure, but I don't know what good it'll do you," Joshua said without allowing the ice to melt.

"I'll contact the vendor and see if anyone remembers selling one of them within the last two months or so," Denise replied, ignoring his cold stare.

Without answering, Joshua vanished into the back of the shop, leaving her free to observe her surroundings. This was the first time that he had left her alone. Usually, he offered her a soda from the little refrigerator behind the counter. This time, he made no such offer.

Joshua had not thawed upon his return. In fact, holding the catalogue in his outstretched hands, he appeared even colder. His entire demeanor was of a man who was very angry and determined to punish the object of the irritation with lack of communication. Denise decided that telling him about bringing Tom to the concert was not a good idea if she wanted his continued support.

"Here," Joshua said as he thrust the catalogue into her hands. "I've marked the page.

Taking it from him with a stifled smile, Denise studied the one page that contained a few baton-shaped bracelets, necklaces, and, of course, pins. The catalogue boasted of being the exclusive supplier of these designs and in any metal. The murderer had to have ordered it either from the manufacturer directly or from one of the merchants who carried his product.

Turning to the front of the catalogue, Denise discovered that the manufacturer would not sell to individuals. She would have to call the company to request the name and address of his distributors in the area. Remembering Joshua's comments about being the only supplier for the company's low-end batons, she realized that she would not have far to look.

"How long has your dad been carrying this product line?" Denise asked as Joshua wiped nonexistent dirt and dust from the counter.

"Not long. It wasn't his idea; it was mine. My father hasn't paid much attention to the shop in years," Tom replied as he buffed out imaginary fingerprints.

"Does anyone else around here sell these little jewelry pieces?" Denise inquired, continuing to ignore the ice that appeared to thicken between them.

Denise watched Joshua dust the trophies and plaques from the board of trade. Each one bore his father's name except the last two. Those carried his name and coincided with his taking over the shop.

"No, only me," Joshua stated without turning to face her.

Joshua continued to wipe with his back to Denise as if she were of no importance in his day. As a matter of fact, the dust received more attention than she did. For once, she would have welcomed the offer of a soda, but it was clear that none would come.

"Do you remember selling any?" Denise inquired, trying to maintain her calm as she became irritated with Joshua's surly behavior.

"Yes."

Feeling her temper shorten in correspondence with his replies, Denise demanded curtly, "Would you happen to know the name of the person who purchased it?"

"Yes."

"Would you share the information with me? It might be helpful to the case I'm investigating," Denise said as she tried to keep tart words from flowing off her tongue.

"No, not without a search warrant," Joshua replied as he turned toward her and rested his hand on the freshly polished counter. He did not seem to notice the sweaty print that he was making.

"Okay, I can get one and return later this afternoon," Denise replied as she picked up her briefcase. She had endured enough of the young man.

"Fine."

Walking toward the door, Denise stopped and turned. "What's the problem, Joshua? Why have you changed toward me?"

"You didn't tell me that you were in a relationship," Joshua replied sharply.

"You didn't ask," Denise stated.

Sticking out his jaw, Joshua responded, "You knew I was interested. Instead, you told me about having a smashed banana in your pocket. You should have told me that you're involved with someone else. I wouldn't have wasted my time."

"Wasted your time doing what? Helping a cop do her job? Making an attempt to stop another murder? What?" Denise demanded, as she no longer held her anger in check.

"All of the above and more," Joshua snarled as he walked toward the back of the store.

"I'll return with the search warrant before closing time," Denise stated as she walked to the door.

Whirling around, Joshua replied with hurt pride and anger showing on his face, "Don't bother. I sold it to myself. I threw that little package at your feet as I helped you search for the lump in the carpet."

Turning again, he left Denise to exit the store without a farewell.

Reaching her car, Denise quickly phoned the Little Gold Warehouse to see if Joshua was telling the truth about ordering the pin. Years of practice had enabled her to commit phone numbers to memory while she flipped the catalogue pages. She would not have needed the search warrant anyway.

Posing as a clerk for Joshua's store, Denise stated that she was checking on the status of their last order. She explained that they had experienced a great turnover in personnel and did not know if the shipment had arrived. The sales department was most helpful and confirmed that Joshua had purchased one gold baton pin. They had shipped it FedEx. According to their tracking records, it had arrived three days ago.

Denise found the latest piece of information intriguing. She had known from her first meeting with Joshua and certainly by the second that he was developing a crush on her. He had proclaimed his interest at the Olney Theater the night of the fall as he invited her to take a drink with him. However, she had not realized then the extent of his crush on her.

It was flattering. Denise found that her ego actually enjoyed the idea that a younger man would find her interesting. Joshua was not much younger, but the age and experience difference was sufficient to Denise that she would not have found him interesting even if she had not been involved with Tom.

So Joshua had made it appear as if the man dressed as the Phantom of the Opera had dropped the box at her feet. Or, at least that was what he said. If that was true, the carpet in the Olney Theater's concert hall could confirm it.

Dialing Tom to tell him of her change in location, Denise said, "Can you believe it? I've reached an age that I'm attractive to younger men."

"I'm not surprised, Dory. You're one hell of a woman," Tom replied with great pride in his voice.

"You really missed working with me, didn't you? I've never known you to talk like this," Denise commented as she pointed her car in the direction of the Olney Theater.

"It's about time that I started," Tom acknowledged with a chuckle. "I've kept my thoughts to myself too long. Give me time, and I'll fill your ears with all kinds of sweet nothings."

"Oh, yeah? Well, I hope they won't really be meaningless. A light stretching of the truth regarding my beauty is okay, but I prefer honest sentiment to fluff," Denise chided as she drove through the park and headed toward the interstate. The hands-free feature of her speaker-phone made it easy for her to talk and drive safely.

"Don't nitpick with me, Dory. You know I'm new at this kind of stuff," Tom growled, laughing at the pleas-ant familiarity of their relationship.

"For an older man, you really don't have much prac-tice in sweet-talking a woman. I bet Joshua could give you pointers," Denise stated as she pulled into the Olney Theater parking lot.

"Don't worry. I make up for not knowing this fluffy stuff by being really good with what I do know. I'll give you a sample of my expertise after dinner tonight," Tom promised in a low voice.

Traveling along the interstate, Denise said, "You can have all the time you want after Joshua's concert. He was icy, but he didn't retract his invitation to hear his group perform. He even said that he had a little surprise for me."

Tom's hackles suddenly on edge, he said, "Be careful, Denise. You don't really know that guy. He might be the perpetrator. He certainly fits the description and has easy access to the batons."

"He's not the type despite his cold behavior today," Denise countered. "I'll see you in the squad room later."

"Be careful!" Tom stressed as the line went dead.

Phoning Mr. Fitzgerald as she pulled onto Russell Street, Denise arranged to meet him at the concert hall doors. At this time of day, the Olney Theater was almost deserted with only scattered clusters of tourists to block her progress. Avoiding the small gathering at the gift shop, Denise walked rapidly toward the man waiting at the foot of the stairs.

"Thanks for meeting me," Denise stated as they shook hands.

"No problem. Glad I could help. This has been a ter-rible experience," Mr. Fitzgerald said as he unlocked one of the massive doors and switched on the lights at the back of the room.

Mr. Fitzgerald stood aside as Denise entered the empty hall. Walking to the corner, she dropped to her knees, being careful not to put too much pressure either on the still slightly sensitive knee or the taped ankle. Shining her flashlight and feeling the carpet, Denise located the ridge that had tripped her, costing her the collar. If she had been a little quicker, she would have caught the man who had dressed as the Phantom and voiced his displeasure at the inequity within the profession.

"Did you find what you were looking for, Detective?" Mr. Fitzgerald asked from his position near the door. He remained outside the room, providing Denise with space to work.

"I certainly did," Denise stated. "You'll need to contact the maintenance crew about this ridge in the carpet. Someone else might take a nasty fall."

"They haven't fixed that yet? I reported it after you took that fall," Mr. Fitzgerald replied, as he studied the raised portion of the carpet.

"How did you know that I tripped?" Denise asked, as they turned out the lights and left the concert hall.

"A man called me with the information," Mr. Fitzgerald replied.

"Did he identify himself?" Denise asked, hoping that the caller had been Joshua. It would make the investigation so much simpler if he had reported the incident.

"No, he didn't. He just said that he saw you fall," Mr. Fitzgerald stated.

"Well, thanks for taking care of it for me and for letting me into the hall today," Denise said, standing at the foot of the wide staircase.

"Come to think of it," Mr. Fitzgerald commented, "the caller gave me a funny name."

"Really? What?"

"He called himself the Phantom of the Opera," Mr. Fitzgerald replied. "At first, I thought that I'd misunderstood. It had been a dreadful night. But, when he repeated his name, I knew that I'd heard correctly. He called himself the Phantom, like in the opera. Strange."

Breathing deeply, Denise said, "Not as strange as you'd think, Mr. Fitzgerald. Thanks again."

Denise left Mr. Fitzgerald standing in the grand hall as she rushed to her car for the return trip to the office. She did not stop to phone Tom from the parking lot. She could hardly wait to see his expression when he learned that the man who had killed so many musicians could have a considerate side to his personality. Not every woman had the opportunity to flirt with danger at the hands of the Phantom of the Opera.

Seventeen

Changing into jeans and a bulky sweater for Joshua's concert that evening, Denise thought about the day's events. For certain, it had not been boring or run-of-the-mill. Tom had given up his new position and returned to the squad room as her partner. Joshua had frozen her out after discovering that she was in a relationship, a great boost to her ego but traumatic for him. And she had discovered that a man dressed as the Phantom of the Opera and the likely suspect in the Music Man Murder case had a chivalrous side. Not bad for a day's work.

The doorbell rang as Denise applied the finishing touches to her makeup. Opening the door quickly, she discovered that no one was there. However, a large bouquet of flowers sat on the floor at her feet. In her secure building, the night watchman had delivered the flowers and left.

Before Denise could finish arranging the flowers in her favorite vase, the doorbell rang again. Looking out, she saw Tom making faces into the peephole. As soon as he entered, he pulled her into his arms.

"Thanks for the flowers," Denise said as soon as she could break from Tom's strong embrace.

"That's just the beginning." Tom beamed.

"Oh really. Well, I could get used to a little spoiling," Denise cooed as she snuggled into his arms again.

"You're going to have so much spoiling that you won't

be able to say no," Tom stated, making reference to the marriage topic again.

"Let's not talk about that now. I've had a wonderful day, and the evening promises to be even better," Denise said with a sigh.

Agreeing with a shrug, Tom said, "Okay, we won't discuss it, but you'll know that I'm thinking about it. I told you that I want you as my partner on and off the job. I haven't changed my mind. In fact, this latest brush with death has convinced me that I can't be completely happy without you. I love you that much and more."

Smiling into his openly enamored face, Denise agreed. "I don't want to think about ever being without you either. I love you, too."

Holding each other close, they stood in the dining room as the fragrance of dinner wafted around them. For the moment, neither thought about hunger. Not even the constant meowing of Max the cat could make them release each other. Only the insistent ringing of the telephone made them part.

Rushing to the phone, Denise listened as the captain explained the intrusion into her evening, saying, "I thought you'd like to know that the real Craig Panns just phoned. It seems he returned home early from his little vacation. When his wife told him about the impersonator, he wanted to touch base with me immediately. He was livid. Good thing the other guy's in jail. I think this man might rip him a new one if he gets his hands on him."

"I'd be furious, too, if someone stole my identity for the purpose of killing a fellow officer who's about to become a new partner," Denise replied as Tom served the dinner.

Clearing his throat, Captain Morton stated, "That's the other reason for my call. Now that Tom has returned with added rank, I'll have to do something with this Panns guy. I've just talked with the chief, and she's finally created a special crimes division. She'll announce it in a few days. You and Tom will be the charter members. You'll be in charge, of course."

"Thanks, but what exactly will the division do?" Denise asked, leery of captains bringing gifts.

Captain Morton replied, "Exactly the kind of work you're doing now, only as a separate division. I've lobbied long and hard for it. The funding has just been approved. It frees up my head count. You and Tom never work anything but special cases anyway, causing the bulk of the load to fall on the others. This arrangement is good for both of us. I get to hire another officer, and you get a promotion. You've got one month to wrap up this case. Make the most of this evening. You've got work to do."

"Captain, I . . ." Denise sputtered.

Putting a halt to her stuttering, Captain Morton replied, "Don't thank me, Dory. You deserve it. Just close that case. You don't need any more murders in this one. It wouldn't look good. Give Tom my regards. Good night."

Denise stood staring at the phone. She had not been expecting a promotion and was not sure that she wanted the responsibility of command. She was very happy with the status quo now that Tom once again occupied the desk behind hers.

"What did he want?" Tom asked, as Denise joined him at the table. Max sat contentedly waiting for one of them to drop him a piece of chicken or shrimp.

"You won't believe any of it," Denise stated, digging into the heaping portion of food that Tom had piled on her plate.

"Try me."

"First, the real Craig Panns has appeared and is hopping mad," Denise began. "The captain actually sounded sorry for the impersonator."

"I can understand his reaction completely," Tom commented between bites. "And?"

"The chief is opening a special crimes division, and I'm to head it. That is, if I ever close this case, and if I accept the job. I won't do it without your support," Denise stated as she looked deeply into Tom's eyes.

"That's great," Tom replied enthusiastically, "as long as it doesn't take you away from me. After all, I gave up the canine corps to be with you although I kept Molly, the best part of it."

"I know, and you'll never know how much I appreciate it. I've even learned to appreciate the dog. The captain said that we'd both become members of the division. How do you feel about the possibility of working under me?" Denise asked as she munched a piece of celery and studied his face.

"Sounds like the status quo to me," Tom replied happily as he planted a kiss on Denise's forehead. "It doesn't bother me one bit and never has. I'm really proud of you, Denise. It's long overdue. When I finally drag you down the aisle, we'll be the highest-ranking couple I know."

"Well, it hasn't happened yet. I have to close this case first," Denise responded as she smiled into Tom's eyes.

Filled with wonderful warmth, Denise turned her attention to the meal. She still was not sure that she wanted the promotion or the responsibility, but she enjoyed the recognition for a job well done. Tom's reception had only made the captain's news sweeter. The evening was off to an incredible start.

Even the weather cooperated to make the night memorable. The stars shone overhead and the full moon competed with the streetlights of Old Towne for brilliance. Finding seats on a bench among the crowd gathered in the park, Denise and Tom watched as the members of Joshua Smithe's group, the Workhouse, tuned their instruments. Although the instruments were electrified this time, she recognized them from the restaurant. Tom also seemed to remember them and appeared ready for the evening's entertainment.

As Denise surveyed the mixture of people gathered to hear the free concert, a small boy of five or six walked tentatively toward her. Holding a little piece of folded paper in his hand, he repeatedly looked over his shoulder as if someone were directing his steps toward her. Thrusting the paper in her hand, he quickly trotted away.

Feeling eyes on her face, Denise looked toward Joshua's group. His eyes met hers and he smiled. Returning his attention to his instrument, he appeared to forget that she existed.

"What's that? A love note from your admirer?" Tom grumbled, peering over her shoulder.

Rolling her eyes, Denise opened the hastily penned note on stationery from Joshua's music shop. Squinting into the semidarkness, she read a simple but direct message. In fountain pen, Joshua had written, *I'm sorry for my behavior. Please forgive me.*

"Humph," Tom snorted with jealousy that surprised even himself.

"Whatever," Denise commented, not wanting to discuss the note. She wanted to savor the boost to her ego that being the object of a man's affection could bring. She liked it. Police detective or not, she was still very much a woman.

Suddenly, silence filled the park, and then delightful music followed. The air filled with electric string sounds that lifted her imagination. Denise involuntarily closed her eyes and allowed the music to flow over her in a flood of colors, to envelop her in silky sensations, and to transport her to a world of mystery and reverie.

Opening her eyes, Denise saw that Joshua's father stood with his back to the audience. He lifted his arms, swayed his body, and controlled the tantalizing sounds that rose on the night air. The musicians and their

instruments bent to his direction and appeared to
hunger for his instruction.

Watching the complete harmony of conductor and
musicians, Denise, for the first time, understood the
power of the conductor. The musicians could play without him, but they could not make music without his
direction. The conductor heard the individual notes and
pulled them together until they produced a single mul-
tifaced sound that thrilled the ear. It was not the little
baton in his hand but the presence of the leader that
pulled the single instruments together into perfection.
She understood the reason that symphony members
considered conductors akin to divinity.

Usually a classical music purist, Denise found that she
enjoyed this electrified version in a primal sort of way.
It was not as sophisticated as the purely classical, but the
notes still rang true and seemed amplified by the elec-
tricity that gave them life. Perhaps knowing someone in
the group added to the appeal, but even Tom sat with his
eyes closed. Tom, an R&B and jazz aficionado, smiled
as the strains of vaguely familiar old chords washed over
him in a new and stimulating way. Little wonder peopled
loved to conduct. They held such creative power in each
downstroke of their batons.

When the last note sounded and the applause began,
Denise did not want to leave. The music had left her skin
tingling and her brain swirling. She wanted more, but it
was over. The musicians had taken their bows and were
packing up their instruments.

Wanting to thank Joshua and his father for a spectacular evening, Denise scanned the makeshift stage, as the
crowd began to thin. Unfortunately, they had already de-
parted, leaving her feeling slightly disappointed. Even
the shop door was locked and the light turned off. When
she saw him again, she would thank him for inviting her,

but it would not be the same. Memory would have dulled some of the impact of the moment.

Denise fairly floated to the car. Although Tom had to admit that the group was good, he was not as overwhelmed as she appeared to be. Thinking that Joshua's infatuation must have caused some of the reaction, he remained silent. He was sufficiently content in their love to allow her to enjoy the admiration of another man without becoming too jealous.

Tom did not realize that Denise, although taken by the music, was also deep in thought. Watching the conductor up close had shed light on the case that sitting in plush concert hall seats many yards removed from the orchestra had not done. She had seen his power and heard its result. Suddenly, she could understand the desire to want to conduct bigger and better orchestras. If Joshua's father could pull this level of performance from this small ensemble of musicians, she could only imagine the energy that would flow from a full orchestra.

The man posing as the Phantom of the Opera had shouted his anger at the inequity of the music profession after the conducting competition. According to the *Post*, he had felt that the competition only whetted the desire to conduct and did not satisfy the individual's need to do it. Few positions as symphony conductors existed. Few conductors would ever feel the thrill of producing music at that level. The Phantom had won the competition but realized the magnitude of his hopelessness.

At that moment, despite the fact that he had killed other musicians, Denise felt sorry for him. He wanted something that fate dictated that he would never enjoy. He had the talent and the skill, but he would never have the opportunity. Guest appearances would not satisfy his desire to control the depths of expression released through music.

"I feel like crying," Denise stated as they drove toward home through the peaceful park.

"Why? What's wrong?" Tom asked in alarm.

"I can understand the murderer's motives, and I feel sorry for him," Denise said as she stared at Tom's face in profile.

"What?" Tom asked incredulously.

Denise tried to explain by saying, "He has always watched others conduct orchestras. They've done something that he's capable of doing but will never have the opportunity to do. He knows that he's as talented as they are, but he'll never be more than a visitor to their world. He's a tragic person, someone who's ruled by his love of music and its power over others."

"He kills other conductors so that he might have their job?" Tom asked as he carefully steered the dark turns of the park.

"I don't think that he expects to take their job," Denise commented. "I think he knows that someone else with better connections is already waiting in the wings."

"Then, why does he do it?"

Struggling for the right words, Denise replied, "He knows that he'll never do more than look into the window of their world, maybe enter for a relatively few minutes, and then leave again. He's obsessed with something that he'll never have."

"He's sick!" Tom exclaimed, pulling from the tranquillity of the park into the busy main street.

"You're right," Denise agreed. "Anyone who can't control desires and impulses has a problem."

They rode in silence as the streetlights lighted their trip home. The houses and trees looked magical with only the sporadically placed lights to illuminate them. Cats slinking after mice looked magical, as they cast shadows on the lawns.

"The killer makes a perfect Phantom, doesn't he?" Denise asked, breaking the silence in the car.

"In what way?"

Denise spoke slowly as she explained her theory. "The Phantom of the Opera obsessed over a woman that he could not have until he finally took her for his captive. The killer obsesses over a life that he can't have and holds it captive by terrorizing the members of that group."

"If he's holding that community captive, haven't his attacks been rather random?" Tom asked, as he pulled into an available space near the pool.

"No, I don't think so," Denise replied. "You see, all of the victims have been connected with music by more than conducting. I think he's purposefully killing conductors who have not been true to their profession. Have you noticed that none of the victims has been exclusively an orchestra conductor? Even Hornblatt, who was the purest conductor, had dabbled in Hollywood film music as a composer, which the killer would have considered heresy."

Unlocking the apartment door, Tom said, "Now, tell me again. Why does he kill the conductors?"

Scratching Max the cat behind his left ear, Denise replied, "I think he's punishing them for not being completely true to the craft of symphony conducting. I think he's a purist who dislikes the idea of one genre of music mixing with the other. He wants conductors, who have the job that he wants so desperately, to conduct and not focus on composing or performing. He doesn't want them to poison music by cross-pollinating the genres."

Pouring a glass of wine for both of them and carrying it to the sofa, Tom asked, "Why does he use ephedra? Why not simply shoot them?"

Sinking into the sofa beside him, Denise replied, "Ephedra is an old natural substance that originally had as its purpose very noble uses. Over time, people learned that it could produce a high as well as cause weight loss.

Rather than working for either by engaging in mental or physical activities, people bastardized the use of ephedra to produce the desired results, just as they've contaminated music by combining activities."

"You're saying that this man is not only obsessed with conducting but an extreme purist who detests mingling of purposes?" Tom inquired, trying to comprehend Denise's thoughts completely.

"That's right," Denise replied, as she sipped the delicious merlot that was their favorite beverage next to Tom's overcooked coffee. "He probably won't take a medicine that was designed for one purpose to cure an unrelated illness. He isn't capable of seeing that, through cross-pollination, both sides benefit from the shared knowledge. He's missing the benefit of community."

"If your theory's correct, this guy can't take in the glory of a sunset with a beautiful woman in his arm," Tom stated as he pulled Denise against his shoulder.

"That's right. Poor guy deserves pity," Denise concluded, snuggling against Tom's warmth.

"He's sick!"

"Whatever."

Conversation ended as Tom's lips found hers and his arms tightened around her body. Putting all thoughts of the Phantom from their minds, Denise and Tom began the slow, tantalizing dance that needed no conductor. The rhythm that they had developed from years of working together provided direction as they let their fingers strum the nerve endings that produced the most exquisite pleasure. They listened to the beat of their hearts and followed the tempo of love that drew them together in blissful harmony.

Pulling away gently, Tom studied Denise's face closely. Her eyes spoke of love. Her lips tasted of love. Her body welcomed love. He felt more for her than he had ever felt for another woman. He needed her as he had never needed another. He must have her in his life forever or perish.

Fumbling in his pocket, Tom extracted a small black leather box. Holding it in the palm of his hand, he whispered, "I love you, Denise, and want our partnership to last forever. Marry me."

Denise's eyes burned with unshed tears. Cradling his face in her hands, she examined every inch of the face she loved so much. She loved the bridge of his nose, the space between his eyes, and the curve of his brows. She delighted in kissing the dimple in his chin, the fleshy part of his earlobes, and the hollow of his cheeks. He was everything to her. Denise could not imagine life without him and did not want to try.

"Oh, Tom," Denise cried, "why must you ask me this? I love you. I'm yours. Isn't that enough?"

Shaking his head, Tom replied, "No, I want to wake up with you in my arms every morning. I want children with you. I want to grow old with you. Marry me, Denise."

"Let's live together. That way, we'll spend all day and all night together," Denise suggested hopefully.

"I want permanence," Tom stated firmly. His eyes glinted the depth of his desire and love for her.

"We're permanent now. I don't want anyone but you," Denise replied as she planted little kisses on his lips.

"Then marry me. There's no reason that we shouldn't," Tom exclaimed as he drew her closer.

"All the marriages of cops that I've ever known have ended in divorce. I don't want that to happen to us. I'm afraid that we'll end up like Calvin and Rita. They were a great couple. They made a great team. They divorced a year after they married," Denise exclaimed with misery in her voice.

"That won't happen to us," Tom protested, wiping the tears that had cascaded down her cheeks.

"That's what Rita said on her wedding day. I was a

bridesmaid. Remember? Right before we started the walk down the aisle, Rita told me that she was happier than she'd ever been and that she knew that nothing would separate them. Nothing but a divorce court." Denise sniffed.

"Take this ring. Wear it for a while. The idea will grow on you," Tom suggested, as he took another direction around the opposition.

Sitting up and ignoring the ring that Tom held in front of her, Denise offered, "Why don't we just live together? You're on a month-by-month lease anyway. This condo is large enough for you and Molly to move in here. We can start looking for a bigger house and put this one on the market. We'll be everything except married. There's no need to fix a wonderful relationship if it isn't broken."

Realizing that compromise was in order, Tom agreed. "I'll move in if you'll wear the ring."

"Why should I wear the ring? It says that we're planning to get married. What if people notice and ask questions?" Denise objected, feeling her resistance weaken.

"That's the only way that I'll move in. Besides, no one will notice. Anyway, I want to call you something other than my girlfriend. We've passed that phase and age. If anyone notices, we'll say that we're engaged with an indefinite date for the wedding," Tom suggested, slipping the ring onto Denise's finger.

"But I don't want to get married. Marriage will ruin our relationship," Denise insisted even as she gazed at the stunningly beautiful two-karat diamond solitaire.

"Whatever," Tom said with raised eyebrows.

Denise broke into gales of laughter that erased any further argument. She was extremely happy, happier than she had been in years. She loved Tom and wanted to spend every minute with him. He would soon move into her apartment. They would look for a place of their own. She could not wish for more.

Walking to the bedroom with arms locked around each other, they switched out the light. The evening had been full of promise and had offered it and more. If only Max and Molly could cohabitate with ease, the living arrangements would be perfect.

Eighteen

When Denise arrived at the office the next day, she inhaled deeply of a different kind of coffee aroma. People gathered around the coffee machine looked up and grinned as she passed. Approaching her desk, she heard first a low murmur and then a succession of whistles and cheers. Finally, the room erupted with Captain Morton leading the applause, holding a drawing of an engagement ring. Denise did not know whether to feel embarrassed or elated.

Contrary to what Tom had said, he made certain that everyone knew about the engagement. He was so happy that, for once, he did not burn the coffee or complain about his cases. He had a woman who loved him and whom he adored. Life looked wonderful.

Even, Ronda, who was usually so calm and unemotional, gushed and cooed over the size of the stone. She hugged Denise and kissed Tom, who almost blushed at being the center of attention. She stated loudly that she intended to handle all of the preparations when the time came. She loved to plan weddings.

Only Molly did not respond to the change. She sprawled at Tom's feet as she had before the engagement. She barely acknowledged Denise's presence except to move her paws to avoid being trampled.

When the commotion finally died down, Denise slid into her chair. She had done nothing on the case and was already exhausted. Her face ached from smiling. Her left hand felt tingly from having been raised and lowered so often as people studied her ring. She had received all of the attention she loathed. Now she could work.

The first order of business was to order theater tickets for the opening of *Annie Get Your Gun*. Although the play opened the next evening, she managed to get two tickets on the aisle at the back of the mezzanine. Knowing that Tom would want to make an evening of it, she made dinner reservations for a little bistro downtown within an easy drive of the theater.

Next, she phoned Mr. Fitzgerald at the Olney Theater. He did not seem at all surprised at her request. He agreed immediately to fax a copy of the biography of each of the leads. Although still shaken, he was more than willing to do anything he could to find the killer.

As soon as the information arrived, Denise placed another call to Mr. Fitzgerald. With his help, she arranged to meet with the male lead later that afternoon. He was busy with final rehearsal but would take time from his schedule to see her. Further, she had arranged to tour the set and Mr. Clay's hotel room. She needed to lay a trap for the killer before he struck again.

Studying the bio, Denise knew that the perpetrator would strike before the next evening. The lead, Clark Clay, was not only a winner of many Tony Awards and Emmys, he was an acclaimed composer and conductor. To a purist like the perpetrator, Clark Clay was a prime target.

Turning to Tom's desk, Denise leaned her arms on the top in her usual way and announced, "I'm going to the Olney Theater to meet with Mr. Fitzgerald and then with Clark Clay, the male lead in the show. If my theory is correct, the perpetrator will strike before tonight's opening."

"Do you want company?" Tom asked, as he closed the folder on which he was working.

"No, but you can treat me to a late lunch." Denise smiled, as she fingered the ring on her finger.

"Too tight already?" Tom teased, watching her intently. He knew that Denise had endured much more public attention that morning than she had wanted.

"No. It's perfect," Denise answered, as the tears burned her lids. Changing the subject, she said, "By the way, we're going to the theater tonight."

"Again!" Tom complained with a smile. "You're increasing my culture level too fast."

Laughing, Denise stated, "You'll like *Annie Get Your Gun*. It's a musical with lots of loud singing and good dancing. I'll see you at lunch."

"Okay. How does Luigi's sound?" Tom asked as Denise packed her briefcase.

"Great! And bring Molly." Denise smiled.

"There's nothing like being a man sandwich," Tom joked, watching her walk away.

Denise chuckled all the way to the parking lot. She had only been engaged a few hours but already the change in Tom had started. To her surprise, she liked it. He was more open about his feelings and more demonstrative in public. Being engaged had its pluses.

Along the route, Denise reflected on Clark Clay's bio. He exemplified everything that the perpetrator disliked. He had performed in many musical genres and received acclaim in all of them. From theater to television, Clark Clay was a star. And now, he was indeed a sitting duck.

Denise needed no escort and wasted no time in reaching Mr. Fitzgerald's office at the back of the Olney Theater concert hall. Since his responsibility covered all of the day-to-day functions of the multifaceted arts center, he made the perfect contact. His emotional attachment to the last victim made him a good colleague.

Mr. Fitzgerald looked up as Denise tapped lightly on his closed door. Smiling, he motioned to her to enter. Standing, he waited until she had slipped into the offered chair. Once she was comfortable, he gave her his complete attention.

"I need to see the sets and Clark Clay's dressing room. I don't know when the killer will strike or where, but I have to prepare for all possibilities," Denise began as she sketched Mr. Fitzgerald's expressive face. Their earlier meetings had not afforded her that opportunity.

"I'll take you on a tour myself. He's in rehearsal now. We can leave whenever you're ready." Mr. Fitzgerald smiled his tired little grin that was more a slight movement of his lips than a real sign of pleasure.

"Good. Let's go," Denise said as she rose and followed him down the hall.

The dressing room was the first stop. The room was comfortably furnished to Clark Clay's specifications. For the six-week run, he had ordered a leather recliner for napping, a chair-side lamp for reading, and a well-stocked refrigerator for munching. Unlike many actors, he had not demanded fresh paint and new carpet. His contractual demands had been few and easy to satisfy.

Opening the refrigerator door, Denise discovered that Clark Clay liked chocolate ice cream and frozen candy bars. The other staples in his diet appeared to be vanilla yogurt and apples. So far, he had not indulged his appetite since the ice cream box carried the original seal as did the yogurt container. However, once open, his selections would be an easy target for the killer, who could easily stir ephedra into the carton of yogurt.

Turning to Mr. Fitzgerald, Denise instructed, "Make sure that no one delivers any more ice cream and yogurt for the next forty-eight hours."

"I don't know if I can do that," Mr. Fitzgerald replied. "They're contract items. We'd be in default if we did. His contract reads that he must have new supplies constantly."

"Then replace them with pint-sized servings. That way,

no one will be able to tamper with the remaining amount," Denise stated, as she handed the cartons to Mr. Fitzgerald. "He won't die without them, but he could die as a result of eating them."

"Oh, my, you mean that the killer might strike again? I don't know how much of this I can take," Mr. Fitzgerald whined as he carried the packages from the dressing room.

"It's possible," Denise advised. "Make sure that no food enters this room without your approval. Everything must be in single-serving containers with safety seals."

"Oh, my. My stomach's acting up already," Mr. Fitzgerald complained as he led the way to the theater. Along the way, he stopped in a rest room and flushed the ice cream and yogurt down the toilet.

Seeing the man's continued distress, Denise commented, "Don't worry. It'll all be over soon."

The orchestra had just cued the female lead, Mary Carter, for her famous number, "Can't Get a Man with a Gun." Although Ethel Merman had made the character and songs famous, Mary Carter was an excellent choice to keep the character of Annie Oakley alive. She threw her head back and belted out the words in grand style. The flaming red hair seemed to give off color as she sang.

Slipping into seats in the front row, Denise sat mesmerized by the energy of the play. She watched as the actors moved through their paces without missing a step, or at least not one that she could see. Denise loved the make-believe of the theater. It was so different from the world in which she lived. Police work often became too real for comfort.

Denise, Mr. Fitzgerald, and the director applauded when the number ended. The actors did not appear to notice but, instead, remained focused on their roles. They were professionals first and always.

Clark Clay entered almost unceremoniously. He was a

tall, handsome man with a rugged appearance that fit the role perfectly. From where Denise was sitting, she could tell that the deep nose-to-mouth lines were real and not makeup. His broad shoulders looked real, too, as they strained against the pseudo rawhide fabric of his costume. He filled the stage as the legendary Buffalo Bill Cody and strutted around with great authority. His Cody and Mary Carter's Oakley looked perfect together.

As the cast took a five-minute break for set adjustments, Mr. Fitzgerald motioned to Clark Clay, who immediately joined them. He was taller than Denise had thought and even more handsome. His eyes sparkled a vibrant blue and quickly surveyed Denise from head to toe. He emitted the aura of a man who was accustomed to receiving the attention of women.

Smiling, Denise introduced herself and reminded him of their meeting. With an almost boyish grin that made her heart flutter, Clark Clay assured her that he never missed a meeting with a pretty woman. She fairly melted as he kissed her hand, bowed, and returned to the stage. She knew that he was all show, but she liked every bit of it.

Willing her heart to stop the adolescent pounding, Denise focused on the stage itself and the props. She could see nothing that the murderer could use to his advantage. Listening to Mr. Fitzgerald's whispered response, she learned that the food was waxed and the canteens empty. Naturally, the guns only fired caps. The murderer would find nothing in the theater that would help him now that Mr. Fitzgerald had thrown out the ice cream and yogurt.

As rehearsal ended, Clark Clay and Denise walked back to his dressing room, leaving Mr. Fitzgerald to return to his office. Once inside, rather than remove his makeup, he gave Denise his full attention. His eyes never left her face as he listened to her instructions.

Holding eye contact, Denise stated, "You're not to

consume any food or beverage that is not in a sealed
container. You must not finish any food that you store in
the refrigerator for later. Do not consume any beverage
that is not in a sealed bottle. Do not drink tea or coffee
in any form. Your life is in grave danger."

"Well, pretty lady, I guess I'll have to abide by your
rules," Clark Clay replied flirtatiously, as he flashed his
million-dollar smile and his capped teeth.

Unable to repress a smile, Denise stated, "I'm going to
your hotel room now. I'll arrange for someone to watch
your room in case you wish to take a nap after lunch."

Clark Clay stated with growing concern, "I'm going to
lunch with Ms. Carter as soon as I remove this makeup,
but I plan to return for a nap in that chair until it's time
to put on this costume again. I should be safe in her presence. I usually return to the hotel before the show, but I
don't have any problem staying here. I'll be very careful.
The last thing I want to become is this man's statistic."

Rising, Denise said, "Good. I'm going to the hotel.
Everything has to look as if you plan to return after rehearsal. I don't want the suspect to learn of any
changes."

"Trust me, Detective, I'm not going to that hotel until
this is over. That chair will make a comfortable bed for
the run of this play if necessary," Clark Clay stated emphatically as he turned toward the makeup table.

"With luck, you won't have to sleep here that long. Mr.
Fitzgerald will return shortly with new yogurt and ice
cream for your refrigerator. Be careful. This killer never
misses," Denise remarked as she walked to the door.
Turning, she added, "By the way, don't touch any conductors' batons either. The killer always leaves them as a
precaution."

"Batons?" Clark Clay repeated. For the first time he
looked a bit concerned about his safety. His careful smile
had faded a bit.

Nodding, Denise replied, "Batons. The killer knows that you're also a conductor. That's why he targeted you. In his eyes, you've tainted the conducting profession. If anyone offers you one, don't touch it. Ephedra poisoning could happen just as easily if you inhale it. Ingesting it isn't the only method."

Growing pale, Clark Clay reached for a long, thin box on his makeup table. Handing it to Denise, he stated in a voice that shook with concern, "This arrived by messenger this morning. It was wrapped in white paper and sealed only with tape. There was no bow. I opened the lid to find that inside. I didn't touch it although I wanted to feel the weight of it. The runner came to drag me to rehearsal. I was holding up progress, he said, and costing the theater extra money."

Lifting the top, Denise pronounced, "You're a lucky man. If I'm right, there's enough ephedra in the handle to kill you simply by inhaling it. We wouldn't be talking now if you'd waved it. You would have died of an apparent heart attack."

Wiping perspiration from his forehead and top lip, Clark Clay said in a voice that shook with emotion, "I guess I owe that runner my life."

Slipping the box and its contents into an evidence bag, Denise remarked, "Let's make sure that you can pay that debt. Remember, no food or drink that isn't sealed and no batons."

As she left the dressing room, Clark Clay stated, "You don't have to worry about me. I've suddenly lost my appetite."

Denise decided to stop by Mr. Fitzgerald's office on her way out. She found her way with ease and soon stood at his door. The obviously shaken man was sipping coffee, but spilling most of it down the front of his shirt as his hands shook violently.

"Oh, my! This is too much!" Mr. Fitzgerald moaned, as Denise entered his office.

"Don't forget," Denise admonished, "you're responsible for that man's life. The killer should strike tonight. I'll be watching the hotel, but you have to be my eyes and ears here. An officer at the dressing room door would draw too much attention."

"This is much more than I bargained for when I took this job. I need a change of profession. This is too much stress for me. My wife has been after me to retire early. I might just do it," Mr. Fitzgerald groaned as he picked up his open bottle of water. Thinking it ill advised, he opened the refrigerator door and pulled out a fresh one. Taking long pulls, he appeared to calm a bit.

Seeing that his color had improved, Denise prepared to leave. Thanking him for his help, she stated, "I'm only a phone call away. Get in touch immediately if you see or suspect anything."

"Okay," Mr. Fitzgerald replied, bobbing his head like a bobble-head doll. "I guess he'll nap at his hotel before the show. I might get a little rest then myself. I'll feel so much better when he's out of this building."

Not seeing any reason to put additional weight on the nervous man's shoulders, Denise did not disabuse him. Instead, she agreed, saying, "I'm sure you will. Tonight should solve all of our problems, and you'll be able to relax a bit."

"Yes, it will be a decisive evening, I'm sure," Mr. Fitzgerald commented, turning his attention to the stack of papers on his desk.

Denise hurried down the hall and into the garage. Along the way, she phoned Tom to tell him of her change in location. Remembering the baton, she added that piece of information before turning her car toward the street.

"Be careful, Denise," Tom advised. "The killer wants you on his tail."

"Don't worry, this is routine. It's not until tonight that he'll make his move," Denise replied as she turned into the park.

"I'd feel better if I were with you," Tom commented.

"I'm fine. See you later," Denise stated and turned off her phone.

The hotel was not far from the Olney Theater; however, with so much to do and so few hours before the play's opening night, Denise felt pressed for time. After showing her badge and explaining the reason for her visit as a courtesy to the manager, Denise made her way to the twelfth floor and Mr. Clay's suite. The opulently decorated halls with the crystal sconces and thick carpet were empty as she padded toward the room. Following the bellboy, she noticed that each nook contained a grand arrangement of cut flowers. Equally impressive was the art that lined the walls. Denise could understand the hotel's appeal to the rich and famous.

To Denise's surprise, Tom waited at the door for her. He looked especially tall and handsome. The smile on his face as he looked at her spoke loudly of his affection.

Beaming broadly, Denise exclaimed, "What brought you here? You think I need backup?"

"I just thought I'd protect my investment. My future happiness rests with you," Tom commented, giving her a quick hug that brought a smile to the bellboy's face.

"In that case, I'm glad to see you," Denise replied, chuckling.

Interrupting, the bellboy said, "If you don't mind, I'll wait here. Take your time."

Her face reddening from his obvious misunderstanding, Denise replied, "We won't be long."

Denise stepped inside and surveyed the room. It was as well decorated as the halls with golden accessories and vases of fresh flowers. A satin spread covered the king-size bed and coordinated with the matching drapes. Reproductions of grand masters lined the walls. Even the bathroom contained impressive art both on the walls and in the shape of the faucets.

Finding the minibar, Denise discovered that Mr. Clay's request for yogurt and ice cream extended to his hotel room as well as his dressing room. Each container was still sealed and did not show signs of tampering. Likewise, the impressive collection of liquor bottles at the bar contained the original seals. The murderer had not as yet made his move.

Looking over her shoulder, Tom asked, "What time will Mr. Clay return to the hotel?"

"After lunch," Denise replied, "but this time, he's staying in his dressing room. I'll assign someone to stay here in case the murderer tries to attack him here."

"I'll do it," Tom stated, as he continued his search of the room.

"No way," Denise declared. "You've already had one close call. I don't want you anywhere near the murderer."

"You need someone you can trust to do this. I'm your man," Tom replied firmly.

"Okay, but be careful. Don't eat or drink anything," Denise stressed, knowing Tom's inclination to consume without questioning.

"I won't drink anything except Potomac punch," Tom replied, indicating the faucet in the bathroom.

"If you do, be sure to drink from your hands. The cup might be contaminated with ephedra," Denise instructed.

"In that case, let's go to lunch now. I need nourishment before the dry spell sets in," Tom ordered as he started toward the door.

Leaving the grinning bellboy in the lobby, Denise and Tom decided to eat at a little bistro on the corner. The place had looked inviting although they doubted that the prices would be within their usual budget. Nothing on that side of town was ever inexpensive.

After ordering pastrami sandwiches on whole wheat, chips, and sodas, Denise sketched out the evening's plans, saying, "First, I'll take the baton to the precinct, and then I'll arrange for someone to relieve you at the hotel so that you can join me at the Olney Theater."

"What baton?" Tom asked.

"The one the killer had delivered to Mr. Clay's dressing room today," Denise replied.

"He doesn't waste any time, does he?" Tom declared, as he attacked his sandwich hungrily.

"No, and he should turn up at the hotel soon, too," Denise said and then added, "Keep your eyes open. You might not want to lie down on the bed, either."

"Why? Are you afraid that I'll miss the show?" Tom demanded.

"No, I'm concerned that he might have dusted the bedding and the towels with ephedra. Everything looked in order, but we won't know for certain until we have the test results on the facecloth I borrowed," Denise stated.

"When did you do that? I didn't see you," Tom asked with pride in his voice.

"I'm quick," Denise joked.

Laughing, Tom agreed, "I'll stay away from the towels and bed. While I'm waiting, I'll sit in the leather armchair and read one of the magazines in the room."

"We'll buy you a new one. The ones in the room might already be contaminated," Denise instructed, licking the whipped cream from the back of the spoon.

"You certainly think of everything. Did you take a magazine, too?" Tom demanded as he watched her tongue seductively scoop up the cream.

"How'd you guess?" Denise teased.

Grinning with pride, Tom stated, "You're one hell of a detective, Detective Dory."

"Not so fast," Denise ordered, holding up her hands. "I haven't solved this case yet."

"You will. That perpetrator doesn't stand a chance with you on the case. No man stands a chance against you, Dory," Tom stated with pride as his eyes twinkled gleefully.

"I don't know about that," Denise answered, as he paid the bill this time. "You resisted long enough."

Walking back to the hotel's parking lot, Tom conceded, "I was hooked from the first meeting. I just didn't let you know. I didn't want you to take advantage of me. I had a bad-ass reputation to uphold."

Joking, Denise stated, "You were about as bad as a kitten with a thorn in its paw."

"You were never fooled by my growl, were you?" Tom asked as he closed the car door.

"Never. I always saw the real you behind that gruff exterior," Denise replied as she laid her hand on his.

Leaning into the open window for a good-bye kiss, Tom said, "I'm glad you did. My life has been all the better for it."

Wiping the lipstick from his lips, Denise advised, "Be careful. We have a lifetime ahead of us."

"Knowing that you'll be with me for the rest of my life has saved me more often than you know. I'll see you tonight. I have my cell if you need to get in touch with me," Tom replied, smiling lovingly into her eyes.

Blowing a kiss, Denise stated, "I have mine, too. Phone if you see or hear anything. Unless the perpetrator returns with poisoned food, I think he has already done his job at the hotel. Keep your eyes open just in case."

Denise waved as she drove away. She hoped that Tom would be safe alone in the hotel room. She would have liked to assign someone else to the stakeout, but he was the only one she could trust on such short notice. Pushing thoughts of Tom from her mind, she made a list of all the things she had to do before returning to the Olney Theater that evening. She only hoped that she had taken enough precautions.

Nineteen

Denise drove straight to the office of her friend in the FBI lab. She did not have time to go through the procedures of sending polite memos and using the department's forensics department. She needed the magazine and facecloth tested immediately. Without telling Mr. Fitzgerald, she had slipped a yogurt from the hotel and one from the dressing room into her bag. Even though both containers had carried the factory seals, she wondered if contamination might still have been possible. Both of these demanded prompt testing for ephedra contamination.

Her FBI contact was, as usual, swamped with work, but he did not hesitate to offer assistance. Indicating the chair next to his desk, Bernard Fields rushed into the inner recesses of the lab, carrying the yogurt, batons, and magazine. He was accustomed to Denise sending a collection of seemingly random items for him to check, and never questioned her reasons. They had worked together on too many cases for him to start second-guessing her now.

While she waited, Denise phoned Tom to be sure that he was safely ensconced in the hotel room. He answered his cell phone on the first ring. He growled happily to hear her voice, claiming boredom and the onset of sleepiness from the big lunch. She reminded him playfully that he was on duty before stating that she would meet him at the Shakespeare bust.

Her next call was to Mr. Fitzgerald. The man had seemed so shaken by the responsibility for Mr. Clay's safety that lay on his shoulders that she had felt sorry for him. However, he did not answer. Thinking that he had taken a late lunch, Denise left a reassuring message on his voice mail in hopes that he would hear it before the evening's opening-night activities.

In addition, she decided to phone Mr. Clay in his dressing room. He answered on the third ring, sounding charming and sophisticated as usual. He had enjoyed lunch with his leading lady and had just settled down for a nap before having to shower and dress for the performance. Despite the restrictions on his activities, he was very comfortable and was looking forward to seeing her again after the show.

Denise's last call was to Joshua Smithe. Feeling that she had not satisfactorily patched up the rift in their relationship, she decided to use the few minutes before Bernard's return to close the unsettled business. Joshua answered on the second ring, probably from his usual position at the front of the store, and seemed happy to hear from her.

"Joshua, I just wanted to make sure that there were no hard feelings between us," Denise began after the initial greetings. "You've been most helpful on this case. I don't want our professional dealings to suffer because of a little bump in the road in our personal relationship."

"No, problem there, Denise. We're cool. Thanks for coming to the concert the other night. I couldn't stick around after, but I appreciated your presence." Joshua spoke casually as if nothing had happened between them.

"Your dad looked pretty good up there conducting your group. You really sounded great," Denise stated.

She was happy that the conversation was progressing so well and that the tension had ended between them.

"We try." Joshua chuckled. "He gets a big kick out of it, and it gives him something to do other than fish and tend the store. Conducting was once a dream of his, too, but marriage and family came along and, well, things change."

"Commitment has a way of doing that," Denise replied, fingering the large, sparkling rock on the third finger of left her hand.

"I'm not rushing into either," Joshua stated with a chuckle. "I have too much to do before I take on the ball and chain. There's too much to see and too many women to love."

Changing the subject, Denise asked, "By the way, didn't you say that you never miss an opening night if you can get away from the shop? Tonight's the opening of *Annie Get Your Gun.*"

Gleefully, Joshua replied, "I'll be there. Dad and I have season tickets . . . third row, center section, aisle seats on the right. Dad's not feeling too well. His arthritis is acting up on him. He might not be able to come with me. I'll look for you at the party after the show, too."

"What party?"

Explaining, Joshua said, "Ask someone to slip you a ticket. I'm sure no one will mind. The Olney Theater throws a big opening-night party for major patrons. Dad and I have attended almost all of them. We're business sponsors."

"I'll do that. I hope your father will feel well enough to attend. Give him my regards. See you tonight," Denise said as Bernard Fields returned.

Tossing her cell phone into her bag, Denise turned her full attention to Bernard Fields. Using her sketchbook as a notepad, she recorded the results of the test on the food and magazine. From the smile on Fields's face, she could tell that the visit to his office had been profitable.

"You were dead on, no pun intended," Fields proclaimed, thumbing through the results.

"You found ephedra in everything?" Denise inquired.

"Yup. Someone had even tampered with the sealed cartons," Fields replied, adjusting the reading glasses that sat low on his long nose.

"How? I didn't see a break in the seal," Denise asked incredulously. "I only brought the yogurt as a precaution."

Leaning back in his chair, Fields explained, "After the yogurt tested positive for ephedra, I emptied the contents of the container into a bowl and washed out the carton. Using a strong light, I discovered a series of tiny pinholes through which the perpetrator must have injected an ephedra solution into the yogurt. He carefully added wax to the surface of the container over the hole. No leak."

"Ingenious!" Denise acknowledged. "Our perpetrator has the ability to poison any kind of food or drink as well as the batons."

"Here's more for you," Fields added. "That facecloth contained ephedra, too. You have a very thorough perpetrator on your hands."

Picking up her cell phone, Denise said, "Excuse me a minute, Bernie. I have to phone Tom. He's in the hotel room now with the contaminated linen. Knowing Tom's appetite, he might decide to partake of the minibar."

Tom answered on the first ring. He sounded sleepy but said that nothing had happened. After listening to Denise, he reasoned, "I don't think anyone will try to enter this suite. It seems as if your perpetrator has already been here."

"That's right," Denise replied. "You might as well go home and change. I'll meet you at the Olney Theater later."

"No," Tom reminded her with a chuckle, "you'll meet me at our condo. My tux is one of the first things I moved in, thinking that I wouldn't need it again. I hadn't planned on attending any more black-tie functions until our wedding reception."

"Okay, I'll meet you at home," Denise replied as she closed her phone and broke the connection.

Before she left Bernard Fields's office, Denise phoned Mr. Clay. Once again, she had to leave a message on the dressing-room answering machine. He must have turned off the phone so that no one could disturb him. She did the same for Mr. Fitzgerald's office although she wondered why he did not answer.

Thanking Bernard Fields for his help, Denise walked to her car. Dialing one last number, she phoned Captain Morton with an update. He seemed genuinely pleased with the progress she had made on the case. However, Denise would not share his enthusiasm until she apprehended the Music Man Murderer and put a stop to this serial killing.

Before driving home, Denise decided to stop at the Olney Theater to check on Mr. Clay's well-being. She did not like the fact that he did not answer his phone. She thought that she would drop in on Mr. Fitzgerald, too. He had seemed so nervous when she left him that she worried about his heart.

She should not have worried about Mr. Fitzgerald. A sign on his door read that he had left for the day but would return in time for the opening night. From the shakiness of his handwriting, she decided that he had gone home early to rest and perhaps see a doctor. His note was so poorly written that it looked as if Mr. Fitzgerald had written it with his left hand.

Walking toward Mr. Clay's dressing room, Denise heard voices coming from Ms. Carter's room and stopped to investigate. She knocked, thinking that the leading lady might know Mr. Clay's whereabouts. Ms. Carter, wearing a satin robe and with makeup streaked, opened the door. Mr. Clay sat on the open sofa bed behind her.

"Come in, Detective Dory, welcome," Ms. Carter stated in a warm greeting, stepping aside.

"I don't want to intrude . . ." Denise hedged as Mr. Clay smiled his welcome.

"No intrusion, my dear," Ms. Carter replied, waving Denise into the spacious, warm gold dressing room. "Clark and I were about to eat a little snack. Would you like a slice of pizza?"

Looking from one to the other with concern, Denise warned, "I don't think it's wise for Mr. Clay to eat that. It might not sit well with you either, Ms. Carter."

Smiling indulgently, Mr. Clay stated, "Don't worry about us, Detective. This pizza's safe. Mary bought the ingredients and made it herself on that little stove. She often prepares our meals."

Looking first at the little stove in the corner of the dressing room and then at Ms. Carter, Denise replied tactfully, "There's a possibility that the ingredients might not be safe. I really don't think that either of you should eat the pizza."

"Nonsense," Mr. Clay commented with a deep laugh. "I know you're just doing your job, but this food is safe. Believe me. Mary has had twenty years in which to poison me if she wanted to do it. She wouldn't have to copy a murderer."

For the first time, Denise noticed the matching rings on their left hands. Ms. Carter interrupted her thoughts by saying, "Carter's my stage name. I've been this guy's wife for half my life. I've learned to live with his snoring and attacks of gout. Believe me, I'm not going to poison him now. He's in safe hands with me."

As Denise munched a small slice of pizza, Mr. Clay

asked, "Why would anyone want to target me? I'm really no one."

Sighing, Denise explained, "You're an actor who also conducts. The perpetrator seems to have a grudge against anyone who crosses over and does both. He's some kind of purist who thinks that no one other than conductors should hold a baton and stand before an orchestra."

Looking worried, Ms. Carter asked, "How does he kill his victims?"

"He uses ephedra, an easily available food additive. He poisons them with it, making it look like cardiac arrest. He had already poisoned all of the food and the bed linens in Mr. Clay's hotel suite," Denise replied.

Looking at his wife, Mr. Clay joked weakly, "It looks, old girl, as if you've saved my life. It I had been single, I would have eaten from that minibar last night instead of joining you for lobster in your suite."

"How long before you catch him?" Ms. Carter demanded with fear in her voice.

Stating with more confidence than she felt, Denise replied, "I hope we'll be lucky tonight. Don't eat or drink anything that you haven't prepared yourself. Sealed products aren't safe either. The perpetrator poisoned the yogurt in a sealed carton as well as the baton in your dressing room."

"Is Clark's dressing room contaminated? He can stay right here if it is," Ms. Carter said as she laid her hand on her husband's.

Speaking carefully to ease Ms. Carter's concerns, Denise said, "The perpetrator added the ephedra to the linens in Mr. Clay's suite but, as far as I know, hasn't touched the dressing room. However, if you have an second costume somewhere, it might be a good idea to wear it tonight as a precaution."

"All right. Is there anything else we should know?" Mr. Clay asked.

Shaking her head, Denise replied, "No, I think you're on board with everything now. Please, for your sake, don't tell anyone, not cast, crew, or Olney Theater employees. You must keep this information to yourself if we're to catch the perpetrator tonight."

Speaking for both of them, Mr. Clay responded, "You can count on us. We'll tell no one and take precautions without arousing anyone's attention."

Denise left the couple and hurried from the Olney Theater. On the way, she stopped at Mr. Fitzgerald's office to see if he had returned. Finding the hastily scrawled note still attached to the door, she rushed to the parking lot. She had to drive home, shower, and dress before returning in the late afternoon traffic. She wanted to be in place backstage before the show began. With Tom's help, she would catch the killer that night.

Twenty

Tom had showered and dressed by the time Denise arrived home. He looked elegant in his tux as he served dinner consisting of Caesar salad with chicken and hot, buttered rolls. As she showered and dressed, he cleaned the kitchen and walked Molly. Checking Max's bowl located high on the washing machine, he made sure that the cat had food for the evening.

Denise emerged from the bedroom wearing a flowing black gown with matching stole. She looked like a model as she glided across the room in the two-inch black-strap sandals with rhinestone ornaments at the toe. Around her neck, she wore a glittering single-diamond necklace that Tom had given her for her last birthday. She felt that the evening would somehow be special. After all, this was their first formal date after becoming somewhat engaged.

The evening was perfect. Stars twinkled, and the moon shone brightly. The fragrance of freshness filled the air. It felt like the eve of a new beginning.

The Olney Theater glowed a dazzlingly iridescent white against the dark sky. The marble reflected the light of the streetlights that lined the driveway. The pillars stretched from the marble entrance to the stars. Inside, the chandeliers sparkled against the red velvet and brocade and gold of the drapes and carpets. Mirrors and windows reflected the elegantly attired guests who looked forward to a night of entertainment and merriment. Waiters in white jackets glided through the crowd, carrying trays of glasses filled to the brim with champagne for the special guests in the secluded area reserved for the special patrons.

Denise and Tom made their way through the crowd to the area in which patrons wearing Halston, Armani, and Mackie sipped Don Perignon and munched the best caviar. Their tickets to the opening-night festivities and the personal invitation of the leading man and lady entitled them to admission to the special room and a sample of the best also. No one seemed to notice that they were not wearing famous-name designers. As a matter of fact, no one even looked at them. Most people in the room appeared engaged in small-group conversation that was exclusive by design.

Smiling broadly, Joshua advanced toward Denise and Tom with outstretched hand. He appeared so very young in his tuxedo as did the woman in a slinky, shimmering white satin gown on his arm. She was glad to see that Joshua had found a woman of his own age.

Introducing her as Janet Clips, Joshua almost gushed, "It's great seeing you guys. I was feeling a little out of place with all these stiffs. It's nice to see someone of my age group.

Chuckling, Denise replied, "I understand completely. The majority of the folks in here look as if they've already reached retirement age."

With his usual direct manner, Tom growled, "They're the only ones willing to dress up like this on a regular basis."

"How's your father? Is he here?" Denise asked in a lull in their conversation.

"No, he's not feeling very well. He decided to stay home tonight," Joshua stated as he accepted another glass of champagne from a waiter, who stopped briefly before moving farther into the crowd.

"That's a shame. It's a good play," Denise commented and then added, speaking to Joshua's guest, "Janet, you look very familiar. Have I met you before?"

Smiling sweetly, Janet replied, "I'm in Joshua's group. He was kind enough to offer me his father's ticket. I couldn't resist the opportunity to get dressed up."

"I don't blame you. Contrary to Tom's opinion, opening night is very exciting," Denise responded with a happy smile.

At that moment, the gong sounded, announcing the opening of the theater doors. The crowd from the special patrons' section mingled with the other guests as they mounted the grand stairway and poured into the theater. Even Tom appeared impressed by the swell of people in their finery.

The theater looked as it had earlier that day. The red velvet seats welcomed patrons, and the chandeliers sparkled brightly. However, the air felt charged with the energy and excitement upon which the actors would soon draw for their strength. Taking their aisle seat, Denise could hardly wait for the curtain to rise.

Before leaving the house, Denise had gained the captain's agreement to station someone in the hotel. As expected, no one had tried to enter Mr. Clay's suite. Reaching him in his dressing room, Denise had learned that the Clay couple had survived the afternoon and were in the process of getting dressed and made up. She had also called Mr. Fitzgerald, who had complained about his fatigue, his nerves, and his need to retire. Everything was as it should be.

Settling into her seat, Denise surveyed the audience one last time. For the duration of the play, she was confident that nothing would happen. After the curtain fell was another question entirely.

The play was excellent. The Clays performed their parts as if they were enacting real life. They teased and argued, laughed and loved with energy and reality. Tom appeared equally impressed. He never once squirmed as he usually did when bored. He sat engrossed, staring at the stage and holding Denise's hand.

The curtain fell to five curtain calls and standing ovations. Gliding up the aisle with the other members of the audience, Denise smiled happily and chatted gaily with Tom. No one would have suspected that they were police officers in search of a dangerous perpetrator who had threatened to strike again.

The Olney Theater had decorated its atrium for the opening-night party. The directors had invited special guests, those who contributed to the arts and those who were political and theatrical celebrities, to attend. The guest list was much more exclusive than at the precurtain cocktail party but no less enthusiastic. Everyone chatted happily about the quality of the performance and the future of the arts in the area. They all looked forward to meeting the cast of the play and expressing their delight and appreciation personally.

A white table spread with elegant gold-rimmed china on gold charger plates surrounded by glistening silver flatware greeted the guests as they walked through the double doors. Fragile intricately carved crystal stemware sparkled in the glow of the chandeliers. A massive arrangement of white roses and candles filled the center of the table with fragrance and beauty. Matching smaller versions continued the elegance for the length of the table. White-brocade-covered high-backed chairs welcomed the guests to the table.

Mr. Clay and Ms. Carter were the last of the crew to arrive. They made their grand appearance dressed in tuxedo and pale pink chiffon evening gown. Looking like Fred Astaire and Ginger Rogers, they floated among

the guests, smiling for photographs, pausing for auto-
graphs, and loosening checkbooks with their charm.
When they reached Denise and Tom, they embraced
them like old friends before moving to the next cluster
of Olney Theater guests.

The white-clad wait staff silently served the soup as the
guests floated toward the table. The gentle tingle of a
tiny bell summoned them to a sumptuous meal of cream
of lobster bisque, oysters Rockefeller, crown rib roast,
pearl onions mixed with baby peas, asparagus, and red-
skinned potatoes. Rolls, still hot from the oven and
dripping with butter, glistened at every plate. The room
smelled enticingly of the mixture of aromas.

Denise had taken the precaution of substituting
friends of hers from the force on the wait-staff roster and
added a few among the guests. She recognized all of
them and made eye contact to confirm that all was well
at the moment. She observed their behavior, thinking
that not even Tom would recognize them.

During the excellent meal, Denise chatted with the
ambassador on her left and the renowned plastic sur-
geon on her right. Both were witty, charming, and very
entertaining. Tom scowled at her from a distance as the
woman on his right plucked at his tuxedo jacket to gain
his attention. Although Denise was not jealous, she had
noticed that he had attracted many admirers. Looking
at Tom in the glow of the chandeliers, she decided that
the women had very good taste.

Mr. Clay and his wife and leading lady, Ms. Carter, sat
at the center of the table. The chairman of the Olney
Theater's endowment fund sat at the head, and the
chairwoman of the auxiliary organizations occupied the
seat opposite. The waiters moved among them, replacing one course with another.

Although enjoying the evening, Denise kept a watchful
eye, remembering that the perpetrator had suggested that

he would strike again that night. So far, she had managed to protect his potential victim and keep one step ahead of her nemesis. However, it was just a matter of time before he would strike.

After dinner, they adjourned to the terrace for coffee, dessert, and drinks as they admired the splendor of the Potomac. Immediately, the guests surrounded Mr. Clay and Ms. Carter. It looked as if someone had removed the constraints of protocol, releasing an outflowing of praise and admiration that they had kept in check during the meal. Because of the congestion around them, the celebrity pair was the last to be served.

Standing at the balustrade and juggling her cake and espresso, Denise allowed herself to take in another natural wonder. Tom looked so handsome that she wanted to throw her arms around him. Unfortunately, the rulebook did not allow such conduct while on duty. However, nothing in the rules prevented her from enjoying his company and appreciating his handsome appearance.

"You were right," Tom stated as he munched a large forkful of gateau, "I am having a wonderful time."

"I knew you would. It was a great play and the food's out of this world," Denise replied as she gazed into his eyes.

"The company's not so bad either. There's one especially beautiful woman whose company I'm looking forward to getting to know better," Tom growled as he fixed Denise with a sexy smile.

"Tom, if I didn't know better, I'd think that you're trying to seduce me," Denise exclaimed, placing her fingers lightly over her heart in feigned shock.

"This is only the beginning. Tonight, you're going to say yes," Tom declared confidently as he fed Denise a piece of his sinfully rich chocolate cake.

Patting her lips daintily, Denise asked coquettishly, "To what? I don't remember you asking me anything."

Immediately, Tom started to sputter and assume the demeanor of a wounded suitor. He knew that Denise often became engrossed in her cases, but he did not think that she would have forgotten the unanswered proposal. The ring sparkling on her finger should have reminded her of their unfinished business.

Before he could speak, a waiter appeared in the glow of the myriad of candles that illuminated the terrace, carrying a silver tray bearing two servings of cake and two glasses of cognac. Heading straight to the play's stars, he did not appear to notice any of the other guests. He had one purpose . . . to reach the celebrities.

Denise appeared frozen in time. She no longer saw or heard Tom, as her eyes followed the waiter. Tingles of anticipation coursed through her body.

The waiter bowed and handed Ms. Carter a slice of gateau decorated with whipped cream and swimming in raspberry syrup, the same dessert that Denise and the other guests had been enjoying. Bowing again, he presented Mr. Clay with a slice of the same cake. He bowed a third time and began his return through the crowd to the serving area inside the building.

Denise sensed rather than knew that something was not right. The slices of cake appeared to be the same, but they were subtly different. Staring through the darkness, Denise saw that a red cherry sat atop the whipped cream on Mr. Clay's slice.

"Grab him! Grab that waiter!" Denise shouted to Tom as she pointed in the direction of the departing waiter who still struggled to make his exit through the thick crowd of people on the terrace.

Immediately, she sprang into action and headed toward the stars. Pulling her gown higher so that she could run, Denise wove her way through the smallest openings until she reached them. People turned and stared at her apparent rudeness. They muttered and gaped at her boldness in disturbing the enchantment of the evening.

Denise shouted, "Don't eat that!"

At first, Mr. Clay did not appear to understand as he stood with his fork ready to enter his mouth. Ms. Carter, however, displayed quicker reflexes. With an upward motion that sent the fork flying, she knocked the utensil from her husband's hands. It fell noiselessly at his feet.

"Why did you do that?" Mr. Clay demanded angrily. "I'm not on a diet. Now I'll have to wait for someone to being me another fork."

"The detective said for you not to eat it," Ms. Carter tried to explain to her petulant husband.

"What?" he shouted, glaring at his wife. He still did not understand anything other than the fact that he could not consume the delicious dessert.

Rushing to join them, Denise explained, "Your cake. I think it's been poisoned."

As Mr. Clay stood slack-jawed, Tom appeared with the angry waiter. He had handcuffed the man's arms behind his back. His eyes smoked angrily as he glared at first Denise and then at Mr. Clay. He said nothing. No words were necessary. The hatred on Mr. Fitzgerald's face confirmed his identity.

"I don't understand," Mr. Clay stated with genuine confusion. His face contained a mirror of emotions, ranging from fear to anger.

"You wouldn't understand, you spoiled, pampered pig of a man!" Mr. Fitzgerald spat angrily. You've polluted the profession. You're not a conductor; you're an actor. You have no right to take up the baton and stand before a symphony. I hate you and everyone like you."

"Why would he want to do this awful thing?" Mr. Clay demanded, looking from the furious waiter to Denise and back.

Again Mr. Fitzgerald interrupted with a mad laugh. Spitting venom, he stated, "You wouldn't understand. You pick up a baton and wave it without any sense of tempo or nuance. Because of your theatrical credits, you're suddenly a conductor. You didn't spend long hours learning the craft. You have no sense of the history of the piece or the composer's motivation. You simply grab a baton and treat it like a flyswatter. I, on the other hand, will never have the opportunity to do something that you take lightly. I've trained and studied for years, but I'll never conduct. The injustice makes me want to puke."

"It's not my fault," Mr. Clay objected. "Do you want me to feel guilty because you couldn't realize your dream?"

"No, not guilty. I want you and your kind to vanish from the musical scene. Go back to where you belong. Leave the conducting to real conductors like me. I'm tired of having to wait on the likes of you. I'm tired of sitting at that stupid desk shuffling purposeless papers while you get all the recognition," Mr. Fitzgerald raved, as he tried to pull away from Tom's grasp.

"He seemed like such a nice man," Ms. Carter murmured as she clung to her husband's arm as if trying to protect him.

Before Denise could respond, Mr. Fitzgerald turned his eyes on her. Smiling slightly, he stated, "I had you going for a while."

"Yes, you did," Denise conceded gently. "Your selection of clues was quite good."

"I was very careful not to leave any prints or telltale signs. I organized everything perfectly," Mr. Fitzgerald stated, seeming almost happy for the attention from Denise and everyone on the terrace.

"Your attention to detail is what made me suspicious," Denise replied gently.

"I don't understand," Mr. Fitzgerald stated, adjusting his posture against the links that bound his hands.

"Your office was such a mess, yet every activity that you organized flowed smoothly. You always complained about the job, but you've been here ten years without taking a day off. You're dissatisfied with you job, yet you left a note stating your plans on your office door. You could have simply left for the day. The two sides of your personality didn't mesh. Besides, I ran a check on schools that offer conducting classes. Your name appeared on one of them," Denise responded honestly.

"That's all coincidental. When did you know that I was the killer?" Mr. Fitzgerald demanded.

"I recognized your legs," Denise replied.

"What?"

"When you conducted the orchestra so masterfully in the Phantom costume, I noticed the shape of your legs. I saw them again when you opened the theater for me and while we sat at your desk. They're very shapely for a thin man," Denise responded honestly.

"So everyone says. I never thought that they'd give me away. Oh, well, I guess I won't be entering any contests any time soon," Mr. Fitzgerald quipped sourly.

"It's too bad that you took this route. You're really very good," Denise stated.

"I know, but it just wasn't in the cards," Mr. Fitzgerald said with a shrug.

Denise felt a strange compassion for the little man who had occupied the cluttered desk and organized so much while receiving so little personal satisfaction from the act. In his own twisted way, he was dedicated to the craft that tortured his imagination while being chained to his job and family. He wanted more but could not have it.

"The car's here. Time to go, Mr. Fitzgerald," Tom

stated, propelling Mr. Fitzgerald toward the waiting officers.

Denise watched as the frustrated little man trotted
ahead of the officers. Turning, she looked at the guests
and the stars. Everyone on the Olney Theater staff appeared shocked that the quiet Mr. Fitzgerald had a
second identity. Denise, however, remembered the saying about the depth of still waters.

Slipping her arm through Tom's, Denise joined the
others as they left the terrace. Mr. Fitzgerald's arrest had
crushed the atmosphere of the evening. As the light of
the wall sconces increased, the guests flowed into the
building. The celebratory mood had ended.

The drive home through the park was, thankfully, uneventful. Denise felt incredible relief at having solved the
case. She could now relax. For the first time in her professional life, she felt tired. She needed a change. The
promotion would take her out of the line of danger and
into administration. It was time.

Breaking into the silence, Tom asked, "Have you given
any thought to my question?"

"What question?"

Bristling slightly, Tom replied, "The marriage question.
Now that we're living together and you're wearing an
engagement ring, can we set the date?"

"The date to do what?" Denise asked, being playfully
obtuse with a serious subject.

"The date to get married," Tom replied with increasing frustration.

"Maybe."

Pulling into a parking space, Tom turned off the car.
Turning toward Denise, he looked at her and demanded
seriously, "Well?"

"Well what?" Denise quipped with a chuckle.

Sighing with frustration, Tom restated the question,
"Will you marry me? There's no reason for you to delay

your answer any longer. You've closed the case. You're up for promotion and won't have as much running around to do when you get it. You've learned to tolerate Molly, who's living with you anyway. I can't think of any objections that you could have."

"I can't think of any either," Denise replied, kissing him gently on the lips.

"Well?"

"Well what?"

Shaking his head, Tom demanded with a laugh, "Will you marry me?"

"Yes, Tom, I'll marry you," Denise responded, pressing her lips gently to his.

"When?" Tom asked between kisses, wanted closure to the topic.

"When what?"

"At what hour, on what day, of what year will you marry me?"

"Whatever and whenever," Denise replied, smothering his face with happy kisses and silencing any further questions.

"Dory, I hate it when you—" Tom sputtered, as Denise kissed him with a passion that took his breath away.

Tom wrapped his arms around Denise and forgot that she had not really answered his question. Maybe some questions simply did not need answers. The responses simply flowed to the music of love.

Dear Readers,

I hope you've enjoyed reading the last installment in the adventures of Denise Dory and Tom Phyfer. They've won a place in my heart as they've solved murder cases and untangled the intricacies of their relationship. They are quite an exciting couple both in and out of uniform.

Let me know your reactions to this romantic mystery. Write to me in care of the publisher or at my e-mail address, courtni@earthlink.net.

Best,

Courtni

Arabesque Romances by *FRANCIS RAY*

__BREAK EVERY RULE   0-7860-0544-0 $4.99US/$6.50CAN

Dominique Falcon's next man must be richer, higher up the social ladder, and better looking than she is . . . which Trent Masters is definitely not. He doesn't fit into her world of privilege . . . but his passion is too hot to ignore.

__FOREVER YOURS   0-7860-0025-2 $4.99US/$5.99CAN

Victoria Chandler needs a husband to keep her business secure. She arranges to marry ranch owner Kane Taggert. The marriage will only last one year . . . but he has other plans. He'll cast a spell to make her his forever.

__HEART OF THE FALCON   1-58314-182-0 $5.99US/$7.99CAN

A passionate night with Daniel Falcon leaves Madelyn Taggert heartbroken. She never thought the family friend would walk away without regrets—and he never expected to need her for a lifetime.

__ONLY HERS   1-58314-181-2 $5.99US/$7.99CAN

R.N. Shannon Johnson recently inherited a parcel of Texas land. There she meets Matt Taggert, who makes her prove that she's got the nerve to run a ranch. She, on the other hand, soon challenges him to dare to love again.

__SILKEN BETRAYAL   1-58314-094-8 $5.99US/$7.99CAN

Lauren Bennett's only intent was to keep her son Joshua away from powerful in-laws—until Jordan Hamilton came along. He originally sought her because of a vendetta against her father-in-law, but when he develops feelings for Lauren and Joshua, he must choose between revenge and love.

__UNDENIABLE   0-7860-0125-9 $4.99US/$5.99CAN

Texas heiress Rachel Malone defied her powerful father and eloped with Logan Williams. But a trumped-up assault charge set the whole town against him and he fled. Years later, he's back for revenge . . . and Rachel.

__UNTIL THERE WAS YOU   1-58314-176-6 $5.99US/$7.99CAN

When Catherine Stewart and Luke Grayson find themselves as unwilling roommates in a secluded mountain cabin, an attraction is ignited that takes them both by surprise . . . Can they risk giving their love completely?

Call toll free **1-888-345-BOOK** to order by phone or use this coupon to order by mail.

Name_____

Address_____

City_____ State_____ Zip_____

Please send me the books that I checked above.

I am enclosing $_____

Plus postage and handling* $_____

Sales tax (in NY, TN, and DC) $_____

Total amount enclosed $_____

*Add $2.50 for the first book and $.50 for each additional book.

Send check or money order (no cash or CODs) to: **Arabesque Books, Dept. C.O., 850 Third Avenue, 16th Floor, New York, NY 10022**

Prices and numbers subject to change without notice.

All orders subject to availability.

Visit our website at **www.arabesquebooks.com.**

Arabesque Romances
by *Roberta Gayle*